MW01126483

CLAIMED AND MATED

DELTA JAMES

Copyright © 2018 by Delta James

Published by Stormy Night Publications and Design, LLC.
www.StormyNightPublications.com

Cover design by Korey Mae Johnson
www.koreymaejohnson.com

Images by Dreamstime/Tanialerro and
Shutterstock/Photographee.eu

All rights reserved.

1st Print Edition. December 2018

ISBN-13: 9781790931606

FOR AUDIENCES 18+ ONLY

This book is intended for adults only. Spanking and other sexual activities represented in this book are fantasies only, intended for adults.

PROLOGUE

It is said that shifters—those who shift between human and animal form—existed long before non-shifters. When the world was a far more dangerous place, the ability to shift from one form to another as needed was natural selection at its finest. It allowed those who could do so to thrive in environments in which a human would have trouble surviving. The shifter's enhanced genetic immunity, rapid healing ability, and long life added to their leap to the top of the evolutionary ladder.

CHAPTER ONE

Three years ago

Marco DeMedici slid behind cover as Taliban forces fired on his unit as well as their Afghan allies. He knew there were those who believed that once the Taliban's stranglehold on the country was broken in 2003 that they no longer held any power in the war-torn area. Marco and the other soldiers that were still in the country knew better. The Afghan government put on a good display of being in control, but that's all it was—a show for the rest of the world at large.

Marco was in a good position to lob a grenade into the small hut where the remainder of the Taliban unit they had been fighting for the past two days had taken refuge and was making a last stand. He rolled up onto his knees, throwing the grenade with deadly accuracy. He watched as it went through the open doorway and then ducked down. He not only felt but heard the explosion and could smell death as the men on the inside of the building perished and the men with him cheered.

When did it come to this, he thought. When did men start to cheer the death of others? Yes, the men he'd just killed were the enemy. He shared none of their beliefs. He believed they had to be stopped. But he did not wish them dead.

Several members of the Afghan force went through the building to ensure that there were no survivors from the blast. They too were cheering.

"What's the matter, Marco? You don't look happy. We routed them today. We won."

Marco smiled wryly. "But what have we won if we have lost a piece of our souls?"

Marco rose from the ground wearily. He couldn't remember a time he had ever been this exhausted. Normally his wolfen physiology allowed him to have more strength and endurance and to recover more quickly than his human comrades. But today he knew it would take more than his wolf-human hybrid composition to restore him to a state of well-being. As others before him had done, Marco knew it was time to go home.

Several hours later he was packing his duffel in preparation for his departure from this land still riddled with war. The general he'd served under for a number of years walked in. He spied the duffel on Marco's cot.

"Something tells me that you didn't just forget to sign the papers to extend your tour."

Marco turned and smiled. "No. I'm going home."

"Look, Marco, I understand needing to take a break. How about you agree to extend for just a year and I'll give you a month's R and R?"

"No, Sam. It's time I went home. My father died last year and the man he left to cover for him has done a good job, but he was always to have been a placeholder. I need to go home to take care of my family, our business, and those who derive their livelihoods from the DeMedici."

The general sighed with resignation. "I can't change your mind?"

"I'm afraid not," said Marco. He closed up his duffel and extended his hand to the human he most respected in the world. "It's been an honor to serve under you."

The general took his hand and shook it. "The honor, Colonel, has been all mine."

There was nothing left for either to say. Marco shouldered his duffel and headed out to catch a ride with one of the Jeeps headed to the airstrip and the plane that would take him home.

A few hours later they had entered Italian air space. Marco breathed a sigh of relief. He glanced at his watch and smiled. In less than an hour he would land at the air base. His plan was to go into the closest city, purchase a good motorcycle, and then head for home.

The thought of home made him smile. The DeMedici pack had held their land for more than a thousand years. It had been a fortress long before that time and had become a vineyard only in the past eight hundred years. The Nebbiolo grape was the predominant grape grown by the DeMedici. Their land and their way of life was well suited to its longer growth season and necessity to be harvested by hand.

Marco closed his eyes and drifted in a light slumber. There she was, the beautiful blonde who haunted his dreams and seemed to comfort him during his darkest nights. That she was his fated mate seemed only logical. He couldn't tell for sure, but he felt she was not Italian by birth. No matter, he thought to himself, once she was mated to him she would be Italian and become mistress to the great DeMedici pack.

She was beautiful—tall, blonde-haired, with piercing blue eyes. Marco longed to get his hands on her naked body. She had beautiful large breasts and a well-defined waist that curved outward to form hips made for bearing his children. And her ass was a thing of perfection. He knew for her to be his fated mate, she would be spirited. His cock began to harden at the thought of bringing her to heel.

Marco's reverie was broken as the plane touched down. He watched as men began to gather their things to deplane. After everyone else was gone, Marco picked up his things and trotted down the ramp. One thing he wouldn't miss was the air travel provided for the Italian Special Forces unit.

As he disembarked, he noticed a large man standing off to the side. It was Giovanni. He smiled, but of course Giovanni would be here. The man he'd grown up with strode toward him opening his arms. Marco put down his duffel and embraced him.

"It's good to have you finally home, Alpha," said Giovanni.

"That designation is still yours, my old friend."

Giovanni shook his head. "No, I was always to be a placeholder. Your father will rest easier and I will be much happier to take my place as your beta until you choose another."

Marco looked askance. "And why would I choose another? Will you refuse your alpha if he requests you to remain at his side?"

Giovanni smiled. "No, Alpha. I would never refuse you."

"Then it is settled and you will remain as beta. But what are you doing here? Is there trouble? I would have been home this evening."

"Obviously you will do as you like, but I brought one of the helicopters to take you to the vineyard. Your pack is waiting and most anxious to have their alpha home."

Marco smiled. "Geared up for a homecoming celebration, are they?"

Giovanni returned the smile. "Yes, Alpha. I thought it might be easier on you if you hadn't been driving all day."

Marco laughed. "Already looking out for me. That is not necessarily part of your responsibilities as beta."

"Perhaps not, but you have no mate to see to it so it falls to me."

Marco laughed out loud. "So, I'm not even home yet and already the pestering to take a mate begins."

"I'm afraid so. There are several girls amongst our number who would be more than happy to assume the mantle of mistress."

"Your mate will have to continue as hostess when needed. I have seen my fated mate and she is not amongst us."

"Then where is she?"

Marco laughed again. "I fear my naughty mate has yet to reveal that to me. But trust me, when she does I will waste no time in making her mine."

"As you will, Alpha. We are truly glad to have you home."

"As am I. I feel the weighted veil of war and death already beginning to be lifted."

The two men crossed the airfield and boarded the luxury helicopter that would take them back to the DeMedici stronghold.

CHAPTER TWO

Two years later

Catherine Livingston boarded her flight on Alitalia in New York City headed to Florence, Italy. She was at peace but more focused than she could ever remember. Catherine had always been the dutiful granddaughter, the dedicated student, and the perfect businesswoman. Her recent reorganization and change in her life was for her. But this trip was for her sister, Shannon.

Catherine was a tall, striking blonde who turned heads wherever she went, but seemed not to notice. Always focused on her own agenda, it took quite a bit of trying for any man to catch her interest. She usually wore her hair loose either naturally curly or pulled back in a French braid. Either showed the length to be well past her shoulders. She had striking blue eyes that changed with her mood. She had often been told that with her temper, she should have been a redhead.

Her parents had died when she was young and she and her sister had been brought up by an indulgent grandfather. He had encouraged her artistic endeavors by giving her private lessons, a large space filled with light to work and more supplies that any one art student should have. He had, however, encouraged her to see her art as a hobby and to study something practical—something she could make a good living at as she seemed disinclined to be a wife and mother and allow a man to provide for her.

She had done as he asked and become a successful corporate raider and business consultant. It seemed her talent extended to both sides of a conflict. She was equally at home destroying a company for a client to be able to gobble up as she was at defending a client from a hostile takeover. More than one CEO had found him/herself quaking in their boots when they realized the opposition had engaged Catherine. She was smart, tenacious, and feared nothing.

The last few years had been difficult. Her beloved grandfather has passed away and her younger sister, Shannon, had gone missing on a dream vacation to Europe several months ago. Their grandfather had specifically willed Shannon the money for the trip as a college graduation present. Shannon had taken off and checked in regularly from London and Paris. She had checked in from Rome. Catherine had spoken with Shannon once more from Rome and then nothing. Catherine had worked through the US Embassy, who had been of little to no help, and then hired private investigators to try to locate her sister—all to no avail. Shannon had simply disappeared. Catherine kept the best of the private investigators on retainer and kept him looking for any clue as to Shannon's death or her whereabouts.

Catherine had begun to feel very much like an orphan. Even though she was an adult she felt the loss of having a family. Her work kept her constantly on the move so meaningful relationships were difficult if not impossible. Mostly she settled for short-term relationships in the various places she had to work. They were finite with a definite beginning, middle, and end. For the most part, Catherine had convinced herself she liked it that way.

But three years ago, she'd been in a freak rollover accident in a town car. She had been thrown free and had escaped with a dislocated shoulder and a lot of bruises. Everyone else in the car had perished. As was her norm, she had finished the job she was on before returning to her SoHo loft to rest and recuperate. It was while she was there that she began to question her life. She wondered if those who had died had been happy or at least satisfied with their lives. She knew when she looked at her own, she would have had to say no.

Catherine also began to believe that if she was ever going to find the answers to her questions about her little sister that she herself would need to find them.

It was during this time of reflection and self-discovery that the mysterious dark man to whom she felt inexplicably drawn began to haunt—no, that wasn't right—to inhabit her dreams. Almost every night she would see him most often with a large black wolf at his side. Some nights they would interact; others she could would merely feel his presence before turning to find him standing with the wolf on the horizon. On several occasions, she had sensed he needed her and had gone close to offer him comfort.

Between frugal living and the income she generated from her business, Catherine had been able to amass a good-sized nest egg. But that was nothing compared to the fortune her grandfather had left her. As she sat in her loft sketching and nursing her injured shoulder she began to wonder what if. What if she hadn't studied business? What if she had followed her passion and studied art? And then the inevitable, what if even after studying she wasn't good enough to make it as an artist?

The latter had led her to explore the careers available in art history, art restoration, and art appraiser. Deciding that any one of the three would feed her soul more than being a corporate raider, she quietly closed shop and enrolled in the prestigious Cooper Union for the Advancement of Science and Art. She was thrilled when she was invited to enroll, as only fifteen percent of those who applied annually were accepted.

Cooper was known to be a daunting experience for most, but with a caring faculty and administration that kept its successful graduate rate above the norm for most colleges. Catherine had thrived there. She had majored in the visual arts, painting to be more specific with a focus on art restoration. She figured if she couldn't create her own masterpieces, she could ensure the survival of others.

Catherine graduated at the top of her class. She decided to reward herself and celebrate with a trip to the fabled city of Florence in Italy. She planned to immerse herself in its culture, its art, and its food. She also planned to begin her own search for Shannon. The private investigator had recently come across some disturbing rumors regarding human trafficking. He had related that young, pretty, single girls like Shannon were easy and tempting targets. He had been able to track her last known sighting to the Ponte Vecchio in Florence.

Catherine's hard work ensured that she could afford to fly first class and her trip to Florence was no exception. After having gotten settled for the long flight, Catherine got comfortable and closed her eyes.

A brief smile crossed her face as the man who had begun to inhabit all of her dreams appeared. Dark-haired, dark-eyed with a massively muscular physique and a regal hawk-like nose. More than one of her fantasies had involved this man and feeling his head between her legs with his nose nudging her outer lips apart so that he could sup on what lay beyond. She had also experienced far more visceral dreams in which he possessed her body completely. She had begun to look forward to seeing him each night and would miss him when he was not there.

Those were not the only dreams in which he appeared. There were others with disturbing imagery. Scenes of war— broken bodies and blood, ravaged landscapes, and the smell of death. She could see him amid the horror. Catherine would often go to him in those dreams and just be with him—absorb whatever she could from him of his pain and mental anguish. That he had caused or been part of the conflict frightened her, but that fear was offset by knowing he took no joy in it and that one day it would be a part of his past.

She began to write in her journal little snippets of the dreams that she remembered. One thing she had found odd was that he was often accompanied by or close to the large coal black wolf. The wolf didn't seem to mean either of them harm. Catherine knew from her research that the wolf was a symbol of guardianship, loyalty, and spirit. It was said that those whose spirit animal was a wolf made strong, quick, and lasting emotional attachments, trusted their instincts, and controlled their own destinies. Once Catherine understood the positive qualities associated with having a wolf as a spirit guide, she decided he could inhabit her dreams as well.

• • • • • • •

Present day

Marco stood on the broad balcony of the villa he called home and watched as the sun made its lazy climb over the horizon. He started each morning this way—alone on his bedroom balcony with a cup of espresso and a chocolate biscotti. He would spend some time just breathing in the rarefied air of his family's ancestral home and vineyard. He would map out his day and then as the rest of the household began to stir, he would descend the stairs and once again assume the mantle of alpha of the DeMedici pack.

When Marco had returned home three years ago after a long stint as a Special Forces operative, he had let the peace and beauty of this place restore his soul. He had been grateful to Giovanni, his beta, for having kept things going between the death of his own father and Marco fulfilling his obligations to the military. He and Giovanni had searched and recruited an excellent vintner who also happened to be a wolf.

Luca had proved to be not only a skilled vintner, but a gifted omega for the pack. He often times had to be reminded that he was not expected to work twenty-four hours a day either as vintner or omega. However, Marco had to admit that under Luca's guidance, both the pack and the vineyard had flourished.

Marco smiled. Today would bring a visit from the Welsh wolf as his people referred to Griffin Owen. Griffin had become a friend many years ago when they had worked on a special black ops mission. Both had recognized that the other was an alpha wolf. Both had put aside their natural inclination to be rivals for the sake of the mission and had found in the other a life-long friend. Since that time, they had shared many adventures—some in the battlefield and some vying for the attention of various women. Griffin often teased Marco that he wasn't a wolf at all but a reincarnation of Casanova, the famous Italian lover. Marco had laughed and merely pointed out that he liked to indulge the carnal side of his nature and that none of the women involved had ever been hurt in any way by him.

Marco finished dressing and descended the stairs. "*Buongiorno*," he said as he walked into the great dining room.

He smiled. While many wolf packs had large dining halls—most often converted from other uses, e.g., ballroom, conference area, etc.—the one at the villa had always been a dining room. It had hosted many a feast over its long history. It was, as was the rest of the villa, breathtakingly beautiful. The walls were all done in hand-painted murals and Marco had replaced the entire back wall with a series of French doors that led out onto an expansive terrazzo.

The members of his pack acknowledged his greeting and many called back to him. They were a self-contained community and company. Most all of those who worked in the vineyards or as part of the villa's staff lived on the main property itself. However, Marco's holdings extended beyond the stone-walled borders to the small town beyond.

Marco joined Luca at the table usually reserved for them.

"Our beta and his mate? It's not like Giovanni to tarry in their bed at this time of year."

Luca chuckled. "While it may be his mate that has his attention at the moment, Marco, I fear it isn't to avail himself of her ample charms."

Marco laughed. Valentina, Giovanni's mate, was a beauty with an extremely sensual nature but a mischievous streak a mile wide. She was forever getting herself into enough trouble that she would find herself face down over Giovanni's knee having her backside peppered until she relented and promised once again to behave herself. Marco idly wondered what she had done this time.

The thought had no sooner crossed his mind than Giovanni entered with his Valentina in tow. He gestured toward one of the chairs at the table. "Sit," he ordered.

"I don't want to," she said petulantly.

Luca and Marco exchanged pointed glances. That tone would not serve Valentina well. Most likely it meant that her punishment had not been sufficient to restore balance between them.

"Did I ask you whether or not you wanted to, *cara*?"

"No." She turned toward their alpha. "Tell him to apologize to me."

"For what?" asked Marco.

"For spanking me this morning," said Valentina in an exasperated tone.

A low, warning growl came from Giovanni.

"Did you not do something to deserve a spanking from your mate?" asked Marco softly but with a voice that brooked no defiance. "Careful how you answer me, Valentina. Lie or play loose with the truth, I will instruct your mate that he is to return with you to your bedroom to

DELTA JAMES

wash your mouth out with soap, spank your lovely backside until he has gotten through to you, and then make you his until you beg his forgiveness in a voice filled with love and desire before he finishes you."

Now it was Luca and Giovanni's turn to exchange pointed looks.

Marco adored women... all women. Those in his pack reciprocated his feelings. He was part older brother and part indulgent father, but all alpha. He would indulge and spoil them in many ways, but never would he place himself between one of his men and the man's mate.

Valentina quickly quieted and glanced back and forth between her mate and her alpha. She walked over to Giovanni, molded herself to him, and stood on her tiptoes to kiss him.

"I'm sorry, Gio. I didn't mean to worry you or make you angry. I won't do it again."

Giovanni smiled and returned his mate's kisses. "Yes, you will," he teased. "Now, do you want to go get a pillow to sit on?"

She nodded.

"Good girl. You do that, and I'll go get our breakfast."

Valentina turned to leave.

"Valentina?"

She stopped to look at her mate.

"What do you have to say to Marco?"

She blushed and walked over to their alpha with her eyes downcast. "I'm sorry, Marco. I shouldn't have tried to drag you into it."

Marco smiled at her and lifted her chin. "That's all right, Valentina. But you mind Giovanni."

"Yes, Alpha," she said quietly. Valentina headed into the adjacent sitting room, brought back a well-padded pillow, and placed it on the chair before lowering herself gracefully and gingerly onto it.

Giovanni brought over plates with hearty breakfasts. "Can I get you anything, Marco?"

Marco shook his head. "No, I'll get something in a minute."

"So when is the Welsh wolf meant to join us?" asked Luca. He'd heard much about Marco's closest friend outside the pack but had yet to meet him.

"I would think he would be here sometime before lunch."

"Is this just a visit or does he have an agenda?" asked Giovanni.

"I think just a visit, but I would like to see if he's heard the same disturbing rumors coming out of the east," said Marco, clearly not wanting to discuss the matter in front of Valentina.

Marco was a firm believer in providing the women and children in his pack as peaceful, serene, and happy a life as he could make. Should trouble ever be headed for their doorstep, he would share what they needed to know. Until then he wanted to allow them to enjoy all that they had.

"What rumors?" asked Valentina.

"Just the usual saber rattling," said Giovanni, glossing over the matter in an effort to reassure her. "Youch," Giovanni said, growling at his mate.

Marco laughed as did Luca. Valentina was well known for kicking her mate under the table.

"It's not funny, Marco," said Valentina, trying to keep her tone to her alpha respectful. "If you aren't going to tell me, fine, but don't assume I'm so stupid."

Giovanni reached over to take her hand. "I'm sorry, *cara*. You are right. There are some ugly rumors starting to come out of the eastern countries. Things we do not want you or any of the others to worry about."

"We will keep you all safe," said Marco.

"Don't you think we know that?" she said. "I'm sorry I kicked you, Gio. I just don't like it when you treat me like I'm an idiot."

He leaned over and kissed her. "And I am sorry for making you feel that way. I promise if the rumors get

DELTA JAMES

confirmed I will share them with you on the condition that you do not share the information with anyone."

She returned his kiss and said, "Thank you, Gio. Anything you tell me I will keep to myself... unless of course our alpha and omega get off their proverbial asses and go find themselves mates."

Giovanni laughed as Marco and Luca only barely managed not to spit what they were drinking.

Marco laughed and shook his finger at Valentina. "You have a very naughty mate, Giovanni."

"I know, Alpha, but what am I to do? I love and adore her and she knows it. It's a dangerous thing for a mate to know," he said, chuckling.

Marco smiled at them. He envied Giovanni his mate. Valentina could be extremely mischievous when she wanted and often tried Giovanni's patience, but she loved him deeply and would do anything to see him happy.

Marco took her hand in his and kissed it. "When I am lucky enough to find my fated mate, I will have her wedded, bedded, and with child before you can teach her to be naughty."

Valentina giggled. "If she is your fated mate, it will be she who is doing the teaching."

Luca and Giovanni laughed. "She's probably right, you know," said Luca.

Marco chuckled. "She probably is. I keep seeing her in my dreams. I will recognize her when I see her, but she keeps evading me—something I will take her to task for down the road."

"Marco, when you're through with breakfast, I'd like a bit of your time before the Welsh wolf shows up and you two start sampling my best wine," said Luca.

Marco grinned. "My time is yours. I just want to ensure the rest of the staff is ready for Griffin's arrival. I think he may be with us for a while. He didn't sound too good when last we talked."

CHAPTER THREE

Catherine's plane landed on time in Florence. She eagerly disembarked and made her way through customs. The Italian officials were quite used to art students coming to Florence to study and see the sights. One of them offered to be Catherine's personal escort but she declined.

She ventured out of the airport and made her way to where she could rent one of the popular Italian scooters. A scooter was perfect for getting around Florence if one wasn't easily intimidated. Catherine had spent some time in Rome the year before. Last year's trip had been both for business and to speak again with the investigator she had hired. At that time, he'd found little information on Shannon. Catherine figured if she could survive Rome and Roman drivers, she could survive anything.

She pulled out her city map and determined the best way to the B&B. She ventured out into traffic and was off. Truth be told, the drivers in Florence seemed far more relaxed than their Roman counterparts. She made her way along the narrow streets and found the residence for her stay. It was all the B&B booking site had promised.

A lovely row home in a clean, pleasant neighborhood. Off-street parking, a private bath, and easy access to all

Florence had offer either via scooter or on foot. She rang the bell on the iron gates and when she answered the questions on the monitor, the lock clicked open. She was instructed to bring her scooter in and park it in the shed and that her hostess would be down momentarily.

Catherine grinned. She believed she had made a good choice. She parked her scooter and grabbed her carpet bag before walking into the courtyard. Catherine wasn't sure what she expected the owner would be like, but Seraphina Vilotti was not it.

Seraphina came into the courtyard and immediately hugged Catherine like an old friend.

"Welcome to Casa Dolce," she said in an American accent. "I'm your host, Seraphina. And no, I'm not a native Italian."

Catherine laughed, feeling very much at home with Seraphina.

"I'm Catherine Livingston. I'm not Italian either, but I can order off a menu with the best of them!"

"*Bene!* Come on in and let's get you settled. New York?"

Catherine smiled. "Guilty as charged. You?"

"Originally? San Francisco; now? Florence, Italy. Moved to be with the man of my dreams. Imagine my surprise when I found he had a wife and kids."

"Oh, my," said Catherine. "I'm so very sorry."

"No worries. I'd left my job and sold everything to be with him, so I bought this place and rehabbed it. Turned it into a nice little B&B. Between that and teaching both English and Italian, I have a nice little setup… and no fog!"

Seraphina walked her into the house.

"Now, I have a room upstairs with a little balcony overlooking the courtyard. And I have a bigger room here on the ground floor with its own private terrazzo. Both have private baths. This is just before our high season and I don't have anyone scheduled before it gets started. Normally I charge more for the one down here, but you can have your choice. Same price."

"No stairs? After hiking all over Florence? Ground floor, please."

Seraphina laughed. "That's what I figured. I don't blame you."

Seraphina took her to the spacious bedroom in the back with the private patio area.

"This is great, Seraphina."

"Sera," she said.

"Sera it is. I'm Catherine." She wandered idly around the room. "This is really lovely."

"Art student?"

"Yes. How did you guess?"

"Right time of the year," said Sera. "And all of you artistic types have a kind of surreal air about you when you reach the Mecca of the Renaissance. Long flight?"

"Yes, but I slept most of the way."

"Hungry? I have some flatbread and some pesto. I'm sure I can put together a quick bite for you if you like."

"That would be wonderful."

Sera smiled. "Well, you get settled in and I'll bring it to you directly. Water? Wine? Soda?"

"I'm bordering on dehydrated so water, please."

Catherine barely had time to unpack before Sera returned with a large glass of ice water, fruit, and flatbread spread with pesto and melted mozzarella. It smelled divine.

Catherine took a bite of the ooey, gooey flatbread, closed her eyes, and sighed in pleasure. "Oh, my God, Sera. This is incredible. That pesto didn't come out of a jar."

"But of course it did," Sera grinned. "Of course, it's pesto I made and jarred myself. So do you have an itinerary or know when you want to get started in the mornings?"

"Uhm, I can be very flexible and I don't want you to go to any trouble. But usually I start becoming coherent about nine."

Sera laughed. "Like me. I'll bet though you're up before then. Why don't I have coffee or espresso and a biscotti outside your door about 7:30 and then you can wander out when you're ready to face the day."

"That sounds perfect. I think I'm going to go stretch my legs and get a feel for where I am in the city."

"Have fun and if you get lost, call me and I'll give you directions home."

"Sounds perfect," said Catherine as Sera left her room.

Catherine finished getting settled and changed into comfortable walking sandals. She headed out the door and began to explore.

Sera's home was on the edge of a residential neighborhood. It bordered on an area that was filled with small, local restaurants, bars, some shopping, and a few art galleries. Catherine spent a very enjoyable afternoon wandering throughout the areas close to Sera's home, and she made it back in one piece in the early evening.

"You're back!" Sera greeted her upon her return. "Do you have plans for dinner? I was going to go hit up one of the local places and I hate to eat alone."

"Sounds great. Am I dressed ok?"

"You're perfect. And if we're not… fuck 'em!"

Catherine laughed. "Oh, girl, I like your style. We're going to get along great."

· · · · · · ·

Marco had met with Luca earlier in the day. The latter had several new wine festivals into which he wanted to enter their wines. The DeMedici wines had always provided a sizeable income for the family, but under Luca's tenure as master vintner, the label had exploded. Not only had sales increased to the point that they couldn't keep up with the demand, but they had become one of the wine critics' darlings—it seemed that there wasn't enough praise that could be given to them.

Luca had found a small boutique vineyard that could be bought for a fair price. The vineyard and label had been in the family for a few hundred years, but the current generation had no interest in wine or in growing grapes. Easily within a day's drive from the villa, Luca had proposed they purchase it. The grapes grown were some he had longed to work with and he felt they would be a nice supplement to those grown at DeMedici vineyard. They also grew some of the variety to be pressed into balsamic vinegar. And the property boasted a large, old stand growth of olive trees. Luca laid out an entire marketing plan for Marco's approval.

Marco smiled. Not only did Luca's plan make good economic sense, he could tell his omega was keen to move on it.

"This sounds good, Luca. Why don't you go to Florence and see if you can't put the deal together."

"No, Marco. You need to do it. You are the DeMedici. That carries weight in Tuscany and I know you will get us a better deal than I could. I appreciate your confidence in me, but you are the far better negotiator."

"Yes, but Griffin will be here later today."

"Take him along. The two of you can talk in the car and Florence is a beautiful city."

Marco laughed. "You're afraid I'll tap into some of those bottles you want to enter into competition."

"There is that, but you will get us a better deal."

"I'll tell you what. If the Welsh wolf is amendable to a side trip to Florence, I'll go. If not, you go and get us the best deal you can."

"Thanks, Marco. I really do think by this time next year we're going to be glad we took this step."

"If nothing else, we can update the residence, if it needs it, and allow our people to use it as a getaway."

They were just finishing up their meeting, when there was a knock on the door. One of the house staff let Marco know that the Welsh wolf should be arriving momentarily. Marco smiled. He'd left Griffin his motorcycle at the airport, knowing Griffin would enjoy the drive and the open air.

"Excellent! Let's finalize plans for this venture and how to get it accomplished at dinner. The more I think about it, the more I think buying this vineyard is in our best interests."

Luca nodded. "I'll get a preliminary meeting set for tomorrow. I'm happy to do whatever you need me to do."

Marco stopped at the door and turned back to him. "I need you to get serious about finding a mate."

"I think the pack is far more interested in our alpha finding his and bringing her home."

"I know none of you believe me," said Marco softly, "but she's out there. I've seen her." He shook his head and chuckled. "She is just being difficult and hiding from me. But never doubt... she will be mine."

Marco left the room with Luca looking after him. No one in the pack doubted that she existed or that whoever this blonde beauty was, she had no idea what her future held.

Marco heard the motorcycle as it pulled up in front of the villa. He rushed down the steps to embrace his good friend and former comrade.

"Welcome! Welcome!"

Griffin Owen smiled at his friend. "It's good to be here, Marco. Thanks for taking me in."

"You know you are always welcome. Juliana has made your usual room ready. It is yours for as long as you like. Are you hungry? Lunch is almost ready."

Griffin laughed. "Marco, you always know how to make me feel welcome. Let me take my things upstairs and take a quick shower to wash the road off and I will happily dig into whatever is being served. I'm starving."

Marco watched Griffin head up the stairs. His friend couldn't fool him. Griffin may have made his voice light and airy but there had been a darkness behind his eyes. If he hadn't yet left Special Forces, Marco meant to urge him to do so. There was only so much a man's soul could take before it would be irrevocably damaged. If Griffin was done, then Marco meant to urge him to stay—here at the villa and if not, perhaps the new vineyard outside of Florence.

Lunch was a lively affair at the DeMedici villa. Marco knew that the sound of happy voices and lots of wonderful food would go a long way to helping the Welsh wolf find his way back to the light.

Griffin joined them within short order.

"God, I'd forgotten what a celebration every meal is with your pack. Don't get me wrong, Calon Onest is home and everyone is lovely, but they're…" Griffin hesitated, looking for the right word.

"Quiet?" supplied Marco. "Dull? Blasé food?"

Griffin started to laugh. "While accurate, that was not what I was thinking."

"But of course not. You are far too kind."

They dug into a delectable meal and enjoyed themselves. Marco asked that the chef be brought out where he was met with a round of applause from his enthusiastic pack.

Griffin sipped one of the wines that had been served. "This is amazing. I swear your wine gets better and better."

"It does," said Marco, "because of Luca here. Not only is he a most excellent omega, but he is a vintner of high regard. Speaking of which, how does a quick trip to Florence sound? Luca has found a small vineyard he wants us to purchase. Not only do they have grapes for wine and balsamic vinegar, but he tells me they also have olive trees."

"I don't think I've been to Florence in years. I think that sounds like an excellent place to start my retirement."

Marco smiled at him. "So you have finally walked away?"

"I didn't have a pack to come home to."

"You did, but chose not to claim it. Ioan would have stepped aside. You know that."

"I do. But he's the right man for Calon Onest. While Wales will always be home, I just don't see myself settling there."

"Home, my friend," said Marco, "is where you bed your

woman on a regular basis and see your children born and raised."

"Really?" responded Griffin with a grin. "Is this your way of telling me you finally found your mysterious blonde-haired mate?"

"Alas, no. She still hides from me, but she is close. I can feel her."

"Well, perhaps we'll find her in Florence."

"She's not Italian."

"Neither am I," teased Griffin, "but apparently I'm going to be in Florence tomorrow."

Marco laughed. "Perhaps. If so, if I see her before Luca's meeting either you or he will need to conclude the negotiations. I will be preoccupied with my mate."

Griffin smiled at his friend. There was no doubt in anyone's mind that when Marco finally found his fated mate, he would move heaven and earth to claim her.

CHAPTER FOUR

Catherine woke to the smell of espresso wafting under her door. She wasn't sure whether to praise Seraphina or damn her. The massive hangover she had from the night before said the latter, but the espresso smelled divine and she knew the biscotti that would accompany it would be homemade. As there was nothing to be done about the hangover, and other than introducing her to an amazing wine bottled about six hours away, Catherine had to admit that the hangover was just as much her fault as Seraphina's.

She cringed as her feet hit the floor. They hurt, but then so did everything else... including her hair. Catherine opened the door and bent down to pick up the tray. She placed it on the bed and picked up the note from Sera.

In this order:
- *Chug the first bottle of water*
- *Eat the banana*
- *Open the second bottle of water and take the pain pills—over the counter!*
- *Dunk your biscotti in the espresso and eat it*
- *Finish the biscotti*

- *Drink the rest of the second bottle of water*
- *Take a hot shower—your room does have a steam shower*
- *Try to take a nap*
- *When you wake again, come join me and we'll have a nice light breakfast.*

Sera

Catherine did as instructed and felt much better the second time she opened her eyes about two hours later. She threw on a pair of leggings and a poet blouse. She pulled back and braided her hair, added earrings she'd purchased the day before, and slipped her feet into another pair of comfortable sandals.

Sera greeted her. "Oh, you look much than I thought you might."

"For the record, I'm taking that remedy home with me. I feel so much better than when I first got up."

"Well, we should both have had a bottle of water, a banana, and some pain pills before we went to sleep, but that's life. Take lots of water with you today and a banana or two. By this evening, you'll be feeling good again."

Catherine smiled. "Thanks for last night. Hangover notwithstanding, I had a great time. But don't think I didn't notice that I didn't see a bill. So tonight, pick a place for dinner and I'm buying. Pick a nice place that locals like."

"I know just the place, Adagio Firenze. Why don't I meet you there? Say 6:30 or so? That way we can avoid the crowd."

Catherine picked up the offered water and fruit and stuffed them in her bag along with the address for the restaurant. "It's a date!"

• • • • • • •

Griffin trotted down the stairs and entered the dining room where he was greeted like family. Marco watched his friend closely. He could tell that even the half day Griffin had been here had started him back toward life. This place, his people had a kind of magic. The DeMedici were reputed to have been founded when a female shifter had become the mistress of one of Italy's most powerful families. Successive generations had both separated themselves from the other and several DeMedici alphas had found their fated mates among the Romany. Marco had never been sure if the stories were true, but he did know his people were warm and protective of those they called pack and those they called friend. In some ways, Griffin was both. Marco worried that Griffin might forever deny himself his own pack.

"Good morning," said Griffin. "I can't remember the last time I slept so well. Dreamless and restorative. Thank you again for inviting me. Are we still on for Florence?"

Marco laughed. "We are indeed. I thought about taking one of the chauffeured cars, but then decided with the beautiful weather, we really should take one of the sports cars with the top down."

"You know me, I always opt for wind in my face."

Marco excused himself to take care of a few things to be handled while he was gone. His weekend bag was already next to the door.

Griffin went out for a short walk and then packed for the unexpected trip.

Once they were ready, they walked out and Griffin let out a low, appreciative whistle.

Parked and ready to go was a red 1929 Alfa Romeo roadster. Griffin shook his head. The DeMedici alphas had been collecting classic sports cars for as long as sports cars had existed.

"Now, that's a ride," he said.

"I know. She takes a bit of tinkering and can be temperamental, but she is my favorite."

"Were you describing the car or your fated mate?" Griffin teased.

Marco thought for a moment. "Both."

They laughed, stowed their bags, slid into the beautiful car, and headed for Florence.

Marco just drove. He knew when Griffin was ready to talk, he would. If Griffin said nothing on the drive to Florence, Marco planned to bring up the rumors either tonight at dinner or on the way back home.

"You seemed relieved that I'd finally turned in my papers," started Griffin.

"I was. How are you feeling about it?"

"Surprisingly good, and yet adrift. I knew you were right the last time we talked, but now I'm just sitting here thinking now what?"

"Whatever you want, my friend. This new vineyard will need a general manager to be on site. If you want, you are welcome to stay and of course you are always welcome at the villa. I know several of my females would love to have a chance to entice you."

Griffin laughed. "I fear they'd be disappointed."

"That is not what I recall hearing from the several women we shared."

Marco was glad when Griffin laughed again. The sound was more well-rounded than when last they had spoken.

"Perhaps. But you and I both know that enjoying the charms of a female pack member when your intentions aren't serious is not good form."

"And you Welsh are all about proper form... except for as I recall a certain little beauty in Germany."

They both laughed at the shared memory. The girl had gotten their names mixed up and when she ended up in Griffin's bed thinking he was Marco, Griffin hadn't corrected her assumption.

"Well, you have to admit she was rather luscious. Oh, God, let's promise never to tell your mate about that."

"What about yours?"

"I'm not sure there will ever be one," said Griffin in a voice full of regret.

"Of course there will. Your fated mate is out there. She's

just hiding better than mine. At least I know mine's a blonde."

"Well, that's good," Griffin said, trying to push the sadness away. "You've always had a penchant for blondes."

"And that is also information you can keep to yourself," laughed the Italian alpha.

"You really believe the woman in your dreams is out there just waiting for you to find? After all we've seen and been through?"

"I know she is. It is because of what we have experienced that I have to believe. It was she who got me through my darkest nights. It was her face I saw when they tortured me and left me to die before you got to me. My *tesoro* saved me. I know you don't believe that. But I could see her. I could feel her stroke my face willing me to live."

Griffin stared at his friend. "I truly envy you, Marco. I can't wait to meet this woman. What an amazing mistress she will be for your pack."

Marco nodded. "So, do not give up. Your woman is out there. I just know it. If you do not believe, then I shall have to believe enough for the both of us."

They drove on in companionable silence for another hour before Griffin finally spoke again.

"Ioan and I have heard rumors…" he started.

"About the packs to the East?"

"Yes. The Ruling Council in Britain is opting to believe it's just the normal saber rattling."

"As is the one here in Europe. But we too are hearing the same rumors and there are occasional stories about female tourists disappearing and never being heard from again or found. Too many for me to discount. And the worst of it is, there are numerous women, mostly tourists, who have disappeared out of Italy—usually Rome, Milan, and Florence."

"That is troubling, but makes sense. All three would be easy ports of call to use. I mean to take you up on your offer and allow myself some time to heal without Bethan fretting…"

"Your sister loves you…"

"As does yours. Has she forgiven you yet for allowing that Irish wolf to force her to run?" said Griffin, smiling.

"She has." Marco laughed, his eyes shining at the thought of his beloved baby sister. "Mainly I think because she has no time to be angry with me. Aidan wasted no time in putting a baby in her belly after he claimed her and she has another on the way. And he dotes on her as does his pack."

Griffin laughed. "And your brothers?"

Marco accepted that Griffin was not yet ready to pursue the disturbing rumors but felt that as he had brought them up they would be able to talk it through.

"Stefano is mated to the daughter of the alpha in Crete and very happy. He will most likely be their next alpha. Tony is happy being beta of the pack in Rome. I think he was disappointed to find that when you are having to discipline women with whom you would never mate there is no sexual component."

Both men laughed.

"But he says now he may have found his mate. He just needs to convince her of it."

Griffin groaned. "Why do the good ones always need convincing?"

"Because they are the ones with spirit and do not lightly give up their independent ways. But that makes their surrender and their acceptance of your authority all the sweeter."

"So, do you think this blonde mate of yours is going to be difficult?"

Marco let out a robust laugh. "What do you mean, going to be? She has been keeping herself hidden from me for a long time. I have yet to decide whether I'll punish her for that behavior before or after I've spent several nights in our bed availing myself of her charms."

Griffin laughed. "Oh, now that, I'm going to tell her."

"By the time you get to speak to her, she will be well aware of where I've spent my time."

Griffin sobered. "Marco, we need to find out if what we think is going on is in fact going on."

"I agree. As you are not true pack with anyone but are attached unofficially to two powerful packs, I wondered if you might go on a fact-finding mission. But only when you have healed. You need to give yourself some time to distance yourself from Special Forces. Spend time here with us and then go visit your sister."

"What do you think the Ruling Councils will do if I find evidence that we're right?"

"Nothing. They are pack of foolish old wolves and will not risk what they have. If we are right and there are women you can help, bring them to me. I will ensure they are safe and will give them time to heal."

Griffin smiled. "Your home and your pack are good for that. I can already feel my soul starting to mend."

"I'm glad. You will always have a place with us... always."

CHAPTER FIVE

Sera was already at the table when Catherine arrived loaded down with packages and a marvelous red cloak thrown over her arm.

It had been a fruitful day. Not only had she found many shops with wonderful things to purchase, but some amazing small galleries with new and emerging artists. She had also found a shop that remembered her sister even after all these months. It seemed Shannon had left something with them to be altered and never returned. They had found it odd that when they tracked her back to the hotel in which she'd told them she was staying, the hotel had no record of her ever having been there.

"I thought you were going to look at galleries?" Sera asked, her eyes glinting with humor.

"Me too… but that Ponte Vecchio is a dangerous place and deadly to one's credit card."

"That it is. I stay away from the place. Way too many talented artisans."

Catherine picked up the menu and accepted the glass of wine Sera had ordered for her. "Seriously?" she said, eyeing first the wine and then Sera.

"Hair of the dog."

Catherine giggled. "Ooh, the same vintner. Is this wine available in the States? I think it may be the best wine I've ever had."

"It's very exclusive and I don't think widely distributed. They say the land has been in the family for over a thousand years and that the artwork in the villa itself is stunning—hand-painted murals, centuries-old tapestries and the like."

"Do they do tours?"

"No. The DeMedici keep to themselves for the most part. Although the head of the family, Marco is well known in Florence and is a patron of the arts here."

"DeMedici?"

"Yes, the De alludes to the story that they are the bastard side of the Medici family."

"How interesting," said Catherine as she perused the menu. "So what's good?"

"Absolutely everything. I've never had anything I didn't think was amazing. And their presentations are downright sexy."

Catherine giggled. She then felt a chill run over her and realized that goosebumps had sprung up all over her arms. She thought it odd as the restaurant wasn't that chilly. She couldn't shake the chill so drew the red cloak over her shoulders, flipping her French braid to the outside of the cloak.

"Oooh," said Sera, "and speaking of sexy… look what just walked through the door."

Catherine turned to look and saw two of the most handsome men she'd ever seen. Both were tall and dark. One had more the build of a thoroughbred or Arabian racehorse, while the other was more powerfully built more along the lines of a quarter horse or warmblood. Both had an air of confidence about them that was unmistakable and very alluring.

"God, please tell me they aren't gay," whispered Catherine, turning her back on them.

"Hardly. The one on the right—the bigger one—is none

other than Marco DeMedici himself. Not sure who the other one is."

Catherine turned to look again more closely at Marco and gasped.

"Catherine, are you all right? You look like you've seen a ghost."

Catherine turned back to her new friend, not wanting DeMedici to see her staring. Unless she was very much mistaken, Marco DeMedici was the man from her dreams.

"It's nothing. One of those moments when you feel like someone is walking over your grave."

"Are you sure? We can go somewhere else if you want."

"Don't be silly." Catherine settled herself back in her chair and tried to slow the rapid beat of her heart. It couldn't be him. He didn't really exist, and yet she'd seen him standing there, felt his pull.

Catherine and Sera ate their appetizers and tried to return to a normal conversation.

· · · · · · ·

Marco and Griffin were shown to the best table in the house by a lovely hostess and then served by an even more beautiful server.

"I'd almost forgotten what it was like to dine with you in Italy. Best tables and women falling all over you."

Marco chuckled. "Yes, but being the gentleman that I am, I will catch her and bring both of us great pleasure this night. You should find a woman and do the same."

"No, I think I'll just sleep. Right now I have little to offer."

"Nonsense. If it's because you fancy our server, I will step aside and go to work on the hostess. She too would make a lovely companion for the evening."

Griffin laughed. "God, I hope your mate has a rampant, raging libido."

"Not until I find and claim her, then I will set that wild

beast in her free to run with mine."

The two men enjoyed the meal. Marco knew that Griffin was enjoying watching his seduction of the waitress, which made it that much more fun. He was just getting ready to give the waitress his hotel room key and ask her to be there waiting for him when he caught scent of her. Not the waitress, but his mate. He had caught a subtle scent when they entered the restaurant. He had dismissed it as nothing more than his desiring the waitress, but there it was again. He inhaled more deeply and smiled.

"What is it?" asked Griffin, trying to figure out what had caught the attention of his best friend.

"She's here," Marco said simply but in an extremely satisfied and peaceful tone of voice. "Finally."

Griffin looked around. "Which one? There are a lot of beautiful blondes here."

Marco scented the air again, his grin growing larger. "Over there. Bad table by the wait station. The short-haired dark girl can see us. My mate has her back turned—as if that would stop me from finding her."

Marco heralded the hostess.

"Yes, Mr. DeMedici?"

"That table with the two lovely ladies over by the kitchen. The short dark hair and the blonde with the French braid. They are to get no bill for their meal. You take them the best bottle of DeMedici wine that you have on hand and find them something decadent for dessert."

"Yes, Mr. DeMedici. I'll take care of it. If they ask for their benefactor?"

Marco thought for a moment. "Just tell the blonde that it is a long-time admirer of hers."

"Yes, sir."

Griffin grinned and watched the hostess do as she was bid.

The two women looked around. Marco and Griffin continued on with their dinner with casual aplomb. They could overhear that the women were perplexed but not overly alarmed as the hostess assured them she knew their benefactor and they had nothing over which to be concerned.

Marco scented the air and frowned. "She is concerned. I didn't mean to alarm her."

"Of course you didn't, Marco. If she is your mate, she should settle quickly."

"Easy, my love," said Marco under his breath. He scented the air again and smiled. "Her fear is abating. Interesting."

"What?" asked Griffin.

"She's not a shifter."

"That could be a problem."

"No, a minor inconvenience. It will require my explaining things to her and having her consent to be turned."

Griffin chuckled. "You think that's a minor inconvenience?"

"Of course. She will feel my pull. I will convince her I am right. It only means I cannot mark her as mine the first time I claim her. But I will claim her before we leave Florence."

Marco watched his mate under hooded lids. When at last she turned and he could see her face, he whispered, "*Bellissima.*"

Marco watched as Griffin stole a look at the woman on whom Marco had focused his attention. "She truly is."

Marco growled.

Griffin chuckled. "Easy, Marco. I mean your mate no harm nor am I willing to tangle with you to try to wrest her away from you."

"You would lose in either event."

"How long have we been friends? Have either of us ever not honored the other one's claim to a woman?"

Marco shook his head and smiled ruefully. "You are, of course, right. Forgive me, Griffin. I fear my impatience in finding my mate and realizing I will have to wait to mark her as mine caused me to take my feelings out on you."

"Perfectly understandable. If I had a mate who looked like that and had yet to make her mine, I fear I would feel much the same."

"We will need to follow them when they leave so I know where to find her."

"Don't you think it would just be easier to walk over and introduce yourself? Or allow the hostess to tell them you paid for their meal?"

"Easier perhaps but I fear not as effective," said Marco. "Tomorrow I will find a way to introduce myself to her with less prying eyes."

They finished their dinner but Marco rarely took his eyes off the beautiful blonde on whom he'd set his sights.

Marco watched as the two women finished their meal and got ready to leave. There was a bit of consternation when they were told that like the complimentary bottle of wine and dessert, their mysterious benefactor had paid for their entire meal.

After realizing that the restaurant had no intention of giving her a bill, Marco's beautiful mate stood and wrapped the beautiful crimson cape more closely around her in order to ward off the chill of the night air. He chuckled when she turned her back to retrieve her packages. Marco made note of several of the shops that she had visited earlier that day.

"What do you find so amusing?" asked Griffin.

"Do you not see my mate's cloak? How appropriate that she dons that which makes her little red riding hood. After all, I as the big bad wolf, intend to gobble her up."

The two women walked past their table. Marco's eyes locked with those of his mate as she looked at him surreptitiously from beneath her hood. He growled softly and seductively and grinned when she shivered in response.

After she had left the restaurant, Marco looked over at Griffin. "Did you see? Even not knowing, she responded to my call."

Griffin nodded. "That she did, my friend. That she did."

CHAPTER SIX

The next morning, Catherine woke after a fitful night of tossing and turning. It seemed that now that she had seen the man from her dreams in the flesh, he was much more persistent in trying to engage her. Several times, the black wolf had howled. Each time, she had felt the sound penetrate her body and take up residence in the marrow of her bones.

Catherine was grateful when she heard Sera moving about and left her room to join her. Sera was heading to her only guest's door with a tray with espresso and a biscotti.

"You're awake."

"I didn't sleep well last night. It might take more than one cup of espresso to get my heart started."

Catherine reached for the cup and the biscotti.

"Chocolate?" she asked.

"Yes, for some reason yesterday when I was making biscotti I just got it in my head to make chocolate."

Catherine laughed. "You say that like it's a bad thing."

Sera grinned. "You're right. Chocolate is never a bad thing."

Catherine followed Sera out onto the main back patio where they sank down into comfortable chairs and enjoyed their biscotti and espresso. They talked of nothing consequential and Catherine followed Sera back into the house.

Sera began to prepare a light breakfast while Catherine grabbed a shower and got ready for the day.

As Catherine came out of her room, the front gate buzzed. Sera answered and then buzzed the person in.

"One of your students?" Catherine asked.

Sera smiled at her before opening the door to allow a delivery person with a huge bouquet of lovely ivory roses with lavender tips. The vessel containing them appeared to be old.

"Which of you is *Signorina* Livingston?" he asked.

"That would be me," Catherine said, coming forward and reaching out to touch the beautiful blooms.

"Compliments of your benefactor from last night. He bids you to remember that fairy tales can come true."

He handed Catherine the card and turned to leave.

"Excuse me?" said Catherine.

"Yes, *signorina?*"

"What kind of roses are these?"

He smiled. "They are sterling silver. We are the only floral shop in Florence that carries them."

"And the vase?" she said, running her hands down it to feel its texture.

"My boss thought that an odd choice as well. It is a piece of Etruscan pottery the gentleman had delivered to us along with his order and instructions."

"And who might this mysterious benefactor be?" she asked.

"We were sworn to secrecy," the delivery man said with a smile.

"Well, I don't accept anonymous gifts. Take them back."

"I'm sorry. I can't do that."

"Of course you can," argued Catherine.

"No, I'm sorry. I can't. Let us just say that I would far rather have you angry with me than your benefactor."

With that, the delivery man tipped his cap and left.

"Hmm," said Sera with a giggle, "it would seem you have an admirer… and one with good taste and a lot of money."

"I don't know about the roses, but if the pottery is real, I could pay my rent with what it's worth for several months. And what the hell did he mean by fairy tales can come true?"

"Who cares? Obviously some wealthy man is courting you in his own unique…"

"Weird," interjected Catherine.

"Unique," corrected Sera, giggling, "way."

"Pfft," Catherine snorted. "But they are beautiful. But what the hell do I do when I go home? How do I value that pottery? And will there be duty when I fly into the US?"

"I have no idea," admitted Sera.

"Well, let's leave them out here so we can both enjoy them. I'm going to head out."

"Where do your travels take you today?"

"I think first the Uffizi Gallery."

Sera nodded. "Good choice."

The two women shared breakfast sitting in the sun-filled kitchen before Catherine grabbed her bag and headed out.

• • • • • • •

The delivery man returned to his shop where Marco DeMedici awaited him.

"Well?" Marco inquired.

The delivery man smiled. "She seemed to like your choices."

"*Bene*," said Marco. "I am in your debt."

"No. We are happy to serve the alpha of the DeMedici. She is very beautiful. Do you plan to take the lady to your bed?"

"She is my mate," growled Marco and then realized the delivery man had meant no insult. He smiled to reassure the man and continued, "Although she doesn't know it yet. Again, my thanks."

Marco spent the rest of the morning visiting any of the restaurants, bistros, and espresso stands he thought she might frequent while during her stay in the City of Florence. He arranged that any and all charges from the beautiful blonde American, for he had learned her name and nationality, were to be charged to him. Marco revisited the stores she had gone to the day before and others of similar quality and arranged for the same thing. Knowing that she might refuse to take the items once she was not allowed to pay for them, he told each shopkeeper to simply charge them to him anyway and have them delivered to the B&B. If she refused delivery there, they were to be sent to his villa.

Griffin questioned him. "I get the dinner last night and the flowers this morning, but why everything else?"

"First, my Catherine—is that not a glorious name—will know that she need never concern herself with finances again. Second, she will know that her mate is a generous man and bent on spoiling her. Third, the less it costs her to stay, perhaps the longer she will extend her stay. And last, let her be intrigued as to how I managed all of this before we even met."

"Careful she doesn't feel manipulated and stalked. You do know the whole thing could blow up in your face."

Marco laughed. "What is love without a bit of fireworks?"

Marco and Griffin spent the remainder of the day at the vineyard outside the city that Luca had wanted them to see. Marco agreed with his omega's recommendation. Even if he hadn't, seeing how much Griffin was enjoying the land ensured Marco would purchase it.

"But I will only purchase it if you agree to stay on for a while and act as my general manager."

"Marco, all I know about the wine business is that you make really good, really expensive wine."

"That is what you have Luca for. Their vintner is a fool. Luca will need to find us someone better to serve under his direction, but until then I need someone here to watch over my interests. Will you do that for me?"

"Why, because you'll be too busy wooing your Catherine?" teased Griffin.

Marco laughed lustily. "No, my friend, because I will be enjoying my Catherine to the fullest extent. It's all I can do to keep a knot from forming when I think of her. I think of little besides bedding her."

Griffin shook his head. "God help that poor girl. She doesn't have a chance."

Marco nodded. "None whatsoever."

They drove back to Florence. The plan was for the sale of the property to be finalized. Luca would gather Griffin's things and join them before heading out to the newest DeMedici property and installing Griffin in the farmhouse to oversee things for a few months. Luca had said they had several workers who had indicated they would like a change of scenery.

•••••••

Catherine had had an interesting but infuriating day. Whoever her mysterious benefactor was, he seemed to have his tentacles throughout the City of Florence. Her money seemed to have no value to anyone.

On top of that when she arrived at the Uffizi Gallery, the director of the museum had come down from his office to offer her a personal guided tour. Catherine had declined and the director had seemed somewhat taken aback.

"I assure you, Ms. Livingston…"

"How do you know my name?" Catherine asked, quite sure she had not given it to anyone.

"One of our patrons asked that I extend to you every courtesy the museum has to offer…"

"I appreciate the offer. But I would just prefer to wander your beautiful establishment on my own… if that won't offend your patron."

"I'm sure it won't. He was most concerned that you have

whatever you need in order to enjoy your visit with us today."

"Let me guess," said Catherine, already knowing the answer. "Anything I want to purchase, I can have but I will not be allowed to pay for it."

"Of course not. Your entire experience here at the Uffizi Gallery has been paid for in full."

"And if I wanted to purchase another piece of Etruscan pottery?"

"We do not have any to sell here at the Uffizi, but I could most likely locate you a piece if you were interested."

Catherine shook her head. "No, the one he gifted me this morning is extravagant enough. Just how much would something like that set you back?"

"Without seeing the piece, it is difficult for me to say, but I can assure you that our patron would have no trouble affording it."

"And I don't suppose you'd be inclined to tell me just who your patron is?"

The director smiled. "He has asked to remain anonymous."

"Of course he has," Catherine said in a dismissive tone. Realizing it wasn't the director's fault and that he was not really the source of her irritation, she added, "I do thank you for your offer, but I will be far happier just to wander by myself."

"As you wish," he said, withdrawing from the foyer in which they had been standing.

Catherine shook her head, trying to shake loose her irritation at the way she was being manipulated. Who was this guy? And what did he want?

Catherine spent the day truly enjoying the museum. While she might find her benefactor a bit highhanded, he did seem to know what she would enjoy. Employees throughout the gallery were quick to answer a question and seemed to genuinely enjoy speaking to someone with Catherine's depth and breadth of knowledge.

As she left the Uffizi for Seraphina's, she had to admit it had been a lovely day. When she arrived back at the B&B, Sera buzzed her in and greeted her at the door.

"I don't know who this guy is, what he wants, or if you've figured anything out, but he's got style."

Catherine rolled her eyes. "Oh, good lord, now what?"

"Well, let's see, there's the case of DeMedici wine; there's the chocolate-covered strawberries; there's some pair of gorgeous earrings…"

"Silver filigree with a ruby in the center?"

"Yep… then there's… Wait, Catherine, what's wrong?"

"I've spent all day not being able to spend money. I saw those earrings yesterday and decided they were too expensive. Then I decided last night to go get them. So today I went back to the shop. The woman who owned it wrapped them up, but wouldn't give me a bill. So I left them. Who the hell is this guy?"

"I don't know but there's this really cool espresso maker that you should go try to buy…"

Catherine shook her head as she started to laugh. "That's not funny, Sera."

"But it is. Some guy wants to shower you with gifts and make your stay in Florence as incredible as he can…"

"Oh, my God, he got to you. Who is he?" Catherine said, stomping her foot and exasperated as she'd ever been in her life.

"I have no idea. Truly. But your bill was settled this morning with a note that if you extend your stay I just have to let the bank know."

"Oh, and at the Uffizi? I was offered a personal guided tour by the director of the damn museum…"

"Whoa. Money and clout."

"Yes, the director there referred to him as a patron. Okay, this guy wants to spend money on me? What's the most expensive restaurant in Florence?"

"I don't know if it's the most expensive, but it's way out of my price range and is considered to be one of the best restaurants in Florence. Enoteca Pinchiorri. But reservations are made way in advance… maybe your last night here?"

Catherine pulled out her cell phone and found the number. "Yes? Hi, this is Catherine Livingston. I'd like one of your best tables for my friend and me… say in an hour? [pause] You can accommodate us? That's so kind. We'll see you then. [pause] Would we like you to send a car for us? Even better." And Catherine gave him the address.

A vintage Rolls Royce pulled up about forty-five minutes later. Catherine and Sera went out and were ushered into the car.

"Do me a favor?" asked Sera.

"Sure."

"Stay forever? I could get used to this."

Catherine laughed. "Tomorrow let's go look at that espresso machine."

They spent an enjoyable evening and as promised the food had been sublime. The chef came out to greet them and the wait staff made sure they wanted for nothing. Both Sera and Catherine made sure to express their gratitude for the food and service before they left.

"That may be the best meal I've ever had anywhere in the world," said Catherine as they exited the restaurant.

Catherine found the next day that again her money was no good. It was maddening, frightening, and amusing all at the same time. The breadth of his reach was mind-boggling. Several times, she would feel something she could only describe as a rumble waft over and through her. The first few times, it was disconcerting to say the least. But the more often it happened, the more comforting she found it.

As Catherine returned to Sera's place, her arms laden down with food she planned to make for Sera, Catherine looked up to see Sera grinning at her and waving a small envelope.

"Look what came for you! And my new espresso machine arrived. Thanks for that. Give me some of these groceries and let's get them put away. You know you don't have to do this."

"Oh, I didn't pay for them. Seriously—got up to the grocer to pay and was told there was no need. Can't pay at a restaurant so if I want to express my gratitude I have to let whoever he is buy the groceries, but at least I can cook it. I can cook it, right? He didn't send some master chef over to do it for me, did he?"

Sera laughed. "Not yet. You'll have to talk to him about that."

"I'd like to talk to him about a lot of things. The main one being what does he expect from me in return?"

Sera tapped the envelope on the counter. "Well, maybe if you open this you'll get some answers."

Catherine crossed over and took the envelope. "Handmade paper. Very nice. And if I'm not mistaken this is pen and ink, not a ballpoint pen."

Catherine took a knife, carefully opened the letter, and removed the paper within. In beautiful handwriting that almost bordered on calligraphy, Catherine read:

Catherine,
I apologize that my work has kept me from your side. I hope I have been
able to provide you with a glimpse of all that our life together has to offer you.
Florence is only the beginning.
I will send a car for you this evening. The driver will bring you back to the
Uffizi where I have arranged for a private dinner.
Marco

Catherine handed the note to Sera.

"Marco? Like I know who the fuck Marco is? This country is littered with Marcos," she said, exaggerating the last word.

Sera laughed. "Catherine, honey, he's been described as

a patron and a benefactor and seems to have a ton of money. With those credentials, there is only one Marco. Don't look now, but I'd bet every dime I have that you're being courted by none other than Marco DeMedici."

"Well, he can bloody well court somebody else. I mean it's been fun and he can spend his money any way he wants, but I'm not going to be summoned to dinner."

Catherine turned away and started cooking dinner for her and Sera.

"Catherine, Marco DeMedici is one of the most eligible men in all of Italy, maybe even all of Europe, and it looks like he's set his cap on you."

"He can keep his cap to himself. I didn't ask for him to start paying my bills, and I don't need him to pay them. I'll send him a note politely declining his invitation and telling him if he'll send me the total of what he's spent I'll reimburse him for his trouble."

"Catherine, that dinner last night alone would pay your bill here for a week. But if you're going to do that, I'll return the espresso machine."

"Sera, there's no need. I made a really good living as a corporate raider, invested wisely, and inherited my grandfather's fortune. I can afford everything he's bought for me. I just don't usually splurge that way."

"But you saw him. Marco DeMedici is sex on a stick."

Catherine laughed. "Well, yeah. He is easy on the eyes, that's for sure."

"Easy on the eyes? Did you see him? Tall, dark, gorgeous. He could have any woman he wanted in Florence and he picked little ole you."

"Well, little ole me doesn't do casual sex or being ordered around."

"Ordered?" questioned Sera. "He sends you a beautiful handwritten note on handmade paper and invites you to a private dinner in the city's most prestigious gallery. You should at least go meet him and have dinner. If you're not interested, then tell him thanks but no thanks."

Catherine shook her head as she sautéed the onions and garlic. "As soon as I get this to simmering, I'll dash him off a note."

Once Catherine had her dinner in a good place to take a quick break, she grabbed a pen and wrote on the back of DeMedici's note:

Dear Mr. DeMedici,
While I greatly appreciate the generosity you have shown to me, I must say
that you have not spent your money wisely. I will not give you a good return
on your investment.
I will not be joining you for dinner. And if you will send me the total of
what has been spent so far, I will be happy to reimburse you.
I would ask that you cease and desist in your pursuit of me and allow me
to enjoy the remainder of my time in Florence.
C. Livingston

Sera shook her head. "Catherine, you're a fool. At least have dinner with the man. Who knows? He could be your soulmate... the love of your life."

Catherine laughed. "No. What he is, is an arrogant prick who thought he could impress me with his wealth and power. I walked away from being a corporate raider because I realized there was a lot more to life than wealth and power and wanted to go find my little piece of it for myself."

Catherine turned back to her cooking. She had just added the pasta to the sauce, when the buzzer at the front gate rang. Catherine tossed the pasta with the sauce, removed her pan from the heat, picked up her note, put it back in the envelope, drew a line through her name and wrote his name on it. She trotted out to the front gate and handed the driver the envelope.

The driver took the envelope and looked at her

questioningly. "You're not coming? But, Mr. DeMedici is waiting."

"And he can continue to wait. He didn't check with me to see if I was interested in having dinner with him or even if I was free, which I am not. I'm cooking dinner for my friend. The note explains it all, but do tell Mr. DeMedici that I appreciate his interest, but that he should refrain from contacting me in the future."

Catherine turned on her heel and walked away, leaving the hired driver to stand with his mouth open. Catherine stole a look over her shoulder. She had to bite her tongue to keep from laughing. The look on the driver's face clearly indicated he felt she was a fool and didn't know who Marco DeMedici was.

CHAPTER SEVEN

Marco paced the empty gallery. He had everything ready. He had indulged her and shown her he was a generous man. He had arranged a romantic private dinner in one of the most beautiful spots in all of Florence. Marco could barely contain his excitement as he heard the door open to the museum.

His shock and flash of anger were palpable when the driver walked in without his Catherine by his side.

"Where is she?" he demanded.

The driver quaked. "She is at the address you sent me to. She sent a note," he said, extending his hand.

Marco snatched the envelope and read Catherine's cold dismissal of all he had done. Marco swore. He saw the effect his anger was having on the poor driver.

"It is not your fault, my friend. My mate is merely continuing in her naughty behavior." He gestured to the table. "Please, my friend, enjoy yourself."

Marco left the museum. Return on his investment? Did she think he was trying to buy her affections? Marco walked through Florence thinking how his well thought out scheme could have gone so awry. He knew his mate was as spirited as she was intelligent and beautiful. He laughed at himself.

What a fool he had been.

Marco had done his homework once he knew his mate's name. Catherine Livingston had enough of her own money to buy anything she liked. What he had seen as trying to spoil her, she had seen as his trying to buy her. He would need to apologize to her for his mistake and ask that she forgive what he was sure she saw as his arrogance.

He marveled at what a long walk through the beautiful city streets could do to restore his good humor and give him perspective. When he had left the museum, his palm had itched to make contact with his Catherine's backside for defying him. Now he could see her perspective and that same hand wished only to caress and fondle that same lovely derriere.

Marco smiled as he recalled seeing her respond to his call. He had to remind himself that she wasn't a wolf and most likely did not understand what those feelings represented. He would have to be patient. He would bring his Catherine to heel and they would have a wonderful life.

Tomorrow he would go about setting things right with her.

· · · · · · ·

Catherine and Sera enjoyed what was mostly a lovely evening. Her pasta dish had turned out even better than she'd hoped. They had talked of their pasts, their current plans, and what their futures might hold. Sera had been none too subtle in pointing out that Catherine's could hold Marco DeMedici.

"Pfft," said Catherine, dismissing the idea. "He doesn't even know me. I'm quite sure if we met he'd change his mind pretty damn quick."

"He's an interesting man. There's the public side, which is well known. But he is just as well known for having a private side. I know that the people who work for him and live in the surrounding town have nothing but good things to say about him."

"Well, then they can have dinner with him. And he's not the only one with a public and private side."

Sera laughed. "Jesus, Catherine…"

She was interrupted by the front gate buzzer. Sera got up to answer and was told there was a delivery for *Signorina* Livingston. Sera turned to look at Catherine.

"Do what you want. I'm not getting up."

"Fine, Miss Stubborn, I'll go get it and bring it to you."

Sera ran out the door and collected the items from the delivery man. She came back in and walked over to Catherine with an enormous grin on her face.

"You do what you like with the notes. But you are not sending these handmade chocolate truffles back."

"You don't know that they're handmade."

"Oh, but I do, Godalpho's only makes handmade truffles that cost the earth and are worth every dime."

She offered Catherine one of the chocolates along with another handwritten note, presumably from Marco DeMedici. Catherine took the envelope and opened it. She read aloud the note enclosed:

Catherine,

I fear my actions, which I intended to delight you, have had the opposite

effect. It was never my intent to make you feel as any sort of investment.

I merely wished to provide you with a wonderful vacation here in
Florence without having to worry about money.

Please accept these chocolates as my way of acknowledging my error
and allow me the honor of buying you a meal or even a drink at your

convenience. I would appreciate the opportunity to allay any concerns

you may have and to offer my sincere apologies for any insult you may

have felt.

Marco

"Well, that just may be the nicest mea culpa note I've ever heard. But how does he expect you to let him know when it's convenient?"

"It won't be convenient," Catherine said to her. "And the address of his hotel is on the envelope. I will have a note delivered to him in the morning."

Sera rolled her eyes. "Catherine, what is the matter with you? The guy goes out of his way to basically give you a dream vacation. Then when you throw it back in his face, he apologizes and offers to buy you dinner... again."

"I don't see it that way. The note is calculated to manipulate and control the situation. His first salvo didn't work, so he's dropped back and means to come at me again. Thanks, but I'll pass."

"Good lord, you're stubborn."

Catherine grinned at her. "You say that like it's a bad thing. Enjoy the chocolates. I'm going to bed."

Catherine went into her room and once again used the back of the paper Marco had used to pen her response.

Dear Mr. DeMedici,

Thank you for your thoughtful note and the chocolates. Neither was

necessary. I will ask again that you send me the total for the expenditures

you have made on my behalf so that I may reimburse you for them.

You asked for a convenient time to meet. I fear there is no convenient

time as I have no intention of meeting with you. I have plans for my

trip, which do not include you. Please turn your attentions toward another. I'm sure she will be more appreciative.

C. Livingston

• • • • • • •

Catherine slept fitfully. Her dreams were interrupted repeatedly by Marco DeMedici and his wolf companion. Doggedly he pursued her in her dreams. She managed to wake herself each time before he reached her only to fall back asleep and find him in pursuit once more. Each and every time as he would close in on her she would hear and feel a low rumbling growl... not from the wolf but from the man.

The next morning she dropped the note off at the front desk of his hotel before heading out to the Bargello Museum. Once again her money was refused for a ticket but she left the cash with the ticket seller any way. She found herself wandering through one of the galleries when she was approached by the director.

"*Signorina* Livingston?"

Catherine turned, pasted a smile on her face, and forced herself to remember that the woman standing before her was not the person with whom she was annoyed. The jerk really didn't seem to be able to grasp the concept of no.

"Guilty as charged. May I help you?"

"There was no need for you..."

"I know," Catherine interrupted, "to pay for a ticket or anything else while I am here. Mr. DeMedici has paid for everything, including asking you to give me a guided tour. I will tell you what I told them at the Uffizi yesterday, I prefer to wander. If you choose not to accept the money I gave to the ticket taker then please give it to your favorite charity or to anyone you wish. Is there anything else?"

"No, *signorina*. Except to say that I have known Marco DeMedici for a long time and I can assure you that he is a man of honorable intentions."

Catherine smiled, this time genuinely. "Warned you that I might not be all that receptive?"

The woman smiled back. "He did mention that if you chose to wander on your own I was to abide by your wishes. Welcome to the Bargello Museum; enjoy your time here."

"Thank you. I will. And I do appreciate the offer of a guided tour by a woman with your reputation."

"It would have been my pleasure."

Catherine spent a good part of her day in the museum. While arguably not as famous as the Uffizi, it was second to none in the quality of its collections and the way they were displayed.

• • • • • • •

Marco saw the note slip under the door of his hotel room. He noted that once again, she had merely marked through her own name and written his own.

"Catherine," he muttered under his breath without looking at her note.

He glanced at his watch. Griffin had agreed to come back into the city this morning to meet him for breakfast and to attend the final meeting on the sale. Marco dressed and bypassed the ancient elevator in lieu of descending the grand staircase into the hotel lobby.

He entered the hotel's restaurant and saw that Griffin had already arrived.

"Griffin," Marco hailed as he joined him.

"Good morning, Marco."

"My friend, already you look more refreshed."

"I am," said Griffin with a smile. "Between the vineyard itself, the people already there and those from your vineyard that joined us, I have found a lovely respite. Best you take care or you may find me a permanent resident."

"Nothing would give me greater pleasure. Well, nothing except for my Catherine to cease her misbehaving."

Griffin laughed. "So you know her name?"

"Catherine Livingston. She is American. A former corporate shark who was in a devastating automobile accident a few years ago. When she had mended physically, she took herself out of the rat race to study art. She graduated just recently at the top of her class."

"And just how did you come by this information? I take it if your Catherine is still being naughty, she didn't tell you."

Marco withdrew the note and read it. He tossed it with irritation to Griffin. "She is being most vexing. I tried to see it from her point of view when she failed to join me for dinner at the Uffizi. You can see the apology I sent her, and still she refuses me."

Griffin laughed, causing Marco to scowl at him. "Oh, she more than refused you, Marco, she ever so politely told you to fuck off."

Marco growled and Griffin continued to laugh until Marco joined him.

Griffin leaned over and patted his friend's shoulder. "Look at it this way, at least you'll know she didn't agree to be your mate because of your wealth."

Marco grinned. "Yes, I suppose that is the best way to look at it. But she is still being most naughty. I followed her yesterday and each and every time I called to her she had a physical response."

"But she's human, Marco. She doesn't even know what the call of an alpha is or that you are her fated mate."

"I will teach her."

Griffin chuckled. "Oh, I'll just bet you will. And your beautiful mate will have either have a very sore backside or a soreness in her most feminine parts to show for the error of her ways."

Marco leveled a look at him. "Most likely both."

"Ah, but which do you desire more."

Marco chuckled. "Depends on which part of my anatomy you're talking to. My palm literally itches to be spanking her beautiful bottom. To have her face down over my knee and begging me to forgive her and stop her punishment. But this damn knot I'm suppressing is insistent on breaching her at the first opportune moment."

"Either way," said Griffin, sipping his coffee, "I believe your Catherine's days of being unmated are in short supply."

Marco laughed. "That they are, my friend. That they

are."

They finished their breakfast as Griffin brought Marco up to speed on the needs of his new property and some more detail regarding Luca's plans. Marco was glad to hear the excitement and peacefulness in Griffin's voice.

They left the hotel headed for the lawyer's office to finalize the paperwork and transfer the deed of sale. They were getting ready to head into the building when Catherine's scent reached him. Marco stopped to scan the crowd for her. He could feel Griffin watching. Once Marco located her, he pointed her out to his friend and then sent a small, focused alpha wave of energy in her direction along with a distinctive growl that only she would be able to hear.

The combination of the two seem to wash over her and caused her to have a visible, physical reaction. Marco watched as she shivered and then looked around. He smiled as her eyes locked with his for a moment before she tried to shake off the effects of his call to her.

"You will not find it so easy to continue to ignore my call, my Catherine."

Griffin chuckled. "I almost feel sorry for her. She hasn't a clue."

"No, but she will," Marco said as he smiled. "And sooner rather than later my Catherine will learn to heed my call or find herself getting her bottom spanked for failing to do so."

Marco and Griffin continued into the building. Marco was interested in concluding this business so that he could focus solely on Catherine.

• • • • • • •

There it was again. That feeling of energy that washed over her and yet seemed to penetrate every fiber of her being. This time she felt it coming from a specific direction. As she followed its path back, she looked up to find her eyes locked with those of none other than Marco DeMedici himself.

Damn the man. What power was it that he had that he haunted her dreams and now seemed to be able to find her across a crowded square in the middle of the bustling City of Florence?

She watched him and the companion who had been with him the other night enter the building. She could feel the loss of his presence. She had to admit, if only to herself, that the man most definitely had a power over her. Several times she had felt that wave of energy yesterday. She now realized he must have been near, watching her. That was altogether too creepy for words.

Catherine turned to walk away and then checked herself. She decided to have a little change in plans. She would go amuse herself walking through some of the open markets and then see if she couldn't confront the man in person at his hotel. Maybe if she told him off to his face in front of others he would finally get the message. Perhaps being dressed down by a woman in public would convince him she had no interest in him.

Several frustrating hours later she headed toward the grand hotel in which DeMedici was staying. Even the open market vendors wouldn't take her money. Over and over again she heard there was no need as DeMedici had provided for her.

As she entered the hotel, she noticed the architecture and artwork that she'd missed this morning when she dropped off her note. It was superb and at another time, she would have liked to spend some time here to study it. But for now, she wanted to accomplish her goal and leave as quickly as promised. The concierge came from behind his desk.

Catherine put up her hand to ward him off. "Please don't. I've heard it all morning. Mr. DeMedici has arranged for, Mr. DeMedici has paid for, Mr. DeMedici has provided for… I'm sick to death of it. Do you have any idea when the great Mr. DeMedici might deign to honor us with his presence? He and I need to talk and he needs to get it through his thick skull that I'm done with his shit."

The words were no sooner out of her mouth than she felt that all too familiar wave of energy wash over her from behind. She felt the goosebumps raise on her arms and a warmth spreading through her being.

She looked at the concierge.

"He's standing right behind me, isn't he?" she whispered.

"Well," said the kind older gentleman, "not *right* behind you."

"You wish to speak to me, Catherine?" came the low grumbling voice from behind.

Catherine whirled around. "Not really; thus the reason I've sent you two notes asking you not to contact me again. But apparently you're having a problem comprehending that. So despite what I would prefer to be doing, I'm wasting my time here having to tell you what should already be obvious."

Marco grasped her gently by the upper arm; when she tried to pull away, he tightened his grip.

"This is not the place for us to talk. Why don't we go upstairs to my room and we can discuss the misunderstanding that still seems to separate us."

Catherine lost what little remaining grip she had on her temper. She stomped on his instep, causing him to momentarily ease his grip. She jerked her arm away. Before Marco could make another grab for her, she stepped forward and into his space.

"Listen to me, you arrogant prick. I have no interest in you, your money, or anything else you think will get you whatever it is you think you want. Leave me the fuck alone. I don't give a good God damn that you're Marco fucking DeMedici. To me you're just some piece of shit asshole who can't take no for an answer. There is no fucking misunderstanding between us. I understand you perfectly. It's you who is too fucking stupid to get it through your thick head that I have no interest in you. Do we understand each other now, motherfucker?"

Catherine found she was out of breath, but feeling quite proud of herself. DeMedici just looked at her.

"Are you quite finished, my Catherine?" His voice was cool, calm, and betrayed no sense of anger whatsoever.

"I am not your fucking Catherine nor will I ever be!"

"Have you said what you needed to say?" he asked in a quiet, concerned tone.

"Yes," she said. "Yes, I have."

"Good." He moved in close, holding her close with the vise grip he now had around her arm. He leaned in to whisper so only she could hear, "That was an uncalled for display of temper. You will learn to control your temper in front of others, or I will control it for you. The language you displayed was far beneath that of a woman with an MBA from Harvard who just recently graduated at the top of her class from Cooper and will soon be the mistress of the DeMedici pack and mother to my children."

A part of Catherine's mind was screaming for her to get away… to break free from Marco. The other part of her brain and everything in her physical being screamed at her to yield to him… to surrender herself to his dominance. She was broken from her quiet reflection and focused on his words when she felt his hand run down her back and slide over her rump, stopping at the lower curve of the swell of her buttock to squeeze it gently.

Marco continued, "If you ever use that kind of language with me again in public or in private, I will wash your mouth out with soap before putting you over my knee and spanking your very beautiful bottom."

He kissed her cheek gently. Catherine felt frozen in time and space.

"I'm going to take you upstairs. Should you decide to reflect on your belligerent and unacceptable behavior and apologize to me when we reach our room, I will take you to bed where I will pummel your pussy with my hard cock as

I have longed to do since I first caught your scent at the restaurant. I would have wooed and seduced you into my bed and made gentle, sweet love to you the first several times. However, as you have shown a need for my dominance, I will provide you with the strength and passion you need. Should you continue in your naughtiness once we are alone, then you will receive the first of what I believe will be many bare bottom spankings before I fuck you long and hard into the night."

She pulled back from him but could only get so far. "You are fucking crazy," she whispered, hoping she sounded more frightened than what she really was... aroused.

Her whole body felt alight with his fire. She could feel his energy crackling over her flesh, raising the fine hair along her arms. A warm sensation settled over her and seemed to seep through the pores of her skin and permeate into the very marrow of her bones.

Confused and unsure of how to extricate herself from the situation and before Marco could anticipate her next move, Catherine balled her fist, pulled it back, and let fly. It connected with his nose in a most satisfying manner. She could hear it crack. Instead of letting her go or retaliating with a blow of his own, DeMedici pulled her closer into his body and bent his head to take possession of her mouth. Catherine would always recall it that way—that he took possession of her mouth, not that he kissed her.

His lips came down on hers and his tongue thrust past her teeth as he pulled her resistant body into his. While strong and passionate, the kiss was also soft and beckoning. He stroked her mouth with his tongue as his one hand continued to fondle her ass.

Catherine could hear and feel what she could only describe was a low grumbling noise that was part growl and part purr. It enveloped her as if a fog had settled around them. She pushed against Marco's chest despite his continued sensual assault on her mouth. He released his hold of her arm so that he could wrap it around her upper body. The other hand continued to hold her close, pulling the lower half of her body into his. There was no mistaking the hard length she could feel pressing up against her.

Catherine could feel her control of her own response slipping away. She couldn't understand why someone didn't do something to help her. And then she realized her body had betrayed her completely and was molding itself to fit his large, hard frame.

Marco lifted his head briefly to gaze into her eyes and smile.

"No," she whispered softly.

"Yes," he growled before capturing her mouth once again.

This time she offered him no resistance whatsoever and gave herself over completely to him. He growled in pleasured response. Catherine rubbed herself like an alley cat in heat against him. She couldn't understand why he kept just standing there kissing her and holding her close instead of taking her up to his room to get naked. She shocked herself with that thought. She knew that in this moment she wanted nothing more than to get naked with this man she had just cussed out and who had just threatened to spank her and feel him repeatedly thrust that hard length into what she knew would be her drenched pussy.

The thought had no sooner actually formed in her mind, than she felt Marco's strong arms swing her up into his arms, cradling her against his chest. He walked toward the grand staircase and took the steps two at a time until he came to the mezzanine level… the most exclusive part of the hotel.

He expertly manipulated the keycard into the lock without ever putting her down or releasing her. She reached down to open the levered door and he smiled. Once inside the room, he leaned back against the door, shutting it firmly.

CHAPTER EIGHT

He placed her gently on her feet and let go, keeping an eye on the state of her fists. That crack to his nose had hurt. His Catherine was a spitfire of the first order. That would not be an insurmountable problem, however. In fact, mounting her on a regular basis would help give her passion a more acceptable focus. Marco smiled, thinking that he was more than capable and looked forward to mounting her frequently.

"Now, my Catherine, do you have something you wish to say to me?"

Catherine shook her head, trying to get it to clear. "Yes, I want you to move so that I can leave."

Marco laughed. "That, my beautiful mate, I will not do. Let us try again. Would you like to apologize to me for your unseemly behavior downstairs or would you like to do so once I have put you over my knee and spanked your bottom to an intense shade of red?"

"Are you fucking kidding me?" she started.

Marco grabbed her by the arm and began to march her toward the bath. He could feel her trying to fight him and reached down and swatted her backside, causing her to yelp but to move in the direction he wanted.

Once they reached the vanity, he tangled a great deal of the hair at the nape of her neck in his fist and pressed her against the vanity with his body. With the other hand, he turned on the water, wetting his hand before lathering it with soap.

"I warned you that should you continue to curse at me that I would wash your mouth out with soap. You will learn, my Catherine, that I do not make idle threats. Now, open your mouth."

He could see her preparing to make what he was sure would be a scathing retort but as she opened her mouth to do so, he inserted his hand, wedging it into her mouth. He had done so in such a way that she could not close her jaws and bite him. He ensured that she got a good taste of the soap so that she would think twice before using such language with him again. When he removed his hand, she coughed and sputtered.

She opened her mouth to swear at him again and Marco switched hands so that the soaped hand now had hold of her hair. The other he used to strip her leggings and panties down to her mid-thigh and delivered several hard smacks to her buttocks.

"Ouch," she screeched. "That hurts, you…"

"Catherine, do I need to add more soap to your mouth?"

She closed her mouth and wisely said nothing. Marco led her back into the sitting room portion of his suite. He sat down on the settee, pulling her into his lap.

"Now, my Catherine, do you have an apology you would like to offer me for your behavior?"

Marco watched her take a deep breath and exhale it slowly. "No. I want you to turn me loose, let me go and never, ever come near me again."

Again, Marco laughed at her show of bravado for that's what he knew it to be. He could smell her arousal and could see the tell-tale signs of it as well. Her thin shirt did little to hide the hardened pebbles of her nipples and as she sat on his thigh he could feel the evidence of her pussy's readiness leaking out to drip onto him.

"In the years to come, my sweet mate, I want you to recall that it was your stubborn pride that led to you getting spanked prior to my bedding you for the first time."

Marco reached between her legs and removed her leggings and panties. She now sat half naked on his lap. He couldn't resist the urge to slip his hand between her legs to caress the hardened nub that was distended and in need of his attention. She tried to close her legs to him and he quickly and accurately swatted her soaked pussy with a satisfying smack.

"You do not ever close your legs to me. Where I choose to put my hands, lips, and cock is where you will have them. Should you be in need of them in between those times I am actively pleasuring you, you may ask. I assure you my answer will almost always be yes. Open your legs, my Catherine."

She clenched them tighter until he growled. Her pussy gushed in response. She sighed quietly, quit resisting him, and relaxed her thighs. She moaned in helpless abandon as he began to explore her outer lips before plunging his fingers into her pussy.

"There's my good mate. See how much better it is when you yield to me so I can see to our mutual need?"

"Marco, please?" she said.

He chuckled and rumbled a low growl at her. He smiled as she shivered in response. He continued to fondle her and kindle the desire he knew was there. He brought his saturated fingers up in front of both of their faces before rubbing them together so that she could see the evidence of her need before licking them clean.

"Stand up," he commanded.

She complied and he stood with her. His massive 6'5" frame dwarfed her even at 5'10". He stripped her of her blouse and unfastened her bra. He stepped back from her.

"Take your bra off, my Catherine, and show me your glorious tits."

She hesitated for only a moment as she removed the

garment and let it drop to the floor. He smiled to reassure her. She was truly magnificent. He lifted a heavy breast in each of his hands, thumbing the hardened nipples as he did so.

"You will suckle our sons and daughters and provide me with great pleasure, my beautiful mate. How I wish you had chosen to mitigate your display of ill-temper downstairs with an apology. You are mine, my Catherine. We belong to each other alone. I will lay claim to you this night, but first I will punish you for your misbehavior."

"What… what do you mean?"

Marco laughed. "You heard what I told you downstairs. I am going to put you face down over my knee and spank your pretty bottom until it is red, swollen, and tender to the touch. Then you will be made to stand in the corner like the naughty little girl you have shown yourself to be. When you have apologized to me and I am convinced you have considered your behavior and found it to be unworthy of you, I will finish with you in the corner. I mean to ride you long and hard and will hear you call my name repeatedly as I bring you to climax several times before seeding your sweet cunt."

"You can't be serious. First, if we're going to have sex, and I'll admit that I'd rather like to have sex with you, it won't be unprotected and it won't be with me standing in the corner with my legs up around your waist. And it sure as hell won't be after you've spanked me."

"You are right in one aspect only, it won't be with your legs around my waist. When an alpha has to punish his mate, he finishes her as she stands with her nose in the corner. He mounts her from behind to reinforce who the dominant partner is. And while there will be great pleasure in it for you, the discomfort you feel every time the cradle of my hips makes contact with your swollen bottom as I am plunging in and out of you will serve as both reminder and reinforcement as to why you do not wish to find yourself on the receiving end of a discipline spanking."

"Marco, no…"

"Catherine, yes. That it is unprotected is of no great consequence. We are mates and will be for life. Should you wish to wait some time before bearing our first child, I am agreeable to that. We can speak with the doctor in Milan to find a form of contraception that you wish to use, but I will never wear any kind of barrier when availing myself of you. Are we clear, my Catherine?"

He saw her blink several times before she whispered, "Don't spank me. If you do, I swear I will never forgive you."

"As you are being spanked in response to your own naughty behavior, I am not the one in need of forgiveness. I assure you, my Catherine, that once I have seen to your punishment and have pleasured us both to restore positive feelings and balance to our relationship, I will forgive you. Now, come, mate, it's time you paid the piper for what you have done. And I am the man who will call the tune."

He rubbed her nipples one last time and dropped his head to give both a lingering kiss and suckle, which caused her to arch her back as she moaned. Marco chuckled as he led her back to the settee. He sat down, drawing her between his thighs. He watched as her downcast eyes spied the hard length of his cock straining against his trousers.

"Come, Catherine, place yourself over my thigh so that I know you accept that you misbehaved and that you deserve the punishment you are about to receive."

"Marco, no one has ever spanked me before."

"I suspected as much. You have nothing to fear, my Catherine, it will hurt but you will be fine. No misbehaving mate ever died from a spanking. Your bottom will be sore, but I plan to love you long enough, hard enough, and as many times as it takes for you to be more focused on how sore I made your sweet pussy than on the fire I intend to light on your backside."

"Please, Marco. I'm sorry."

"The time to apologize to avoid your spanking has long

past, sweetheart, but I'm happy to hear that you are acknowledging you were naughty. Now, place yourself over my knee and let's get this over and done with."

Marco saw her stiffen her resolve. His Catherine was no shrinking violet easily cowed by the idea of getting her bottom blistered.

Before she could say something else that would make him have to harshen the spanking she was due, he preempted whatever it was she planned to say. "Catherine, behave yourself. If you go back to fighting with me, you will only make the spanking worse. Is that what you want?"

He saw her soften before she whispered, "I don't want to be spanked."

"Good, then next time you think to disobey me or misbehave, you think of that and modify your behavior before you earn yourself one. I'm asking you for the last time to be a good girl and put yourself in position. I promise it will go better for you if you do."

He waited and watched her fight with herself. He felt that human males had done their counterparts no favor when many of them had abdicated their leadership in their relationships. He understood why—most were lazy and did not want to carry the burden of leadership. There were still some who used the tried and true method of holding their mate accountable just as there were wolves who had abdicated true leadership and used their societal norm for their own pleasure.

He patted his thigh and gently tugged her hand to encourage her compliance. With a stifled sob, she gave herself over to his care. He knew that not fighting the spanking was far beyond her. Truth to tell he had never been one to expect a female to simply lie there and take her spanking with no reaction. He closed his other leg so that it was snug up against the back of her thighs and placed his left hand on her upper back.

He rubbed her quivering bottom as he asked, "Were you naughty, my Catherine?"

She said nothing and his hand came down hard on her upturned bottom, making her screech. He only swatted her once. She hadn't lied to him. Her reaction to his first swat indicated that she had never been spanked.

"When I ask you a question, sweetheart, I expect you to answer me with yes, sir or no, sir. Do you understand me?"

He allowed her a moment.

"Yes, sir."

"Good girl," he crooned. "Now were you naughty, my Catherine?"

"Yes, sir," she said. He could hear she was trying to hold back her tears.

Marco understood that her tears were from her apprehension of the unknown. She would learn that there was nothing for her to fear from him, but would also learn to respect and yield to his authority.

"And do you accept that it is within my responsibilities to you as your mate that I punish you for that behavior?"

"Yes, sir," she said, losing the battle with her tears.

"Very well. Then let us dispense with your need for a spanking."

Marco brought his hand up and brought it down with a sharp staccato swat to the cheek he had failed to target with his first swat.

"Marco, please, don't do this to me."

"No, Catherine. I will not fail in my duty to you."

He began to spank her with hard, sharp swats targeting each of her cheeks precisely. He covered her entire bottom with handprints, causing her to squirm and try to kick her legs. He knew this to be part of the process. She needed to be spanked through her resistance until she had acquiesced to his authority and asked for him to forgive her bad behavior.

While Marco had no mate of his own, he had chastised more than one female member of his pack for misbehaving. Part of his responsibility as alpha was to keep his people, especially the women and children, safe and secure. Often times the women needed a reminder that their role was to yield to their male counterparts and that not doing so had consequences that made sitting uncomfortable.

Again and again he swatted her ass. For the most part he concentrated on the fullest bloom of her cheeks, turning them a dark red. Once or twice, he directed his hand to her delicate sit spots, which made her yowl in protest. Her bottom became heated to the touch and he knew that it would be red and begin to swell before long.

The longer and harder he spanked her, the harder his cock became. He had to stifle his chuckle as it was difficult for him to believe it could get harder than it had been when he brought her to their room. Marco knew if he chuckled, it would hurt Catherine's feelings and undermine her surrender to him. He could also scent that her own arousal was increasing and knew that when he went to mount her, he would find her more than ready.

Marco continued to punish her backside until finally, she slumped over his thigh and began to cry in earnest.

"I'm sorry I was such a bitch, Marco. I'm sorry I cussed you out. Please be done. Please?"

Marco stopped mid-swing. "Have you had enough?"

"Yes, sir," she sobbed.

"Do you understand that when you misbehave I am going to spank you?"

"Yes, sir. Please be done."

"As this is your first spanking, I will let this suffice although I am not sure I left enough sting in your pretty tail for it to have done as much good as it should."

"No, you have. I will never sit down again," she cried.

This time he did chuckle. He let her up and brought her onto his lap. She winced as her bottom made contact with him. "There, there, my sweet, you will be fine. And see how your body reacts to my dominance of you?"

He reached up to play with her nipples before sliding his hand back between her legs. When she started to clench them together, he growled.

"Do I need to spank that pussy before sending you to the corner?"

She quickly opened her thighs. "No, Marco," she said as she guided his hand between them once more.

He dipped his fingers into her soaked pussy and brought her natural lubricant back up to rub onto her engorged clit. He rubbed that sensitive bundle of nerves with her own fragrant viscosity, making her moan with desire.

"There will come a time, my Catherine, that I feast on the honey you keep between your legs, but not this night. This night I will claim you repeatedly with my cock sheathed in your pussy. Now you get up and go stand with your nose in the corner."

"Marco, please. Can't we just go to bed?"

"No, Catherine. You will do as you are told or I will put you back over my knee. Do you yield? Or do I put more sting in that sore bottom?"

He watched her scan his face to see if he would back down. He could tell that she recognized he would not.

"No, sir. I'll go stand in the corner."

"Good girl. You stand facing the corner with your hands on the wall and push your bottom out."

"Why?"

He chuckled. "Mainly because I told you to."

"Yes, sir," she said with resignation lacing her voice.

"But also, because it puts your pretty red bottom and your very wet pussy on display for me to admire."

He watched her blush profusely. "No woman may have died from a spanking, but did one ever die from humiliation?"

"No, my Catherine. And you will not be a first. Now go stand in the corner."

She got up and went to the corner. Marco followed her. Once she was standing as she'd been told, he ran his hand down her back and lightly fondled her punished backside.

"Good girl. I'm very proud of you. You stand here until I tell you otherwise."

CHAPTER NINE

Catherine couldn't believe she was standing as she'd been ordered. And the tone of Marco's voice left no doubt that she had been ordered. But there were worse things, she told herself. Worse was almost preening when he had praised her. Worse was how much her ass hurt. Worse was how incredibly turned on she was. But worst of all was that she was quite certain he knew all of it.

"Such a beautiful ass you have, my Catherine. And it has such a lovely feel to it—firm and smooth yet enough give and bounce when it is spanked that your mate can tell you feel it. And you felt it, didn't you?"

"Yes…" she said a bit sullenly.

"Yes, what?" he queried her as a reminder.

"Yes, sir."

"Good girl," he said again in his low rumbling voice.

Catherine could feel her nipples contracting even more tightly and danced lightly on her feet. She hoped partly that shuffling back and forth might reduce some of the sting and partly because she had to do something to try to alleviate the growing need she had to feel him do as he'd promised—mount her from behind and take her long and hard. She had no doubt that he was quite capable of making good on that promise as well.

She heard Marco chuckle. Catherine was quite sure he knew the state she was in… both in terms of pain in her ass and the fire that was spreading throughout her body. She heard him growl and once again felt the sound as well as heard it. It caused her to shudder in response. She heard him chuckle again. He knew what that sound did to her.

"You do that deliberately," she accused as she whirled around to face him.

"Catherine, you turn back around and put yourself in position. This is the only time I will remind you without there being consequences."

The easy charm and lust had been replaced by command. This was a man used to issuing orders and having them followed with no questions asked. Well, he'd have to get used to plenty of questions and a lot of not having his orders followed. What was she thinking? She wasn't going to be with him. This was a one-night stand… two at most. But he had talked as though he planned to be with her.

She flashed back on what he'd said—suckling his sons and daughters? And when had his calling her his mate begun to sound normal? On second thought, this was a 'just as soon as he fucks me and falls asleep' stand. She meant to get out of this hotel and out of Florence. She didn't think he'd much care for his plans being thwarted and did not wish to bring any trouble to Sera's front door.

She wondered why he couldn't just come over here and fuck her. She'd begun to ache. Her pussy seemed to be throbbing in time with her heart. She desperately needed him to take that hard length she'd felt and use it to ease her need.

"Marco?"

"Yes, my Catherine?"

"I thought you were going to forgive me."

"Have you apologized and asked for my forgiveness?"

"I apologized," she whined and hated the sound of her own voice.

"You told me you were sorry. You were only sorry that you were about to get your bottom spanked. Would you care to apologize and ask to be forgiven?"

She jumped as his finger ran down the side of her neck. How had he joined her so quickly and so quietly?

"Marco, please. I'm sorry. I did apologize for being a bitch…"

She yelped as his hand connected once again with her very sore backside.

"Listen to me, my naughty mate, you do not use curse words of any kind and you do not refer to yourself in any derogatory manner. You are my beautiful Catherine. You are exquisite beyond measure and I will not have anyone denigrate you in any way… including you. Have I made myself clear?"

"Yes, sir."

"Try again."

She stomped her foot, which made him chuckle.

"I'm sorry for whatever you need me to be sorry for so you'll quit fu… messing around," she corrected herself, which also made him chuckle. "This isn't easy for me," she said as she started to lose control of her emotions and tears began to threaten to fall from her eyes again.

She felt him nuzzle her neck as he wrapped his arm around her and stroked her side.

"Shhh," he crooned. "I know, but you have to learn to behave. I have no wish to punish you, but I will when you are in need of correction. Now, try again."

"I really don't know what you want me to say."

"I want you to apologize for refusing to allow me to apologize for insulting you…"

She waited and then realized he expected her to repeat what he said.

She took a deep breath. "I'm sorry for not allowing you to apologize to me."

"And for using foul language."

"And for using foul language," she repeated.

"But mostly for failing to heed my call as your mate."

"What do you mean by that?" she asked, confused. "I mean I can say it, but I don't understand."

Marco growled low and she felt her whole body respond with a shiver of pure desire.

"My call, my Catherine. That fire you feel running across your skin and seeping into the marrow of your bones. You are my fated mate. I have been waiting for you… as I believe you have for me. Haven't you?"

Catherine felt panicked. How did he know? Did he know about her dreams? What did he mean by fated mate?

"Catherine, you will apologize for not heeding my call."

"All right, Marco. I'm sorry. I didn't know that's what it was."

"But you felt wildly attracted to me and I have haunted your dreams, have I not? As you have haunted mine?"

"Yes," she whispered.

"Yes, what?" he gently chided.

"Yes, sir. I have seen you in my dreams for years so when I saw you at the restaurant, it was unsettling."

"But I am here now, my Catherine. You are my fated mate. Now finish your apology."

"I'm sorry I didn't heed your call."

"Such a beautiful mate. Shall I forgive you and take care of that fire between your legs?"

"Please, Marco. But seriously, I haven't been seeing anyone and so haven't been on the pill."

"And this would be a problem because?"

"Because I could get pregnant."

"And that would be a problem because?" he chuckled, nuzzling her neck and running his hands up the front of her body to gently grasp her breasts, flicking his thumbs over her nipples.

"Shit. Can't you just use a condom until I can get protection?"

"No, my Catherine, if my seed strikes fertile ground, your belly will swell with the glory of our lovemaking."

She couldn't repress her shiver. He made it all sound so easy… so normal… so right.

He moved directly behind her, maneuvered her lower body, and spread her legs apart so that he could mount her. She heard him unzip his fly and felt the hard head of his cock begin to probe between her legs, seeking the entrance to her core.

She felt him grasp her hips and hold her steady as he lined up his cock with her pussy and then thrust home. She was surprised with her climactic response to his possession. One of his hands continued to hold her steady as he began to pump in and out of her. The other he wrapped around her waist to support her as her knees began to buckle.

"Oh, my God, Marco," she said, trying to catch her breath.

"My glorious mate; how sweetly you respond to me."

His rhythmic thrusting was strong and steady. Catherine felt her pussy contracting around him as she enthusiastically made his cock welcome within her warm sheath. She thought she'd never heard a sweeter sound than when Marco groaned and then growled in pure pleasure. Catherine used one hand to lean heavily against the wall. With the other she brought his hand up to her breasts.

He chuckled as he began to rub her nipple between his thumb and finger, causing her to gasp again. He moved his hand so that now his arm stretched across her torso and caught her other nipple between his fingers as he pinched and pulled her. His other hand quit grasping her hip but slid across the lower half of her body to trap her more fully and to allow her even less movement as he pummeled her pussy with his cock.

"Brace yourself, my Catherine, I mean to finish hard in you."

She did as he ordered and felt herself open even further to him. He rammed her with his cock over and over. She felt her pussy start to contract in orgasmic spasms. But more than that, she could feel Marco reach his own finish and begin to pump her full of his seed. For the first time in her life, she understood what it was like to be taken by a man, what it felt to be used for her intended purpose, and more than that, what it felt like to be loved.

Loved? Where had that thought come from? He'd said nothing of love. But he growled low and long in her ear as he continued to pump his cum deep into her core. She felt the warmth of his feeling embrace her completely.

Finally, she felt him finish filling her. He snugged up against her bottom, making her wince. He pressed himself even more tightly against her. She had lost herself to his passion while he was fucking her, but now was reminded this same man had spanked her to tears before he'd taken her without any protection whatsoever. She knew instinctively that he was pressing against her to seal the entrance to her womb, trapping all of his essence within her. Even though it hurt, she settled her ass back against him within the cradle of his pelvis.

Marco continued to nuzzle her and make low growling noises, which only increased her sense of well-being. Why had no man ever thought to growl at her before now? Why had she never known what it was like to be possessed so completely and when she wanted it so badly? She found herself weeping silently.

"It's all right, my Catherine. I'm here. I have you now."

He withdrew from her with a loud groan, and her legs started to give way. She quickly found herself swept up into his arms and taken to the bed. He set her on her feet but held her steady as he turned back the covers. Once again he lifted her in his strong arms and cradled her against his chest before kissing her deeply on the mouth and then gently on each eye. He laid her down on her side ensuring she was comfortable and then tucked her in.

As he went to leave her side, she reached for him. "Marco?" she said quietly.

He smiled down at her and sat on the edge of the bed. He stroked her hair and leaned down to kiss her again.

"Do not fear, my Catherine. I will not leave you. I am just going to get undressed and arrange for dinner to be brought up to us in a few hours. Then I will join you in our bed and we will sleep and let your body recover."

He ran his hand down her back and gently across her punished ass. She smiled. The caress was at once possessive, soothing, and a reminder of his dominance.

She watched him as he stood and began to remove his clothes. There was a grace and elegance to his movements that transcended his wealth and power. He was primitive and wild. He would expect and demand nothing less than her best. She knew he would support her in all ways and yet he would demand her surrender to his will.

He walked around the end of the bed, turning back the covers as he did so before joining her. She felt the mattress give with his weight and then felt his arm snake out around her middle and draw her to him. He kissed the back of her neck.

"Rest, my Catherine. I will use you hard and well this night."

She shivered in response to him but snuggled more closely into his body as she shut her eyes and slept. Her dreams no longer contained the man who held her close, but the black wolf remained.

CHAPTER TEN

Catherine woke rested but a bit disoriented. Then it all came flooding back to her—being carried up the stairs of a grand hotel ala Scarlett O'Hara, having her mouth washed out with soap, getting spanked, being made to stand in the corner, and then being fucked there, all by a man she hadn't even known existed a week ago.

Marco sensed her sudden restlessness and pulled her closer, offering her comfort even in his sleep. Once he'd settled down, Catherine extricated herself from both his embrace and their bed. Quickly and quietly she picked up her clothes and began to slip on her top and leggings. Sandals, bra, and panties could be added later after she got out of this room. And she knew she had to get out of this room and escape the web of seduction Marco was weaving.

She had flipped the deadbolt and was just reaching for the door when someone from the other side knocked, calling "Room service." Catherine jumped back from the door and whirled around to see Marco had come fully awake. He looked pointedly at the bed and at Catherine. He said nothing but pointed to the corner.

"No," she whispered.

"Yes, Catherine, or I will strip you first before I let the

boy in with our meal."

Catherine looked at the door and calculated her chances. If she could get to the door, perhaps the confusion of the room service person would give her time to get into the hall. Surely Marco wouldn't chase her down in public.

"You'll never make it and even if you did, I'd have no trouble catching you before you reached the stairs," he said as if he could read her mind.

He got out of bed, crossed the room to her, and took hold of her arm. He cracked the door open and said, "Just leave it, I'll bring it in the room in a moment."

"Certainly, Mr. DeMedici," the staff person said with appreciation as Marco slipped him a tip.

Marco closed the door and looked Catherine in the eye. "Naked. Corner. Now. Do not make me regret my largess in not allowing the boy to see your lovely backside as you stand in the corner."

The low rumbling growl overtook her. She was becoming used to the sensation and could now distinguish between when the sound was angry, lustful, or just generally pleased. She shook her head.

"No, I won't. I can't explain what happened earlier, but I'm not up for a rematch."

He surprised her by chuckling. "What happened earlier, my Catherine, was that you sought to deny and defy me and ended up with a backside full of my red handprints and a pussy full of my cum. The same thing that is going to happen to you once you have stood in the corner and we have something to eat."

"I'm not going to stand in the corner."

Marco said nothing but somehow managed to strip her clothes off her without any problem. He turned her toward the corner and marched her into it, accentuating each step with a hard swat to her still sore bottom.

"Now you stand there until I tell you different."

She whirled around, her own anger flaring. "I won't."

Marco turned her to face the corner again before

delivering several well-placed and hard swats to her sit spots, causing her to yowl in pain.

"You will."

He let go of her but watched her for a moment. Catherine knew he meant to ensure she stayed put this time.

She heard him walk to the door and wheel the heavily laden trolley in. The smells coming from the food it contained made her stomach grumble.

"It seems my mate is hungry. I had planned for us to enjoy each other's company while we dined. But I find myself wondering how best to use the food to reinforce the lesson it would appear still needs to be learned. Care to share your thoughts with me, my Catherine?"

"Quit calling me that. I'm not your Catherine."

"But you are. And what's more is that you know you are. As you once again seek to deny that, I fear we will need to repeat the entirety of the first lesson and add to it."

Catherine turned around. "Look, I really don't know who you think you are or why someone hasn't come to check on me after that little stunt downstairs, but I've had enough. I'm leaving."

With as much dignity as she could summon, Catherine boldly walked out of the corner. Marco caught her by the arm then wrapped it around her waist, bending her slightly before he landed a flurry of hard, well-aimed swats to her still very sore and now swollen buttocks.

"Ouch! God! Marco! Stop it! I'll scream!"

"Go ahead," he said in an amused tone. "I'm sure many a naughty mate before you has and many who come after you will. The walls are thick and the soundproofing insulation excellent. No one will hear you."

He let her up and forced her to look at him. His smile was predatory and intimidating. He finished turning her back to the corner, pushed her gently and landed another stinging slap to her bruised derriere.

Catherine found herself going to the corner and standing quietly. She wondered how this had happened and why it felt perfectly normal. She also noted that her show of bravado had accomplished nothing more than getting her spanked.

"Marco?"

"Yes, my Catherine?"

"May I please come out of the corner and eat something. I'm hungry and haven't eaten since breakfast."

"I would like nothing more than to share a meal with you. But do you have something to say to me first?"

"I'm sorry."

"What for?"

"I don't know. For pissing you off?" she replied in a tone of voice that clearly showed her irritation.

"Temper, temper, my Catherine. Losing yours with me will not serve you well. Let's try having you repeat after me again as that seemed to work for you last time. You are sorry for leaving our bed without waking me."

She took a deep breath and exhaled it slowly, hoping to stem her rising anger. "I'm sorry I left our bed without waking you."

"And you're sorry for getting dressed without my permission."

"Are you kidding me?"

"No, my Catherine. In the future a repeat of either of those will earn you a trip over my knee. Say it." The last he growled and smiled as she shuddered.

"And I'm sorry for getting dressed without your permission."

"And you are sorry that you thought to yet again deny my call and sought to sneak out of the hotel."

"And I'm sorry that I didn't listen to your call and didn't get a chance to get away from you."

"Naughty mate. Are you really wishing to add to your punishment by continuing to misbehave?"

"You are not going to spank me again."

Marco laughed. "I most assuredly am. What I'm trying to determine now is whether or not I will use my belt on you and leave a trail of welts across your beautiful ass."

"You wouldn't," she cried as panic started to settle on her.

He nodded. "I will if I believe it to be in the best interest of correcting your behavior. Behavior earlier today you led me to believe I wouldn't see again. Tell me, my Catherine, did you knowingly lie to me earlier today?"

The question was asked softly, but she could hear the steel that lay beneath it.

"I never said I wouldn't try to get away."

"That is true," he said, chuckling. "I assumed when you admitted you had failed to heed my call that you understood you were my fated mate and that being with me was implied. But, as you say it is not, let me be clear. You are my mate. Your place is at my side and in our bed. You will not leave our bed without waking me to tell me you are doing so. If you do, you will be spanked. When you enter our bedroom you will strip naked and naked you will remain unless I give you leave to cover yourself."

"Should I kneel in your presence and bring you your slippers?" Catherine muttered sarcastically.

"Careful, my Catherine. You have already earned yourself a spanking. Were I you, I would be trying to soothe my mate's anger, not encouraging it to grow. You implied that I had not been clear in my expectations. I am attempting to remedy that."

"So you expect me to give up my life and stay with you. And when we go in our room I'm to get naked. And what, you'll fuck me whenever you like?"

Catherine watched as he raised his head and sniffed the air before replying. His smile was at once predatory and lascivious.

"Yes, and given the state of your arousal, I do not believe that you find the prospect of my taking you again to be unwelcome. Now where was I? Ah, yes, being more clear about how I expect you to behave. You will mind me and be respectful…"

Catherine couldn't help herself. She started to laugh.

"Can you hear yourself? Do you actually believe the crap you're spewing? First, I'm not even convinced I believe in this fated mate bullshit. Second, I don't know that I want you for a fated mate. Third, I'm not going to wake you up in the middle of the night if I have to pee. Fourth, I'm not getting naked for your fun and amusement. And as for the rest of that claptrap—not happening."

Catherine was now on a roll. She could feel her strength and belief in herself and her abilities come surging back to the forefront of her being. She strolled out of the corner. It occurred to her that it would probably be more effective if she had clothing, but she had a point to make.

"And let me tell you another thing," she continued. "I'm not sure what came over me earlier when I allowed you to spank me and then fuck me without any kind of protection, but neither of those things will ever happen again. As far as you dictating to me what I will or will not do, that would probably be more of a concern if I were planning to be anywhere around you, which for the record I won't be."

Marco watched her quietly. When she took a breath, he growled long and low. As always it wasn't so much the sound that rattled her as it was the feeling it evoked throughout her entire being. And as she had a few other times, she also felt a wave of energy that felt a lot like a gust of wind knocking her back.

She watched with a kind of fascinated horror as Marco sat down and spread his legs.

"Are you quite finished with your tirade, my Catherine?"

"I am not your fucking Catherine, you arrogant jackass," she shouted.

He said nothing but patted his thigh.

Catherine could not explain the sudden burst of apprehension that started to gather in her belly. As she noticed that feeling, she could also feel the well of desire beginning to pool below it.

Marco patted his thigh again and growled at her.

All of the power, energy, and determination she had been building deflated like a balloon that had been pinched shut and now was opened. In its place was a feeling of dread, which only fed the feeling of arousal that was coursing throughout her entire body.

She shook her head, "No, Marco."

"Yes, my Catherine."

"I'm sorry I lost my temper."

"I'm glad to hear it. Apologizing without my having to prompt you is a step in the right direction. However, apologizing after the fact will not negate your punishment for doing so in the first place. And I would have thought that a taste of soap would have given you pause before using foul language with me again so quickly."

Again, he patted his thigh.

"No, Marco," she said as she walked toward him like a man on his way to the gallows.

She stopped to stand between his legs. He said nothing more; didn't pat his thigh; didn't offer to take her hand to help her into position; just waited. He never took his eyes off of her.

"Marco?" she asked quietly, trying to keep from pleading.

"Now, Catherine." His voice was quiet but the command in it was unmistakable.

"Help me, please?"

Something about the tone of her voice must have broken through his steely resolve. He took her hand and instead of guiding her over his knee, he pulled her from between them, closed his legs, and helped her to sit on his lap.

She didn't realize she'd begun to cry until he took a handkerchief and wiped the tears from her cheeks.

"Tell me why you're crying?"

"I... I don't know. I don't seem to know anything anymore."

With that confession the tears started to fall freely.

Marco wrapped his arms around her, pulling her close into his massive frame. She snuggled into him and had her head tucked under his. He rocked her quietly and just let her weep. He seemed unconcerned about time and sought only to comfort her. Finally, she was able to regain her composure.

She was still unsure as to what to do, but seemed content just to sit in his lap and accept the solace that he offered. Her quiet reflection was interrupted when her stomach rumbled again.

"I think, my Catherine, that before we do anything else, I should feed you. I want you to stand up and go back to your corner. Yes?"

She nodded. "Yes, sir."

He helped her stand and she went to stand quietly in the corner. She could hear him roll the trolley from just inside the door to what sounded like over by the settee. She could hear him lift the cloches from over the plates. Wonderful, tantalizing aromas wafted across the room to her. She wanted to turn around to see what he was doing, but refrained from doing so.

"Catherine, come here."

She turned and saw that Marco had resumed his place on the settee with the trolley full of food within easy reach.

"Come and sit on my lap, *tesoro*."

"I don't suppose I could put something on."

He said nothing, but merely quirked his eyebrow at her.

She sighed. "That's what I thought. You do know I find all of this extremely embarrassing, right?"

"There is no reason for you to be embarrassed. You have a beautiful body and it gives me great pleasure both in how it feels and how it looks. I think you spending some time unclothed will remind you to behave yourself and that you are no longer in charge. Now come sit with me."

She walked over and made to sit beside him.

"No, Catherine—on my lap."

"Fine," she said, sitting delicately and reaching for the

trolley.

The light tap on her hand made her draw it back.

"No, Catherine. I will feed you."

"I don't want to be fed."

"Then you can go back and stand in the corner until I have eaten. When I'm finished, I will give you your spanking, followed by having your mouth washed out with soap and perhaps, depending upon how you act from this point forward, another spanking."

Catherine inhaled deeply. "No, Marco, please?" she cried forlornly.

"Yes, Catherine. Before I claim your beautiful body again, you will get your mouth washed out with soap and be spanked to tears again. And this time, my mate, I will ensure that your spanking is harsh enough that you remember that minding me and behaving is a much better choice. Here, try the bruschetta. It is especially good here."

He held up the bread and offered her a bite. She was hungry and knew the only way she was going to get any food was to allow him to feed her. She took a bite and sighed with immense pleasure.

"Oh, my God, that's good. Wait, I can say that without getting my mouth washed out, can't I?"

Marco chuckled. "Yes, my Catherine. You can also appeal to the Gods when I am pleasuring you."

He offered her another bite and then popped the rest in his mouth.

He fed her the rest of their meal, always offering her the first bite and insisting she take at least one bite of anything with which she was unfamiliar or said she didn't like to eat. She was full before he was but was content just to sit curled up on his lap as he finished. They'd shared half a bottle of wine, DeMedici of course, but only used one glass.

She nuzzled the hollow of his throat.

"Marco, can't you just accept my apology and take me back to bed?"

"I could if I was not the mate you need. If I did not care

for you and wish to see you at your best, then I would simply let you do whatever you want and just fuck you when the mood suits me."

"Sounds good," she said and made to hop up off his lap and make a beeline for the bed.

His hand reached out to stay her and brought her back to his lap. The thought that at least she was sitting on it and not face down over it did occur to her.

"Catherine, you wound me. I am not such a man. You are my fated mate and I will see you at your best… always. You were not raised in a pack and therefore do not understand. I will make allowances for that, but there is a baseline I will insist you recognize and abide by. That includes the use of vulgar language, losing your temper in front of others, and being unclothed when we are alone in our chambers."

She looked at him incredulously. "You're serious, aren't you? You just expect me to fall into line and do what you say or else you'll beat my ass again."

He smiled benevolently at her. "No, my Catherine, I do not expect to you do anything of the sort. Yours is a wild and free spirit—one which I will cherish and never see squelched, but that does not mean you will not submit to my authority over you. I am worthy of your love and respect and will keep you safe and loved. When your behavior requires correction, I will provide it."

She shook his head. "Do you hear yourself? What did you just step out of, some time travel machine? I don't need you to keep me safe and loved. I can take care of myself and I have a life I love waiting for me back in the United States."

Marco looked at her, his dark eyes starting to glow. "You have no mate; in fact, there is no man who has ever made a claim on you."

"Because I didn't want one. I was perfectly fine living my life the way I wanted and when I wanted to get laid, I found someone suitable and we enjoyed each other's company."

"And is that what you think this is?"

"Well, I'll admit it was a bit more intense... okay, a lot more intense than usual and I wouldn't mind spending more time with you provided you don't spank me again. My ass still hurts."

"So, when you told me that you accepted you were my fated mate and as such understood that when you misbehaved, you would be punished, you were lying to me?"

Catherine realized that she may have just backed herself into a corner. Why was he able to throw her so off balance and why did she care?

"No, I just... I can't do this, Marco."

His body lost its angry tension as did the look on his face.

"What is it you feel you can't do, my Catherine? Answer me truthfully."

"I can't do this... this whatever this is. You just make me feel unbalanced. You throw off my equilibrium. I don't like it."

"Ah," he said, nodding. "That is to be expected. You have not had a man worthy of your submission and so have withheld it. That was wise of you. But I am your mate. I take my responsibility to and for you seriously and it will always be uppermost in my mind. It may take you a while to learn and to settle in as my mate, but I will help you. And when you go awry, I will help you modify your behavior so that you can embrace all that our life has to offer."

"I'm not going to make a life with you."

Marco laughed. "Of course you are."

He brought her face to his and kissed her softly but with intense passion. She felt him coax her mouth to soften and yield and accept the sweet gift he gave to her.

"I must apologize to you. It would seem that I forgot that to you this must sound very strange. Like something you have longed for all your life but feared would forever be denied you. You will need time to learn to trust that our way of life is better. I will help you learn and try to be clear about what I expect of you. But I will also always answer your questions or ease your concerns. But you must be honest and open with me."

"Marco," she started.

He kissed her again. "No, my Catherine. I will accept that the greater part of the fault for this latest misbehavior lies at my doorstep. Had you been born to a pack, you would have understood. You would have been raised to see yourself in your proper light. That you were not is something of a mystery, but one that can be remedied. I fear I was not clear before we rested and then overreacted when you were attempting to sneak away. For the record, even had you gotten outside the hotel, I would have found you before you ever left Florence."

"You can't just keep me in your hotel room."

"Of course not. As soon as I can conclude the last of my business here in Florence we will go home to the villa. But between now and then I am going to insist that you remain here in our room. I believe your proud spirit needs to be redirected, not eradicated. As I feel that your latest misbehavior is as much, if not more, my fault as it is yours, I will forego your punishment if you apologize for using foul language and acknowledge that you now understand that you are my mate."

"You can't just expect me to give up my life," she said, feeling as though she were losing the argument and uncertain as to how she felt about that.

"Not giving up your life. You will simply be building a life here with me and with our pack."

"What pack? What are you talking about?"

He chuckled, the sound rumbling from within his chest. "Ah, that may require a longer, more detailed conversation. But it can wait for a later time. Do you want to apologize to me and acknowledge what you know to be true… that you are my mate?"

She shook her head, not trusting her voice.

"Catherine, you know it is true. I have haunted your

dreams as you have haunted mine. You have heard me call to you. And when I do so, you feel it deep within you and every part of you wants to respond and yield to me. Will you lie to me... to yourself?"

"No," she whispered.

"No, what—that you will not yield or that you will not lie?"

"You... you weren't supposed to be real. You were only supposed to exist in my dreams."

"Is it not better to have me be flesh and bone?"

"No."

"Once again your mind is in conflict with your body. For I am quite sure when I possessed you earlier, your body was very glad I was not just an apparition. Explain to me why you believe you would choose me to remain a mere specter," he said quietly.

"Because in my dreams I could wake and you'd be gone. I could go on with my life as before."

"But did you not choose to change the course of your life when you were injured? You have great courage, my Catherine, you have shown that you have the ability to change your destiny. What if all you have come through was only leading you to this greater path before you? The path you will share with me."

"But you expect me to be some subservient, meek woman who does your bidding."

Catherine was surprised as Marco began to laugh out loud.

"It's not funny, Marco. Not to me."

He stifled his laughter, but his eyes retained their amused light. "I adore you and believe you are capable of accomplishing anything you choose to do. But it is not in your nature to be subservient or meek and I would never expect that of you. You are wild and free, proud and fierce and I love you all the more for it."

"But you've said repeatedly that if I don't mind you, you'll spank me."

"Which I will, but I expect to have to correct you. Can you imagine a woman such as you describe being happy with me? As you have pointed out on more than one occasion, I am an arrogant, overbearing what was it you called me? Ah, yes, either a prick or a jackass. Both of which are probably apt descriptions but inappropriate. I would never want my mate to be frightened of me. A meek and subservient woman would never suit me. Besides, as you have now experienced, a good spanking often leads to intensely pleasurable feelings."

"But you said I was to be naked when we are in our bedroom."

"Yes, at least for a while. You are extraordinarily beautiful, my Catherine. Gazing upon your naked body gives me great pleasure and arouses me. Besides it makes you a bit uncomfortable and I believe will serve to remind you that you are not the dominant one."

"So you just expect me to wait around in our bedroom until you join me, get a hard-on and fuck me?"

She had become relaxed sitting on his lap and the swat he landed between her legs, catching her sensitive lips and inflicting more than a bit of heat and sting was unexpected.

"Mind how you speak to me, my Catherine. Are you in need of another taste of soap?"

"No." She started to struggle to get off his lap.

The growl that accompanied her trying to extricate herself from him stopped her cold and she could feel the pool of her aroused state begin to drip on his leg.

"No, what?" he asked calmly.

"No, sir," she said sullenly. "Then what do you expect?"

"I expect us to be happy. What had you planned to do with your degree from Cooper? Do you wish to paint? There is a salon at the villa that has excellent light that we could easily turn into a studio for you."

"I don't know that I'm good enough. I had really thought I might try my hand at restoration."

"If that is what you want, you can easily do that at the

villa. I'm sure there are environmental concerns and conditions you would need to institute but we can do that. It isn't that I don't want you to have what you want. I merely want you to share it with me."

"Really? You don't want me to give up my life?"

He chuckled and captured her mouth with his. "No, *tesoro*, I want you to be happy and fulfilled. There are things I will need for you to do for me, such as act as hostess when we need to entertain, but you will have a large staff and can delegate much of the mundane work. In addition, I sit on several boards that deal with the arts. I haven't a clue most of the time what they are talking about. I believe both our interests and those of the institutions would be far better served were you to undertake those responsibilities."

The life he described didn't sound so bad… especially if having sex with Marco on a regular basis was part of the bargain. "Really?"

He nodded. "Really. But I don't want you to give up painting. It has been a part of you for most of your life and if nothing else provides you with an outlet for your creativity and brings you joy, does it not?"

"But I don't want to be spanked. My ass still hurts."

"And probably will for another day or so. If you wish to avoid being spanked, then behave yourself. Let me be clear, when you misbehave, I will hold you accountable and you will get your pretty bottom spanked."

"But you've decided that it's your fault I didn't wake you and tried to sneak out?"

He chuckled again. "I have decided that while the naughty behavior is yours, that my not being clear led you to act out and so I will forego spanking you this time."

"And my language?"

"For that I should still give you a mouth full of soap suds."

Catherine smiled seductively and rubbed her hardened nipples along his chest, tickling them with his chest hair.

"I can think of something we'd both prefer you fill my

mouth with," she said, nuzzling his neck.

Marco inhaled and growled low at her. This time though there was nothing angry or commanding about the sound. It was merely a reflection of his own growing arousal.

"Can you," he said, running his hand up between her legs. He smiled as she parted her legs eagerly. "I believe, my Catherine, that we would both prefer that I fuck your pussy as opposed to your mouth."

Marco stood, lifting her as he did so and carried her back to what she now thought of as their bed.

CHAPTER ELEVEN

Marco spent the rest of the night and the next few days weaving a web of seduction around Catherine. He made love to her repeatedly, each time bringing her to multiple orgasms before seeking and finding his own release. She fussed once or twice about not being protected, but he was able to soothe her protestations.

Catherine woke to find herself once more spooned in Marco's strong embrace. She smiled as she recognized that he always had his arm wrapped around her, ensuring she could not leave their bed without his waking.

She felt him nuzzle her neck as he realized she was awake. She wiggled around so that she could roll over and face him. She wrapped her arms around his neck and molded herself to his body and smiled as she felt his cock becoming rigid and trying to poke between her legs.

"Good morning," she purred at him.

"My Catherine," he sighed. "I always fear when I wake in the morning I will find you were not real and that these last several days were merely an intense dream."

She giggled. "Ask my ass or my pussy. They would be quick to tell you otherwise."

"You did not complain so much about the latter."

"No, you made sure that each and every time you mounted me I was screaming your name. You really don't fight fair."

"I have been a warrior too long. I always fight to keep what I hold dear."

Catherine saw him smile as she hooked one of her legs over his and lined her sheath up with his hard, heated staff.

"Please?" she said softly. "What was it you said to me the last time? Ah, yes, I have need of you, mate."

Marco smiled broadly. "Mate, is it?"

She nodded quietly. He kissed her.

"Then there is little I could deny you," he said as he reached down to cup and lift her buttocks before sliding into her and groaning as her pussy contracted around him.

Marco rolled her onto her back and held her close as he gently thrust in and out of her. Catherine could feel his length and breadth. She clung to him with desperation and committed each movement and its resulting feeling to memory. As much as she desperately wanted to believe he was her mate, she didn't believe they could make a life together. She knew she had to leave him as soon as she could.

If nothing else, she had to find Shannon. Even though the private investigator would no longer take her money and had tried to tell her that her sister was dead, Catherine believed Shannon was still alive, that she could find her and that she could bring her home.

Catherine knew that Marco planned to leave her today to finish up some business and she had decided to take what she had with her, which included her passport, and flee the city, maybe even the country, while he was gone. At some point, she'd contact Seraphina and have her things shipped home. As much as she wanted to stay with Marco, she knew there was too large a gulf between them and her sister was depending on her.

Marco's repetitive thrusting consisted of long, slow, powerful strokes that began at the entrance to her core and were stopped as the tip of his cock reached her cervix. As was his norm, he held her close while he fucked her, never allowing her to move her hips in rhythm to his. She had come to recognize and respond profoundly to this act of dominance on his part.

She came apart in his hands more than once before she began to rake his back with her nails. She didn't want him to stop and seemed unable to keep herself from making him. He groaned each time she did so and then answered her moaning with a growl that would make her whole body come alive and respond even more fully to his possession.

When at last he whispered in her ear, "Come for me, my Catherine," she was helpless to do anything but what he commanded.

Catherine could feel him continue to spurt his cum within her depths even after her pussy stopped contracting. As had become his habit, he settled deep inside her and kissed her with a soft and abiding passion.

She had tears in her eyes as he lifted his head. "What distresses you, mate?" he said with great concern.

"Nothing," she lied. "I'm just going to miss you when you leave to sign that paperwork."

Marco made a rumbling noise that was half sated growl and half self-satisfied chuckle. Catherine knew she would miss that when she was gone.

"We will have breakfast and then you should rest. I fear my need for you grows with every time you surrender to me."

He nuzzled her one last time and allowed himself to slip from her body. Marco sat up and dialed room service, ordering them a hearty breakfast. He leaned over and kissed her and then went to take a shower. He was just coming out of the bath when room service knocked discreetly. Marco ensured that Catherine was covered up and allowed the boy in directing him to set up next to the bed.

Catherine grinned at him. "Planning to keep me naked and feed me again?" she inquired sweetly.

The waiter tripped as Marco growled at her and then seeing the merriment in her eyes, chuckled.

"Careful, mate, before I show the boy here how a man deals with a naughty minx of a mate."

He tipped the waiter generously, who couldn't seem to get out of their room fast enough.

Catherine threw back the covers, revealing to Marco the aroused state of her body. He grinned broadly and came to sit next to her. He bent over and sucked one of her taut nipples deep into his mouth, making her inhale sharply.

"Would that I had time, my Catherine. But if you wish, when I return I will take care of that need. You, however, are not allowed to pleasure yourself unless directed by me to do so."

"Greedy bastard, aren't you?"

Marco reached down and pinched her nipple, and she gasped in both surprise and discomfort.

"Language, mate, and yes, I am. I do not share what is mine and mine alone."

"That hurt, you know," she said petulantly.

When all he did was quirk an eyebrow at her, she softened her tone.

"You could offer to kiss and make it better."

He laughed. "What an excellent idea," he said as he suckled the offended nub. "Now, let's share breakfast and then I need to be off. Where would you like to go to dinner tonight? Shall I show you off or would you prefer I simply feed you between ravishings?"

"Planning to ravish me again, are you?" she teased.

"Repeatedly. And when I get you home to the villa I will take you into seclusion in our rooms and rut with you until your legs will not support you without my assistance."

She giggled. "Promises, promises." Realizing that she did not plan to be here when he returned, she sobered. "The past few days have been very special to me. I will remember it always."

"Pfft," he dismissed. "That was nothing compared to

the memories we shall make together."

Catherine sat up in bed, grimacing as she did. "Don't you dare laugh at me. This is your fault."

"I'm not laughing. It was my responsibility to correct your behavior. That is a duty I take seriously to ensure your safety and happiness."

"Hot news flash… women don't find happiness face down over a man's knee getting their ass spanked."

He leaned over and kissed her. "No, but they find great happiness afterwards when their mate is thrusting himself in and out of their sweet pussy hearing her call his name."

Catherine closed her eyes and leaned back. "I can't even dispute that. Well, I can, but you'd get after me for lying to you."

Marco grinned. "That might be one of those times I filled your mouth with something other than soap."

She giggled. "I promise you'd find it far more satisfying… as would I."

They finished eating and Catherine watched him leave. She went over to the window and watched him depart from the hotel. He turned to look directly at her, and she raised her hand in a wave.

Catherine went in, took a shower, gathered her things, and then discreetly exited the hotel from the back entrance. She hailed a cab and had the driver take her straight to the airport. At the airport she found there were no outbound flights until that evening. Knowing Marco would be on her trail long before then, she bought a train ticket out of Florence on the first departing train. It was headed toward Milan.

• • • • • • •

Marco met Griffin as they both arrived at the lawyer's office to finalize the purchase of the property.

Griffin grinned at him. "Now that is the look of a man who has spent the last few days in the arms of his beloved."

Marco laughed heartily and clapped his friend on the shoulder. He leaned in so that only Griffin could hear him. "No, my friend. This is the look of a wolf who spent most of his time between his little red riding hood's thighs doing just that... riding her. My God, Griffin. My Catherine was magnificent. Such passion and fire. She will keep me warm for the rest of my life."

"Have you talked to her about that minor inconvenience? You know where you're a wolf and she isn't? You know where you're going to overwrite her entire DNA and then, oh, there's the whole knotting and tying her, not to mention marking her as yours."

"No, I want to get her home first. But I must say she handled being disciplined extremely well. I think once it has been done, she will welcome my knot and the resulting tie, but the alpha's mark may be a different discussion. She will come around and will bear my mark with pride. After all, she will be mate to the alpha of the DeMedici pack."

"My best wishes for a long, happy, and peaceful joining. Your Catherine is a bit of a spitfire and may not be brought to heel as easily as you imagine. Truly I'm happy for you... and just a wee bit envious."

"You will find your Catherine. Of that I have no doubt."

They proceeded up the stairs to finalize the purchase.

Once it was complete, Marco was convinced that the sellers were idiots. According to Griffin the land was incredibly rich and could be producing far more than it did. The workers seemed relieved that someone with an outstanding reputation was taking over and that their jobs would be secure.

Once their business was concluded, Marco called one of the better restaurants in Florence and secured a table. Knowing that Catherine had nothing with her at the hotel that was appropriate and doubting she had brought anything to Florence with her, Marco went to one of the high-end boutiques Catherine had visited and found a dress and shoes he thought would be an excellent choice and suit her taste. He then headed to one of the jewelry artisans to find the perfect accessories.

Pleased with himself and the conclusion of his business dealings, Marco returned to the hotel and had to harness his energy to keep from having a knot form and from taking the steps up to their room two at a time. He felt as giddy as a schoolboy.

He could feel the lack of her presence before he even entered the room.

"Catherine," he growled as he spied a piece of the hotel stationery resting against the pillows. He read the note:

Marco,
I have nothing to say other than to ask you to forgive my cowardly exit from your life. You will find another who is far better suited to the life you can give her than I.
I'm sorry,
Catherine

Well, at least she had dropped the coldly stiff language of her first two notes. As for being sorry… she would be more so once he caught up with her. He would teach her once and for all not to run from him.

CHAPTER TWELVE

Catherine was pleasantly surprised that Marco had not anticipated her needing a train ticket. She decided on a private compartment. She was in no mood for idle chitchat or the company of anyone... including her own. The porter was old school and had questioned her lack of baggage. She decided to be polite but vague, answering that her things were back in Florence as this was just a day trip. He arranged for refreshments to be brought to her.

She leaned back against the seat and closed her eyes. She ached, not from the spanking he had given her and not from the dominant lovemaking they had shared over the past few days. No, she ached for Marco himself—his presence, his voice, his touch, his very essence.

Catherine stifled the beginnings of a sob. How was it possible that she could miss him so much when she'd known him for such a short period of time and hadn't even known he existed a week ago? A little voice at the back of her brain reminded her that the latter wasn't true. The man had been haunting her dreams for a long time.

The voice was persistent, if she missed him, why was she running? She told the voice to shut up.

Catherine drifted between drowsiness and wakefulness.

She looked out her window as the beautiful countryside rolled by. The train made frequent stops but they were brief and often in very picturesque towns. She was still drowsy when she suddenly felt as though a huge gust of wind had blown through her being.

"No," she whispered. "It couldn't be."

The door to her compartment flew open and Marco entered, turning to close and lock the door and pull down the shades.

She could feel the heat of his anger rolling off of him.

"What do you think you're doing?" she stammered as he turned to face her and the train lurched as it started on its way again.

"Did you think if you ran that I wouldn't chase you down?"

Catherine went on the offensive. "You can't just come in here. I was under no obligation to stay in Florence, much less your hotel room."

Marco shook his head. "I was under the distinct impression, my Catherine…"

"I am *not* your Catherine," she cried.

"You are most definitely *my* Catherine. And therein lies the fundamental issue we must settle between us. I had thought that as of last night we settled this, but apparently not. I assure you it will be settled once and for all by the time I am through with you."

"If you think you're going to spank me here on this train… think again. The walls don't have the soundproofing that hotel did. Someone will hear."

"Interesting that you already accept you are going to be spanked. I suppose that's a step in the right direction. Not much of one but a small start."

"No, Marco, you can't."

"Yes, Catherine, I can and will. I don't care that anyone hears you cry when you are getting a spanking. Let them come in and watch for all I care. What they will see is a man taking his woman to task for being naughty and trying to run away. Anyone who might challenge me is either enough of a chauvinist prick himself to understand that there are times a man must discipline his mate regardless of where he finds her, or would get a vicarious thrill to watch me spank your beautiful bottom, innately understanding that when I'm through, I will most likely plow that furrow between your legs."

She backed as far into the corner of the seat as she could get, shaking her head as she went.

"No, Marco."

"Yes, Catherine. And while I prefer to have you naked when I punish you, I will have to settle for stripping your leggings off so they don't interfere."

He removed his silk handkerchief from his pocket. He offered it to her.

"What's that for?"

"I thought you might want to bite on it to keep from crying so loud there will be no doubt in anyone's mind that you have been naughty and are being punished for it."

"You can't."

"I think we've already established that I can and will."

"Marco, not here."

"Here, my Catherine."

Catherine watched as he took a seat across from her and reached out to bring her out of her seat. What was most shocking to her was that she didn't resist him, not even the tiniest bit. She got to her feet and went to stand in front of him. She felt the cool, recirculated air in the compartment waft across her buttocks as Marco bared them. She shivered as his hand caressed them as he removed her leggings.

"Can't this wait until we get back to the hotel?"

"No. Let this be a lesson to you that should you think to run or hide from me when you have been naughty that I will spank you wherever I find you. You will learn, sweetheart, that disobeying and angering your mate is never a good idea."

He pulled her across his knee and once again offered her

the use of his handkerchief. Catherine calmly took it from him and stuffed it into her mouth with as much dignity as she could. Marco's hand braced her upper body while the other stroked her quivering backside gently.

"Good girl," he crooned. "This could have been avoided had you chosen to mind me and stay where you were told."

She hated the fact that when he told her she was a good girl it seemed to matter to her so much. That thought was fleeting as his hand made a sudden sharp connection with her upturned seat. She took note that the handkerchief did seem to muffle the sharp cry she tried to bite back.

Marco began to spank her, his hand slapping her ass in a sharp, hard rhythm. Catherine could feel the fire burn as it spread across both of her cheeks. The spanking seemed worse than the one he'd given her previously and she wondered if it was because she actually felt guilty this time or because it was covering the same area he'd left reddened and swollen from their first night together. Oh, God, and did she have to start getting so aroused?

Dual sensations assaulted Catherine. On the one hand, Marco was peppering her backside with hard swats designed to leave a lasting sting. On the other, her pussy was soaked and beginning to spasm in rhythm to the spanking. What was it about this man that he so completely dominated every part of her being? And why did it feel so right that he did so?

Marco scolded her as he spanked her. "Your beautiful bottom will thank you if you remember that you are my Catherine. You will learn to mind me and when you don't you will find yourself in the position you are in right now. You are not to run away because you are frightened of your feelings or because you are throwing a tantrum. In either event, I expect you to come to me so that I can reassure you of your importance to me, my commitment to you, and our feelings for each other."

The hard, repetitive blows to her still tender backside interrupted any profound thoughts she might have had. She was now crying in earnest and grateful for the handkerchief that kept her from crying so loud the whole train would know she had displeased her mate and he was taking her to task for it.

After what seemed an eternity, he stopped spanking. He rubbed her bottom soothingly. With his other hand he reached down and removed the makeshift gag from her mouth.

"Whose Catherine are you?" he said quietly but with an underlying growl.

"Yours," she said.

"Say it again."

"I am your Catherine, Marco."

"Good. Should you refute that again, you will earn yourself another well soaped mouth as well as a hard spanking. And if you are so foolish as to run away again, my Catherine, I will take my belt or a special strap to your bottom and leave a trail of welts across it. Do you understand me, mate?"

"Yes, Marco. I'm sorry."

"Not as sorry as you will be when I get you back to the hotel. And there, my sweet Catherine, I will endeavor to make your pussy as sore as your backside. I had thought when I finished my business that by this time I would already have had you beneath me and brought us both great pleasure. You may get up."

Catherine seemed unsure and rose unsteadily to her feet. Marco brought her onto his lap. Catherine was quite sure he enjoyed seeing her wince as her punished backside made contact with his hard thighs.

"But aren't you going to… you know…"

"Fuck you?" he laughed.

She nodded.

"Is there a corner where my naughty mate can be stripped and sent to stand naked while she contemplates the error of her ways?"

"Well, no."

"Then," he said, sliding his hand between her legs and slipping a single finger into her drenched pussy. "Your need to be completely forgiven for this latest bit of nonsense will have to wait."

Catherine groaned. Marco smiled. He knew exactly what he was doing to her. She supposed he was owed a little payback. He played with her gently, slowly bringing her to the edge of her orgasm and then stopped.

"Let's get you back into your leggings. You are entirely too enticing this way."

She reached for her leggings and Marco helped her back into them. He brought her back to his lap and made her comfortable there.

At the next stop, Marco and Catherine got off the train. Catherine wasn't overly surprised to find a driver waiting for them. Marco helped her into the limo before instructing the driver where to go. They spoke in Italian and Catherine could only understand bits and pieces.

As Marco got into the back with her, she asked, "Will you teach me to speak Italian or can I get Sera to?"

"And you think you will learn to speak my native tongue?"

She leaned over to nuzzle him. "I suppose if I'm staying and will be sharing your life, it might be nice to understand conversations that are being had around me."

Marco smiled and Catherine was happy to see the last of his anger begin to fade. "So, my Catherine…" He hesitated to see if she registered any protest at his assertion that she was his. Catherine said nothing but nuzzled him again. Marco smiled. "If you want to learn to speak Italian, we will teach you. And your friend Seraphina is always welcome at the villa."

Catherine shook her head and Marco growled. "Oh, hush. I'm merely shaking my head because it seems so normal to be sitting on my sore ass on your lap planning a future. A few days ago, I thought you were arrogant and manipulative."

Marco chuckled. "I would plead guilty to both. But I was manipulating things only to make your time in Florence more enjoyable and to show you what life with an indulgent mate could be like. I was never trying to buy you, my Catherine." He took her hand in his and kissed her palm. "I never thought you were for sale."

Catherine could feel tears welling up in her eyes. "Now why'd you have to go and say that? Now I feel like a total bitch…"

"Catherine," he growled. "I will not warn you again."

She smiled. "Regardless, I feel like one for ever doubting your intentions."

"Then why did you leave Florence?"

"Can we not talk about that?"

"Answer me."

She took a deep breath. "Because you scare the hell out of me. You make me feel things I've never felt before and even if I'd felt something similar, the feelings I have for you are far more intense. I worry that I'll lose myself in you."

And Catherine knew that while that was true, it was not the only reason she had left. Part of her wanted to confide everything in him, but she feared he would look at the evidence rationally and conclude there was no hope of finding Shannon and would prevent her from continuing her search.

"Would that be so bad?" he said softly. "I have already lost myself in you. That is the nature of fated mates."

A single tear started to roll down her cheek.

"Do not weep, my Catherine. There is nothing to fear."

Trying to lighten the mood, she quipped, "Why does a single tear bother you, but when I'm crying my eyes out when you spank me, it does nothing to move you?"

He smiled. "The single tear shows the depth of what you're feeling. Your caterwauling when I am expressing my displeasure at your behavior is simply part of your tantrum throwing."

"Tantrum throwing?"

He nodded. "Yes. But it is of no consequence. It is, after all, supposed to hurt enough that you refrain from doing it a second time."

"And what if a woman doesn't have a mate to discipline her?"

Marco leaned over and kissed her. "If she is part of a pack, then she has her alpha and her beta to provide her with the structure and correction she needs. If she is allowed to be on her own, as you have been for far too long, she becomes unsettled and unruly. It is then up to her mate, when he finds her, to give her boundaries within which to live happily and to correct those bad habits that have been allowed to flourish."

"Pack? Alpha? Beta? What the hell are you talking about?"

"Calm yourself, my Catherine. That is a discussion best left for a better time and location."

"And what if I want to discuss them now?"

Catherine wasn't sure why, but she knew the answer to those questions was important and would impact her life greatly. She wanted answers and she wanted them now.

"Do not fret, *tesoro*. I am here now and will give you what you need…" He laughed. "Even when you don't want it. I will not allow you to merely twist in the wind or to be blown about and not be able to enjoy all the sweetness that our life will give you."

"You know, Marco, I'm pretty damn good at taking care of myself."

"Are you? Then why are you not already mated? Why has no one ever given you the loving guidance you so desperately need?"

"You're a few years older than me. Why aren't you already mated… or are you? Sera said you had plenty of secrets… is that one of them?"

"I am not mated because you have been good at staying hidden… just enough out of reach that I couldn't find you. I knew you were my fated mate and would settle for nothing less. And that had best be the last time you ever accuse me of infidelity."

"See what I mean? You make me unsettled and then I get nasty. I just don't think this will work."

Marco growled low and seductively and watched as her body responded. She softened and her body quivered in response. He knew if he scented the air in the backseat of the car he would be able to smell her arousal.

"Shhh, my Catherine," he said as he pulled her unrelenting body closer to his. "It will be all right."

Catherine struggled, but could not get away. Marco did nothing but hold her in his arms and gently rock her as though she were a small child to be comforted. His gentleness... his somehow knowing what she needed even when she didn't were her undoing. Once again, she started to cry.

"There, there, sweetheart—your mate is here. I have you. There is no need for you to fight any longer. That is my duty and responsibility. I will keep you safe whether the danger be physical or emotional, real or imagined."

Catherine gave up whatever fight she had left in her and nestled deeper into his lap, burrowing into his chest and seeking his comfort. Part of what left her feeling a bit disoriented was how quickly she vacillated from one extreme to the other. One minute all she wanted was to feel his cock thrusting in and out of her like a battering ram and the next all she could think was how to get far, far away from him.

Catherine wasn't sure when she'd fallen asleep or for how long she'd slept. She started to stir as Marco got out of the limo with her cradled in his arms. She felt him enter the hotel and once again climb the grand staircase. This time he negotiated the door on his own, closing it before laying her on the bed.

"Why are we back here?"

"There are a few remaining things I need to do. That will be more easily accomplished if I am here in Florence and they can bring papers for my signature here to the hotel. I will not leave you again, sweetheart, to worry and fret. I will be here to reassure you and see that you get what you need—whether it be food, spanking, or my cock stroking your pussy. I'm going to order dinner. Is there anything special you'd like?"

"No," she said quietly. "Whatever you want."

He leaned over and kissed her, igniting the spark of passion they both knew he would fan into flames later. "What I want is for you to get naked. You will remain so until we leave for home."

Marco watched her undress and demanded she surrender her clothes to him. She had resisted but acquiesced as soon as he growled at her. Once she was naked, he ran his hands over her body possessively. He smiled at her shivered response and then sent her to stand in the corner to await his forgiveness for running away.

He sat back and observed her demeanor. He was learning to read her body language quite well. When she was first made to stand in the corner her spine would be straight, her shoulders back, and her overall posture rigid. As he continued to watch her and she accepted not only her punishment but his authority, her body would soften, her shoulders would slump, and often she would lean against the wall.

It was only then that Marco knew she was ready to be forgiven.

• • • • • • •

Catherine felt him close in on her. She felt his hands come up to reposition her body to be more easily mounted. This very act—putting her body where he wanted for his use—was both humbling and arousing at the same time.

He fondled her breasts and nipples with a degree of roughness that served only to inflame the arousal that had begun as he watched her undress. She swore she could actually feel her body producing the amount of lubrication he would need to mount her without causing either of them any physical distress. He nuzzled her neck and she moaned in response. It seemed so easy for him to produce his desired effect. She wondered how he could make her body respond to him by seemingly doing so little.

Her nipples were beaded and hard and her breathing was more shallow and erratic. Having his body so close to her, feeling his cock probe between her legs and nudge the entrance to her sheath made her go weak at the knees. She leaned against the wall to help hold herself up, but it was Marco's strong embrace that kept her where she needed to be.

"Please, Marco."

"Are you ready to be forgiven, my Catherine?"

"Yes, please."

"Then ask me," he commanded quietly.

"Marco, please forgive me."

"What for? Were you a naughty mate who got her bottom spanked and now needs to be fucked to know she is forgiven and reminded that her mate loves her above all else?"

"Yes," she cried.

Catherine knew it to be true. She had disobeyed him and found herself beginning to accept that she needed him to punish her for that and then to forgive her and reestablish the sensual dynamic that existed between them. She needed to know she could rely on his strength and love and that she could surrender to both.

With no further preliminaries, Marco powerfully thrust home, causing her to orgasm in response.

She heard him make the provocative half growl/half chuckle that made her feel as though the sound itself skittered across her skin. She knew that he knew she had a primordial response to that sound and to the dominant way he possessed her, taking them both to heights of sexual bliss she had never experienced before.

His thrusting was strong, deep, and practiced. If nothing else, the man knew how to fuck a woman to complete and total satisfaction. He never even began to seek his own release until he was assured she'd climaxed at least twice and usually more than that. Catherine found she was becoming used to being a bit tender in her feminine parts… and was enjoying that.

Anger gnawed at Catherine's insides. She wasn't even angry at Marco. She was angry with herself. She should be looking for Shannon and instead she was falling hopelessly in love with a man she knew very little about. She could hear her heart and soul cry out that the latter wasn't true. She knew Marco the way he knew her—in a way she had never experienced and had come to believe didn't exist. But why then did she feel the need to hide her true reason for coming to Florence from him?

CHAPTER THIRTEEN

Marco had been as good as his word. He had rarely left her side. Catherine had basked in his attention. Her emotions had continued to fluctuate wildly. One minute she wanted to escape and to find her sister and the next she wanted to tell Marco everything and beg him to help her.

Through it all he continued to speak of the villa, the business, his past, and his extended family. In some ways he was an open book willing to share anything. But she felt that there was a lot he wasn't telling her. Things that were important and that she needed to know. He would typically brush off her concerns and then divert her attention with his commanding lovemaking. Whatever fears she might have would be pushed aside the moment Marco began to seduce her—heart, mind, body, and soul.

Catherine felt him nuzzle her. She snuggled back into his body, seeking his warmth. They most often fell asleep either with him spooned around her or with Marco on his back and her being snuggled under his arm with her head on his chest. This morning they were spooned together. It never ceased to amaze her that she had become so used to sleeping with him. Not just having sex with him, but actually sleeping with him.

Catherine smiled. So far she'd been able to avoid a face-down over-his-knee spanking since the train, but had earned the occasional swat here or there. She had put his shirt on one morning and he'd told her to remove it. When she sat down instead, she found herself pulled off the couch, the shirt stripped off of her, and her bottom swatted hard several times. Marco had warned her that if she disobeyed him again, she'd earn herself a true punishment spanking. He seemed to understand that accepting his authority and leadership was new for her and not necessarily a natural fit, but insisted it would come easier for her in time.

"Marco?"

"Yes, my Catherine?"

She smiled. He rarely used her name that the possessive 'my' wasn't in front of it. The thing was it no longer bothered her and in fact now seemed perfectly normal.

"If I am your Catherine, does that make you my Marco?"

He chuckled—the deep rumbling sound she always felt surround her completely.

"But of course. Who else's Marco would I be?"

She giggled. "Why does that make me so happy to hear you say that?"

"Did you doubt it?"

"I don't know that I doubted it, but it's nice to hear you say it."

"As you no longer seem to object to being my Catherine, I will tell you that I have waited a long, long time for you. I love you, my Catherine. Now and forever."

Catherine wiggled around in his arms until she was facing him. She searched his face for any sign of deception. There was none.

"You do?"

"Do you doubt me?" he asked softly.

Catherine thought for a moment. "No. No, I don't. But I do wonder what it is you aren't telling me."

"As there are things you have yet to tell me… including, I might add, that you love me too."

"Are you sure that I do?" she teased gently.

Marco smiled. "Yes, my Catherine. I am sure you do. If you are not ready to say it or even admit it to yourself, I can be patient. But know that all of your secrets are safe with me."

"But you don't think that I can be trusted with yours?" she chided.

Marco thought a minute and seemed to make a decision.

"Do you still see me in your dreams?"

"No," she said. "Ever since the first time we were together you no longer inhabit my dreams, but your buddy the big black wolf is still there. He is usually off on the horizon, but always watching."

Marco smiled and chuckled again.

"Do you remember the first night we saw each other?"

She nodded.

"You were wearing the red cloak with the hood?"

Again she nodded.

"The very embodiment of little red riding hood."

"So, what does that make you? The big bad wolf? Because for damn sure you aren't my ailing grandmother." She laughed as she said it and then realized Marco wasn't laughing. She tilted her head and looked at him closely.

Marco kissed the tip of her nose and then each of her eyelids. "I am the one who gobbled you up, am I not?" he teased.

"Marco, don't tease. What is it?"

"The wolf is a part of me."

"What do you mean? Like he's your spirit guide/animal? I didn't think that was a part of the Italian belief system."

"I am not pure Italian. The blood of the Romany flows through my veins as well. But no, the wolf is not my spirit guide, but he is a part of me."

Catherine sat up and looked into his seemingly bottomless eyes.

"I don't understand."

Marco sat up and pulled her into his embrace, arranging

it so her head was against his chest.

"For thousands of years, there have been two types of humanoid lifeforms inhabiting the earth…"

Catherine pushed off his chest, sitting up again. He allowed her to pull away but not to put any real distance between them.

"What are you saying?"

"What I'm trying to tell you is that humans such as yourself are not the only humanoids who evolved on earth."

"Of course they are."

"No, my Catherine. There is another line that can shift between their purely humanoid form and their animal form. In my case, the wolf."

"That's fantasy or science fiction… I can never tell the real difference between the two…"

Marco shook his head. "It is neither. It is simply something that my kind have hidden as best we could from your kind. There are those of your kind who have known and in much earlier times, my kind was more widely known and accepted by some."

"Your kind? What the hell do you mean by that? You're human. Hell, Marco, I've seen you naked. I've had my hands on every part of your body. There's nothing not human about you. I don't think this is funny."

"It is not meant to be funny. And I realize it is difficult to understand, but in our human form we are outwardly indistinguishable from humans. But we have the ability to shift to an animal form. In my case, and that of my pack, wolves. The wolf you have always seen with me in your dreams and who now continues to stand vigil is me."

"That is complete and total bullshit."

"Catherine, I realize what I'm telling you is difficult to accept, but you mind your language."

"You want me to believe you have the ability to change into a wolf and you're worried about my fu… freaking language?"

Marco's growl had cut off the word she had been about

to use and caused her body to shiver in response to him as it always did.

"I will not warn you again, my Catherine. Remember how much you disliked the taste of soap. As I was trying to explain, in ancient times, the ability to shift between human and wolf gave my kind a definitive advantage. We were able to adapt to less hospitable environments. We were also gifted with enhanced genetic immunity, rapid healing ability, and longer life."

"You want me to believe you can just blink your eyes and you change into a wolf? Or is it more that there's a full moon and you go through some horrific, painful change where your clothes get torn asunder."

"None of the above," he said with a smile. Marco kissed her softly and then got out of bed. "Normally we remove our clothing as it gets in the way, but as I am already naked…"

He moved so that he was positioned between Catherine and the door.

Catherine watched him with a combination of horror and fascination as his body shifted smoothly from that of the man with whom she had experienced the most incredible sex and intense emotions of her life to the black wolf of her dreams. She tried to scream, but no sound came out.

The wolf approached her cautiously. He was larger and appeared to be more powerful than the wolves she had seen in the wild or in the zoo. In fact he was much larger.

"Marco?" she said quietly as she tentatively reached her hand out to him.

The black wolf nuzzled her hand and rubbed his head against it. His eyes never left hers and his tail wagged slowly.

Catherine brought both of her hands up and put them on either side of his head. She lowered her forehead to his and again he rubbed against her.

"It really is you," she said in a whisper filled with wonder. "Can you understand me?"

She giggled as his tail wagged with more enthusiasm.

"Holy shit!"

The wolf growled.

"Hey! I get a pass on that. It is way outside of the norm for the man you love to change into a wolf. Can you change back that easily? Is it easy? It looked easy. But does it hurt?"

The wolf backed away and she watched again as the wolf became her lover. He smiled at her and then stood to his full height.

She shook her head. "I say again, holy shit."

"That, my Catherine, is the last pass on your language. And am I?"

She looked at him with confusion.

"The man you love?" he whispered.

She nodded and then started to giggle. "Apparently man and wolf. Okay, that's going to take some getting used to."

He drew her out of bed and into his arms. "I didn't frighten you?"

"Not frightened, but it's kind of a lot to take in."

"I know. It's not an easy subject to approach with someone who has no point of reference. And there are certain ramifications that we will need to discuss."

"Like are you housebroken?" she giggled again and then started to laugh when he did. "I'm sorry… I'm just not sure what one says in this situation."

"To answer your questions, yes, I can understand you and we retain all of the information we learn whether as wolf or man. Once you have learned to shift, it is very easy and doesn't hurt at all."

"Are there female werewolves? Do you call yourself werewolves?"

"No, primitive man labeled us as such to differentiate and classify us as some kind of demon. We refer to ourselves as wolf shifters or just shifters."

"Are there other kinds of shifters? Are all shifters male?"

"There are other kinds of shifters—bears, eagles, lions, horses, elk, just about any animal. And not all shifters are male, although for some unknown reason we are seeing fewer and fewer female shifters born."

"So will your kind become extinct?"

"No, our two species can interbreed and in much earlier times it was far more common. Humans can be turned or changed so that they too become shifters. It is never to be done without their informed consent. Unfortunately there are starting to be some disturbing rumors about missing human females."

"How does a woman get turned?"

"From a wolf bite or blood transfusion. Our blood or saliva can infect your blood creating a virus that overwrites the human DNA."

"Oh, my God, did you turn me?"

"What?" he asked angrily.

"Well, God knows I've had enough of your saliva from kisses and when you go down on me."

She felt his anger fade as quickly as it had risen.

He chuckled. "No, my Catherine. It has to be introduced into your bloodstream. I would never turn you without your consent and without you knowing all that it entails."

Understanding started to dawn. "That's why you have a mysterious side. That's why you referred to your family and the people who live at the villa as a pack. Is there a true pack structure?"

"Yes. I am alpha of our pack."

She giggled and pushed him onto his back, throwing her leg over him to straddle his body.

"Of course you are. You couldn't be anything but the alpha. So can a woman be the leader of the pack?"

"No. Ours is a male-dominant society. The men are in charge and our women…"

"Get ordered around and spanked when they don't do as they are told," she said archly.

"Our women are loved and protected above all else," he corrected. "But yes, my Catherine, as you have found, they answer to their mate's authority and when they choose to be naughty, get their pretty bottoms spanked in order to correct the behavior. Do not get comfortable up there, mate. It will be a rare occasion that you find yourself in anything resembling a dominant position with me."

"I don't know," she said, pinning his shoulders to the bed. "I think I've got you right where I want you."

Catherine was shocked at the speed with which he moved and she found herself flat on her back with Marco towering above her.

He chuckled as she struggled and could not get away from him. "Enough, my Catherine. Yield to me and I will release you. Continue to struggle and I will keep you where you are until you do. Continue for too much longer and I will think you need your backside rewarmed to remind you who is dominant between us. You, my beloved, are mate to the alpha of the DeMedici pack. We have held our land and our territory for more than a thousand years. And you, my beautiful, spirited mate, will learn to behave."

He watched as she balled her fist. He leaned down and kissed her.

He whispered against her lips, "Strike at me again, mate, and I assure you that the spanking you receive will be more painful than all the others."

Catherine relaxed her fist. "Wouldn't do me any good anyway, would it?"

"Doubtful. Do you yield?"

"Yes, Marco. I yield… for now."

He laughed and released her, allowing her up but pulling her into his lap as he too sat up. "Now and forever, my Catherine. Now and forever."

CHAPTER FOURTEEN

The next morning, Marco felt as though an enormous burden had been lifted from him. Not only had he found his beloved mate, but she had accepted that he was a wolf and not been repulsed by it. He reminded himself that while she knew humans could be turned, they had yet to discuss his desire to turn her so their spirits could truly be one.

He had left Catherine sleeping peacefully and well sated. She had a healthy libido—one to rival his own. He stood in the shower and allowed the steam to penetrate his skin and make him feel renewed.

Marco felt the knot begin to swell at the base of his cock. He chuckled to himself. That was another topic he had yet to bring up to his mate. He desperately wanted to mount her and force his knot deep within her, sealing her to him before rocking her and ultimately tying her. While he knew that in human form the initial breach was painful for a woman, he knew most felt that the rapture experienced after that was more than worth it. He closed his eyes and focused on getting the knot to release.

He also knew that he needed to explain their custom of alphas marking their mates. While the knot had tried to form repeatedly, Marco found it far easier to suppress the knot than the almost overwhelming need to mark her as his own. On numerous occasions when he had been inside Catherine, stroking her powerfully and feeling her experience the ecstasy that had become an integral part of their lovemaking, he had felt his canines elongate in order to allow him to mark her.

He was drying himself off and chuckling, thinking he was certain he could entice Catherine to accept his knot, but that the discussion around her accepting his mark might be an altogether different story.

The final papers for the acquisition of the vineyard would reach him today. He planned to invite Griffin to join them for lunch at the hotel before taking Catherine home to the villa. As he contemplated the drive in the vintage sports car, it occurred to him that might be an opportune time to discuss any of the three sticky topics that needed to be addressed.

Marco heard a soft knock on the door to their suite as he exited the bath and saw a slip of hotel stationery being pushed under the door. He turned to ensure that Catherine still slept in their bed. He walked to the door and reached down to pick up the paper. What he read enraged him.

Catherine,

It is imperative that we speak. I had expected to hear from you before now.

I understand you have allied yourself with Marco DeMedici. I would urge

you not to discuss our relationship or the reason for our need to meet.

Salvatore

How dare this Salvatore presume to speak to his mate and keep that information from him? Marco had been well aware that there had been others before him, but Catherine had indicated there was no one with whom she was currently or recently involved. If this Salvatore thought to take his Catherine from him, he would find himself grievously injured and most likely dead.

• • • • • • •

Catherine was awakened by a feeling of unrest. Marco had explained to her that fated mates could most often feel if the other was experiencing an emotion that was especially intense. She looked up to see him scowling in her direction.

"Marco? What has you upset? I couldn't possibly have done anything between now and when you left me in our bed. I was asleep the whole time."

"Who is Salvatore? And why does he have a need to meet with you?"

It was then that she spied the note in his hand.

"Is that for me?" she asked, a note of irritation creeping into her voice.

Catherine knew what he was thinking. She knew him well enough to know that he didn't really believe there was anyone else, but also knew that she had secrets she had not shared with him. So while she was a bit annoyed that he'd read the note meant for her, she also knew that were the situation reversed, she would be feeling the same way.

"It was not in an envelope nor was the outside of the paper addressed to anyone in particular. Answer my questions—who is Salvatore and why does he want to see you?"

"Tell me… in your wolf society is it only a man's integrity or honor that can be insulted?"

"Of course not. Answer me, Catherine."

"Your tone and your accusation are insulting mine."

She let that sink in for a moment. Marco crossed over from the door and sat beside her on the bed, handing her the note.

"I am not angry or upset with you, my Catherine. And if I made you feel like I was then I am very sorry. But I do not appreciate men I do not know or have ever heard about from you seeking an audience with my mate and trying to keep it secreted from me."

Catherine set the note aside without even looking at it.

"I was going to tell you if you wanted to be forgiven you needed to go stand naked in the corner. Then I realized you'd have to be facing outward and the logistics of my trying to mount you there were just too much for me to figure out at the moment. So I just thought fuck it."

Marco smiled slowly. "I see," he said, his pronounced accent becoming even deeper.

He drew the covers away from her body. He chuckled as the reveal showed her body flushed with desire, her beautiful nipples as hard as diamonds, and her legs parted so that he could see and scent her arousal. He dipped his head down, sucking in one of her nipples as his hand came up to pay attention to the other.

"I, however," he said as he nibbled and kissed his way up her body, "am more than capable of figuring out how to properly forgive my naughty mate after she has been punished. The logistics as you said are quite easy as I have been forced to do it before."

"Wait a minute. You're the one who jumped to conclusions and all but accused me of having a thing with Salvatore."

"No, you jumped to the conclusion that I had done so when I never doubted your commitment to me. And you, my beautiful mate, not only thought to try to be dominant with me but used language unworthy of you."

"Shit, Marco, that isn't fair."

Marco silenced her with a kiss. He had a hand on either side of her body.

"On your belly, Catherine."

"Why? Are you going to take me from behind again?"

"You wish that were what I had in mind. Do as you're told or I will put you over my knee."

He waited. Catherine thought seriously about going on the attack and then realized that tactic had never served her well with her mate. Reluctantly she rolled over as he'd told her to do. She didn't have to wait long for his hand to spank her hard three times, making her cry out.

He leaned down and kissed the side of her neck.

"That's one swat for each word. The next time even one curse word passes your lips, you will get your mouth washed out and your bottom spanked properly. Yes?"

She nodded. "Yes, Marco."

He rolled over and she saw out of the corner of her eye that his cock was engorged and seemed to be swollen at the base.

"Marco? Are you all right?"

Marco glanced down and realized there was a knot forming rapidly.

"Yes. That is a knot and we will discuss that later. Now who the hell is Salvatore?"

"Are you sure? That thing looks like it hurts."

"It is decidedly uncomfortable unless it is lodged within your mate's pussy."

"Uhm, Marco, you can barely fit all of you inside as it is, I don't think that will fit."

Marco dragged her across the bed and into his arms.

"When the time is right, my Catherine, I assure you I will make it fit."

She giggled and eyed the knot again. "If you say so."

"I do. Now who is Salvatore and why does he want to meet?"

"Is that what the note says? I didn't read it."

"Catherine," he growled. "If I have to ask you again, it will be once you are draped across my thighs with a very warm, red bottom."

Catherine managed to straddle him as he reclined on the bed, rubbed her hardened nipples along his chest, and kissed him passionately.

"To be honest, I have no idea what he wants and am far more interested…" She stopped short and caught herself. She swung her leg back over Marco and tried to get up without him hearing the sob caught in her throat.

Marco caught her around the waist and hauled her back into bed. Even though she struggled, she found herself forced into his embrace where he used one finger to tilt her head up so he could see her eyes.

"Listen to me, my Catherine," he said in a voice as smooth as silk with an underlying seductive growl. "There is nothing you could say to me that would change who and what we are to each other. Whatever secret it is that causes you such pain, share it with me so I can ease your burden."

"You can't fix it," she said softly, trying to keep from crying.

"I couldn't change into a wolf either," he said, teasing her.

She giggled. "Yeah, well, we both know I was wrong about that."

"Even if I can't fix it, at least sharing it with me would allow me to help you carry the burden of whatever this sadness is. Please, *tesoro*, won't you tell me?"

He drew her leg back over his torso so that once again she was straddling him. He kept his hands on her hips but waited for her to decide.

"I have a sister," she said softly.

"How did I not know this?"

"Because she's been missing for months."

"Is she in hiding? Did run off? How can she be missing? How could she worry you like that? She will have a lot to answer for when we find her."

For the first time in a long time, Catherine felt a light begin to shine in that dark part of her heart that feared the worst for her sister.

"She wouldn't worry me like that, Marco. We were close. She graduated and went on a long-planned grand tour of Europe. She last checked in with me when she arrived in Rome. She left Rome to go to Milan and then Florence via train. She was last seen at the Ponte Vecchio here in Florence and then… nothing."

She could see Marco thinking.

"The embassy did nothing?"

Catherine nodded, not trusting her voice to speak.

"Your country's embassies are rarely of any help in these situations. I take it Salvatore is someone you hired to find her?"

"Yes. So if he does want to speak to me, I have to meet with him."

"I will meet with him. I will have questions he will need to answer. But we will begin a search for your sister."

"I've been searching…"

"Yes, my Catherine, but you are human and do not have friends in Army Intelligence and Interpol. Also Griffin has begun to do a bit of investigating about rumors that have surfaced over the past few years involving human women going missing and being turned without their consent."

"Oh, God, Marco, you don't think…"

"We don't know what to think at this point, but we will meet with Salvatore and then we will find the answers you seek."

"Thank you," she said, kissing him. "Thank you."

"We haven't found the answers yet, but we will. Is this the cause of the sadness I often sense from you?"

"Yes," she said, speaking so softly it was barely audible.

"That's all of it?"

"You don't think she's alive either, do you?"

"I don't know what to think, my Catherine. But I believe the answers—whatever they may be—will give you peace and allow the grief you feel to heal. Whatever we find, I will be by your side. You will also have the love and support of our pack. You are no longer alone."

Catherine leaned forward, taking his face in her hands to kiss him and then yelped as his hand connected with her behind.

"That had best be the only secret you ever try to keep from me," he said, grinning at her. "Keeping secrets from one's mate is a spankable offense and the next time your magnificent ass will sorely regret your tongue's decision to hold itself."

"You're such a jerk," said Catherine, laughing. "Now can we go meet with Salvatore?"

"No. I will meet with Salvatore and Griffin for lunch after we have signed the final papers on the new property. I want Griffin to hear what he has to say as well."

"I'm going to be there."

"No. I will meet with him and see what he has to say."

"Marco, this is my business and she is my sister."

"Yes, and it will be far easier for him to fool you than Griffin and me. I will get to the bottom of what he knows. As I said, I'll see what my contacts can find."

"Marco, do you think my sister's disappearance has anything to do with those rumors you've been hearing?"

She got up and tried to move away from the bed. Marco caught her arm and gently pulled her back. He was sitting on the edge of the bed and drew her into his lap. The sad, guarded look in his eyes was all the answer she needed.

"You do," she said in a voice filled with anguish. "I should have done more… why didn't I do more?"

Marco softly embraced her. "You did all you knew to do. But yes, I fear your sister may have fallen victim to my kind. Promise me this won't turn you against me or our pack."

"Don't be stupid. I'm sure there are bad wolves just like there are bad humans. Do you think they've turned her?"

He nodded solemnly. "I fear if they took her, she was turned without her consent. The change can be difficult on one who did not choose it for themselves."

"Do you think she's dead?"

"I don't know. If she has even a fraction of your strength, she yet lives and we will find her."

"Is Salvatore a wolf?"

"I detected the slightest hint of wolf scent on the paper. It could have come from anywhere. But if Salvatore is a wolf and has been stringing you along, it would go a long way toward explaining why he didn't want me to know."

Catherine searched his face; there was more. "What aren't you saying?"

He smiled. "You are too smart by half," he said. "A beautiful woman with means, but all alone in the world…"

"You think he was going to make me disappear too."

"If he is wolf and if he is mixed up in all of this, then yes, I do."

"If he's been leading me on, I'll kill him," she whispered.

"You won't have the chance," he said grimly. "Griffin and I will find out the truth and go from there. You, my Catherine, are to remain in our room."

"She's my sister, Marco."

"And you are my mate, Catherine. You will remain here where I know you will be safe or I will meet alone with Salvatore and send Griffin up here to keep an eye on you."

"Is Griffin…?"

"Yes, Griffin is a wolf as well. He too is an alpha, but with no pack at present. He is a long-time and trusted friend. He will be on our new property ostensibly to help with the transition, but really I want him to have a place to heal. He's only just left Special Forces."

"Were you in Special Forces?"

"Yes. It's where I met Griffin. I left before he did and came home to take my place as alpha. Tell me about your sister. She is your only family, correct?"

"Yes. Her name is Shannon. She is younger." She closed her eyes and bit back a sob. "Tell me about your family."

"I too am the eldest. Next is my brother Stefano. He is mated to the daughter of the alpha of Crete and will likely be their next leader. Then there is Tony. He is beta for the pack in Rome. We will talk to him as well about your sister. And last is the baby of the family, Gianna or Gia as we call her. She is mated to an Irish alpha and has one son and another on the way." Marco laughed. "My sister was none too happy when I allowed Aidan to force her to run and he claimed her. I swear he put a baby in her belly the night he marked her and now less than two years later she carries another."

"What do you mean, forced her to run and marked her?"

He laughed again. "Hmm, let me think. Which answer will incur less of your anger?"

"Let's go with forced her to run."

"I'm not sure that is the correct one, but nonetheless I will answer you. In our society if a man is certain a woman is his fated mate, he can try to convince her alpha of that. If he succeeds and she is being difficult, he can force her to run. If he catches her, she will have no choice but to accept his claim."

"Let me get this straight," she said, starting to get angry. "Some jerk convinces you he is supposed to be with Gia. She says no, he forces her to run... like literally?"

Marco couldn't help but enjoy the fire he could see igniting in Catherine. "Yes, the custom is that the woman shifts to her wolf form and her mate takes off after her. If he catches her, he can claim her in wolf form, although most allow their mate to shift back and accept the claim as a human."

"And what if she's not a wolf?"

"There are other ways naughty mates who are being difficult can be convinced to heed the call of their fated mate... as you are well aware."

"Oh, that's so not happening on my watch. I'll take a shotgun to any male wolf who tries it and if you allow it, you'll be sleeping by yourself."

Marco chuckled. "The women of our pack are going to be so happy I waited for you to lead them. But you will not fire on a fellow pack member and the only place I will ever sleep is by your side."

"Marco, that's barbaric. Does your sister even speak to you? Did your brothers do anything?"

"They wished Aidan well as he chased after her," he chortled.

"It's not funny. What if he'd hurt her or been abusive after the fact?"

"Then I would have slit his throat and brought my sister and her sons home. While males are dominant in our society, most will not tolerate abuse." He pulled her closer and kissed her. "And it is a known fact that many spirited women, the best women, resist the call of their mate. For instance, there is a story of one of the DeMedici mistresses who got her bottom spanked on a train when her mate had to chase after her."

Catherine blushed. "Do *not* tell that story to anyone."

Marco laughed out loud at her. "And I suppose you really don't want them to know how frustrated and upset you were when you found out I was not going to have my way with you on the train or in the car coming back to Florence. Or how ready you were for me when I got you back to our room. As I recall, my Catherine, you climaxed as I mounted you and drove my cock deep within you on the first thrust."

"So tell me, how many mistresses of your pack have you had?"

"You misunderstand, my Catherine. Mistress or Madonna is the honorary title given to the mate of the alpha. The latter is Italian and only used in rare instances when the alpha's mate is of exquisite beauty, intelligence, and kindness, has earned the love and respect of the pack, and is seen as an absolute necessity to the happiness of their alpha and thus the happiness and security of the pack itself."

"I'm human. I'll be lucky if they don't refer to me as that horrible American gold-digger you dragged home from Florence."

The signs of amusement left Marco's face. "Any male referring to you with anything less than the utmost respect will find himself without a pack. Any female will be punished and made to apologize. If her mate or our beta do not see to it adequately, I assure you that I will. You are my mate and will be treated with the respect that is due you. Besides, once they see you are my fated mate, they will fall at your feet."

"Have I mentioned I can be a terrible klutz? I'll just trip over any bodies lying around."

Marco threw back his head and laughed. "And that, my Catherine, is why they will love you almost as much as I do."

CHAPTER FIFTEEN

Marco had finished freshening up. Catherine was sulking on the settee. He smiled as he crossed to her and leaned down to kiss her. She shoved him away.

"Catherine, behave yourself."

"I want my clothes, Marco. I'm meeting with Salvatore."

"You are not and, therefore, have no need of your clothes unless I am going to have to send Griffin up to watch over you."

"Why can't I go?"

"Because you did not give me enough time to check this Salvatore out. I don't know who or even what he is. Without that knowledge, I cannot assess how much of a threat he is to you. I will not put you in a situation with that many unknowns. Now do I need to send Griffin up or can you do as you're told?"

"Are you always going to be this intractable?"

"Where your safety is concerned? Yes. Now is Griffin coming up or not?"

"No. If Salvatore is a threat, I'd rather you have backup. And don't you dare croon at me that I'm a good girl. I swear I'll punch you."

Marco leaned down and kissed her. "Save that fire for

later, my Catherine. And see that you mind me."

Marco left her and Catherine went into the bathroom and showered. She came out in a towel and thought about remaining naked awaiting her mate's return.

"Fuck that," she said.

She got dressed and headed downstairs. She was intercepted by the man she had seen with Marco at the restaurant... Griffin.

"I thought you might think to defy Marco, given your spirited nature. That would be a decidedly bad idea," Griffin said, grinning at her.

"I don't recall asking for your opinion."

"You didn't," he said agreeably. "But I've known your mate far longer than you. He doesn't take it well when his orders are disobeyed, especially where the safety of his mate is concerned. Go back to your room, Catherine, and this stays between us. If not, I fear your ride home will be none too comfortable."

"There won't be any need to tell him anything. He'll know because I plan to join them. Now get out of my way."

Catherine pushed past him and trotted down the grand staircase with Griffin in her wake. She spied Marco at a table with a man she assumed was Salvatore.

"Marco, my beloved," she called as she crossed the room to him. "I do hope you apologized to Salvatore for my tardiness."

Marco stood and intercepted her as she tried to skirt around the table from him. "I explained to Salvatore that my mate would not be joining us."

The inference that Salvatore was a wolf by Marco referring to her as his mate was not lost on Catherine.

"Griffin, I'm glad you're here. Do me a favor and have a little chat with Salvatore here. Find out what he knows and then see he is paid for any balance due. Apparently my mate and I need to discuss more pressing matters upstairs. Also if you could have my car brought around, I would appreciate it."

"I'm under no obligation to speak to anyone other than my client," Salvatore said, starting to rise.

Marco pressed his shoulder until Salvatore yielded and sat back down. "The only obligation you have is to yourself and to stay alive. Give me the information I need and you will remain so. Refrain from anything less than complete and candid disclosure, Griffin here will rip your lungs out. And if you leave this place, tell those who employ you that Florence falls under my protection and from this moment forward anyone caught hunting or trespassing in my territory will be dealt with in the harshest of manners. And if I catch any of you hyenas sniffing around my mate, I will hunt each and every one of you down and ensure that you meet a slow and painful end."

Catherine watched as all of the blood left Salvatore's face.

"Griffin, may I impose on you to get the information we need?"

"But of course, old friend. That won't be a problem. Before I leave the hotel, I'll have the information. I take it you'll just leave your things?"

"Yes, Catherine and I will sort it out the next time we are here."

With a death grip on her elbow, Marco led Catherine out of the dining room and back toward the stairs that led to their suite.

"Do you always stay here when you're in Florence?" she asked conversationally.

"Naturally, we own the hotel. I keep our suite and several rooms here for our use and the use of our pack and friends."

"You own a hotel? Just how rich are you?"

"We," he said, stressing the pronoun, "are quite wealthy."

"You do not get to order me around," she hissed.

"But I do. And you, my Catherine, are about to be reminded as to why you should learn to do as you are told

136

and what happens when you don't."

He ushered her up the stairs and into their room. She could feel the anger rolling off of him in waves. She had assumed her would be annoyed with her, but not to this extent.

Once inside he spun her around and pressed her back into the wall, his mouth descending on hers in a feral kiss. She pushed at his chest. Her resistance lasted only a moment before it melted in response to his passion. Catherine found her body almost immediately answering the call of his and she responded with a hunger of her own.

When Marco finally released her mouth, she said shakily, "I take it he's a wolf and is implicated in my sister's disappearance and that of others?"

"Yes on both counts. He knows far more about your sister than he has ever let on. If I am correct, and Griffin will now see to verifying that, you were to have been his next prize—taken and sold to the highest bidder to be mated and used for breeding by your new alpha."

"I would never have agreed to that."

"You miss my point," growled Marco. "The choice would never have been yours. You are an unclaimed female, beautiful, wealthy—few alphas using Salvatore's service would have given your choice a second thought."

He moved away from her, leaving her aching for his touch.

"Now, my Catherine," he whispered seductively, "you will strip and go stand in the corner to await your punishment."

"What? You can't be serious. You drag me upstairs, kiss me until I'm breathless pinned up against a wall, and then think you're going to spank me? I don't think so."

"You do not have a say in the matter. Or rather the only say you ever had was whether or not you obeyed me, which you chose not to do. Show me you are remorseful for your choice by getting naked and accepting your punishment."

She searched Marco's face for any inkling of softness to

his resolve and saw none. He growled and her whole body shook with trepidation and the re-ignition of her ever increasing sexual response to him.

Resigned, she removed her clothes and moved to the corner. Catherine stood there, acutely aware that he was watching her. She knew that he would be able to sense her growing apprehension at the spanking she knew he intended to give her and at the annoying evidence of her arousal that knowledge produced.

Catherine was startled when she felt his hands skim down her sides.

"Such a beautiful mate."

He ran his hands up and cupped her breasts, rolling the nipples between his fingers. Catherine pushed her tits further into his hands, enjoying the possessive yet tender way in which he was fondling her. He ran his hands down her ribcage and spanned her waist with his hands.

"And such a tiny waist."

His hands dropped lower.

"But then we come to my mate's wide-set hips made to cradle a man as he fucks her face-to-face and to hold her steady when he is pounding her from behind. Not to mention her beautiful ass that fills his hands as he drives into her or bounces so prettily when she is being punished for her latest misbehavior. Do you know which of your assets I intend to utilize first?"

"Marco, please, I don't want a spanking. I just got angry and lost my temper."

"At least you now understand why you are being chastised without my having to tell you. It will serve you better if you can remember that before you earn yourself a red bottom."

He took her gently by the hand and led her back toward the bed. She didn't resist with any true effort but she did not come willingly. He chuckled and sat down, drawing her over his lap so that the fullness of her lower cheeks was at the highest point.

Before she could make another protest, Marco brought his hand down with a resounding swat, making her yelp. He proceeded to cover her entire backside with blow after blow. Catherine could feel the sting and heat from each one compounding on the ones before it. She could well imagine that once again it would be red and swollen when he was done.

She needed to remember that while Marco loved her dearly he would not tolerate her disobedience and each and every time she sought to defy him, she would find herself face down over his knee on the receiving end of a disciplinary spanking. She briefly considered if loving him and being with him was worth accepting that as a part of her life. She realized that she'd never had a choice. From the first time she felt his call reverberate through her body, she was lost. The God-saving grace was that as he had told her, Marco would always find her and would love her completely for as long as fate allowed them to breathe the same air.

Catherine tried not to struggle or squirm. Partly due to pride and not wanting him to know how much it hurt, but partly to try to acknowledge that she was accepting his authority and discipline with good grace. But good lord, it hurt.

She lost the battle of not fighting and began to cry and tried to kick her legs, which were trapped between his. She heard him chuckle as he merely tucked her more securely in place and continued to rain swats all over her bottom, now covering ground he had already spanked.

She began to cry and promise incoherently that she would behave in the future and beg him to stop.

"Had enough?" he asked pleasantly as he rubbed her backside soothingly.

"Yes, Marco," she said between tears.

"Try to remember that it is best to do as I ask."

He allowed her to get up and merely pointed to the corner. He followed her there and lifted her hair, rubbing several strands through his fingertips. He nuzzled the back of her neck and she could feel her nipples begin to draw into stone-hard pebbles and her pussy begin to clench in desperation to be filled with him.

"You, my mate, disobeyed me and left our room against my express orders. That is the last time I will use just my hand to reprimand you for blatantly disobeying me. The next time, I'll warm up your bottom with my hand, but then you will feel the sting of my belt as it lays welts across your backside. And as you chose to be naughty in public, part of your punishment will also be witnessed by those who work for us. They will be reminded that their alpha is not a man to be trifled with."

"What do you mean public?"

Marco chuckled. "You will find out soon enough."

Marco pulled her away from the wall, opened his fly once again, freed his cock, and thrust into her waiting pussy. As she had feared, she climaxed immediately upon his possession. Catherine found it very annoying that he could make her respond so forcefully and so immediately when she was so angry with him. She had no doubt that Marco found it appropriate and fitting that she did so. He began to plunge in and out of her pussy, seemingly focused on producing a dramatic response from her.

She braced against the wall and tried not to wince each time his groin made painful contact with her well-punished backside. She likely would have tried to move away from him, but he had a hard hold on her and seemed intent on driving home his point that she would not disobey him and that he was the dominant partner between them.

He hammered her pussy, making her come numerous times, each climax seemingly more intense than the last. Finally she surrendered to him—not just physically, but mentally and emotionally. She knew he felt it as his thrusting became more loving, coaxing her response as opposed to demanding it. That was her undoing. She could handle his anger, but this acknowledgement and acceptance of her capitulation to his dominance seemed to produce an intense well of pleasure for him and she caught her breath to keep from crying.

He thrust hard one last time and surged forward, shooting his cum deeply within her.

Catherine was completely spent and barely noticed when he withdrew from her and lifted her in his arms and then deposited her on the bed. He made short work of rolling her in the bedsheet before hoisting her over his shoulder and heading out the door.

"Marco, no."

"Yes, my Catherine. You saw fit to give reign to your temper and acted out in front of others. Those same people will now see you spent and wrapped in a bedsheet tossed over the shoulder of your mate to be taken home. They will be correctly presuming that you have had your bottom spanked and are leaking my cum from your well-used pussy. Those who are wolves will assume I have claimed you, which with the exception of marking you as mine, I have."

She began to struggle and he landed a large hard swat on her derriere. Even though there was padding from the bedsheet, it still stung. Catherine ceased to fight him and only hoped her hair hung down over her face hiding her embarrassment.

He headed toward the door. She heard Griffin offer to get the door for him and thought not only would she extract her vengeance on her mate but on his good friend as well.

The car was waiting for them and Marco chuckled as he saw the added pillow to the passenger seat. He gently put her in the roadster before going around to the driver's side. Catherine tried to ensure the bedsheet stayed up, covering her nudity as best she could.

"You will thank Griffin for his thoughtfulness the next time you see him."

"I will do no such thing," she said petulantly.

"You will," Marco said calmly but firmly. "Your choice is only whether or not you will have a freshly spanked bottom and a pussy full of my cum when you do so."

They rode for the next several hours in silence.

"Marco?"

"Yes, my Catherine."

"Are you done being angry?" Her voice was small and quiet.

He found a place to pull over on the side of the road.

"I was done being angry, my *tesoro*, when I felt you surrender to me. And you did surrender, did you not?"

She nodded. He leaned over and kissed her with a mixture of passion, abiding love, and reverence.

"Do I have any clothes in the car?"

"Not that I know of."

"Jesus, Marco, I can't meet your…"

"Our," he corrected.

"Our pack wrapped in a bedsheet and smelling of sex with you."

He laughed. "By the time we get home, the story will have already arrived. Several of those who work at the hotel have friends or family who live and work at the villa. That their alpha has found and claimed his mate will trump any circumstances surrounding the manner in which he did so. They will most likely be waiting to meet you and thrilled that you are finally home."

CHAPTER SIXTEEN

They drove on with Marco pointing out various landmarks along the way. Catherine asked him questions about their home, their people, and their business. Marco assured her once again that if she wanted to pursue a career in art restoration he would ensure that she had all that she needed. When he saw the shadow of grief pass over her eyes, he caught her hand, bringing it to his mouth to kiss it. He reassured her that they would find out what had happened to Shannon. And that if she still lived, she too would be brought home.

"Marco, what about my things at Sera's?"

"I will send someone to collect them. I will also, if you like, invite your friend to come to the villa and make sure she knows it is an open invitation and that she is always welcome."

"Is Sera a wolf?"

"No. And it is often best not to tell someone of the difference unless she is your fated mate and you wish to claim her, but she is your friend and I will leave that decision to you."

"In other words, best to remain silent on the subject of wolf shifters unless you're a man and wish to spank and fuck her silly?"

He laughed. "In not so many words."

"Marco, promise me you won't ever let anyone force Sera to accept his claim."

"That I cannot do. If she is the fated mate to a wolf, he will eventually find her and even though I will let it be known that she is under my protection, I would be obliged to listen to a man who believed she belonged to him."

"But he can't make her run if she's human, right?"

"Correct, but he can still force the issue."

"How?" she asked, fearing she knew the answer.

"He can claim her in front of the ranking members of the pack—just the alpha or any combination of the alpha, beta, and omega. The alpha must always be present."

"Claim her how?"

"One of two ways."

Once again, he pulled the car over and stopped.

"He can put her over his knee and spank her or he can put her on her back and fuck her until she yields. So you see, my Catherine, you were always going to surrender."

"If anyone tries to force Sera or any other woman who seeks *my* protection, be prepared for one helluva a fight. Truly, that is barbaric."

"That is tradition."

"Fine, it's a barbaric tradition."

He laughed. "Only from a woman's point of view."

"From any point of view."

"No. For a man with a fated mate who is being difficult, it ensures he has a way to bring her to heel. Never doubt, my love, had you not willingly surrendered to me..."

"I'm not sure how willing I am," she said, grinning at him.

He chuckled. "Nevertheless, always remember I was more than prepared to claim you in any way I had to. The interesting thing is that it seems those alphas who must force the issue with their mates have the happiest of pairings."

"Then we should be deliriously happy."
"My point exactly."
They got back on the road.

• • • • • • •

Several hours later they crested the top of the hill that marked the outskirts of the vineyard proper. Marco had pointed out to her the boundaries and explained how their entire estate was set out. When he drove through the automated gates and stopped the car so she could see the entire vineyard laid out before her, she couldn't help but gasp at not just the sheer size of the operation, but its incredible beauty.

"Marco, this is amazing. I don't think I have ever seen a place more beautiful."

He smiled at her and kissed her hand again. "It pales in comparison to its mistress."

"Then can its mistress please have clothes so she can meet her pack in something other than a bedsheet?"

"No. There is nothing in the car."

"Marco! How can you do this to me? If there truly is nothing in the car, then what am I to wear at the villa or should I just run around nude?"

"Don't be absurd, Catherine. For the next little while you and I will spend our time in seclusion where we will discuss whether or not you wish to become a wolf. By the time you decide, there will be clothes for you to wear provided you behave. Now cease your tantrum."

"I am not throwing a tantrum, but I will if you don't get me something to wear. I am not going to meet your pack or family dressed in nothing but a bedsheet."

Catherine opened the car door and got out.

"Catherine, get back in the car."

"Not until you get me some clothes."

"Catherine," he growled. "Get in the car."

"No. I am not going to walk into the villa like this."

"I was never planning for you to walk. Would you prefer to be carried into the villa over the threshold in my arms? Or would you prefer to be carried up to our room slung over my shoulder in the same state as when I carried you down the stairs at our hotel?"

"Neither. If you want these people to respect me, I need to be dressed when I meet them. Damn it, Marco, if there really are no clothes in the car, take me somewhere where I can buy something to wear."

Catherine watched as he slowly exited the car and shut the door firmly. Looking at his face, Catherine realized she may have once again pushed him too far. She turned to run, but was too late. As she spun, she got caught up in the bedsheet. She started to stumble and fall, but Marco was there to catch her.

"You caught me," she said, surprised that he had been able to react so quickly and keep her from injuring herself.

"I will always catch you, my Catherine—either to keep you from falling or when you are trying to avoid a spanking."

"You can't be serious. You're going to spank me?"

"Did you return to the car when I told you to do so?"

"Well, no," she admitted.

"Did you cease your tantrum when I warned you to stop?"

"No," she sighed.

Marco gently fisted her hair. It occurred to her that it was odd that he could tangle his hand in her hair giving him control and yet do so in a manner that didn't cause her any pain. And then she realized that any shot she'd had at any dignity whatsoever upon first entering her new home had vanished when she disobeyed him and then tried to run.

She shook her head—what made her think she could outrun a wolf in his own vineyard wrapped in a bedsheet?

He used her hair to guide her into position over the hood of the car. He pulled the bedsheet up. Catherine could feel the cool breeze brush over her bared bottom like a lover's caress.

"Marco," she pleaded.

Marco said nothing but quickly began to pepper her backside with light stinging swats that made her dance to try to get away from him.

"I'm sorry."

"Are you?" Marco asked her.

"Yes. Please?"

Marco stopped and stepped away from her. Catherine wisely stayed where he had put her. Out of the corner of her eye, she saw him come close again. He slowly and deliberately reached between her legs and chuckled as she responded by spreading her legs and giving him easy access to her throbbing clit and gaping pussy.

"Please, Marco."

"What is it you want, my Catherine?" he growled, allowing the lust he too was feeling to rumble through her.

"I want you not to be angry when we get home."

"You want to be forgiven?" he said as he stroked her clit, dragging his fingers through her wetness, only barely dipping his fingers into her sheath.

"Please," she sighed.

"And how do I normally forgive you when you have forced me to spank you?"

Wisely, she decided not to argue the point that she hadn't forced him to do anything. "You mount me from behind and fuck me until you've made me climax so many times I lose all sense of time and place."

He chuckled. "But you like my way of forgiving you, don't you, *tesoro*?"

"Yes, Marco, please. Those swats hurt and left a lasting sting, but it's nothing compared to the ache I have to feel you inside me stroking."

She saw him open his fly and his cock spring free. Taking hold of her hips, he positioned himself behind her and thrust home strong and hard. She had come to expect that after he spanked her that his possession of her would cause her to orgasm and this time was no exception. She had ceased to think about the fact that they were standing on what amounted to a very long drive way up to their home or that the first time her pack would see her would be tossed over his shoulder carried up to their room. All she cared about was Marco's passionate and all-consuming lovemaking.

He thrust in and out, groaning with pure animal satisfaction as he did so. She moaned in obvious, oblivious pleasure. She took one of her hands off the hood of the car, grasped the hand holding one of her hips, and brought it up to push aside the bedsheet to fondle her breast.

Marco began to piston his hips, ratcheting up the power and speed with which he fucked her. Even though every time he surged forward, her punished backside made painful contact with his pelvis. It caused a mixture of discomfort and profound lust. Catherine found she reveled in the way he made her feel—both physically and emotionally. Whenever he finished with her she was completely sated and was content to bask in the love she felt envelop her.

He groaned loudly as his cock began to spurt into her. She could feel her pussy being bathed with his creamy essence. Her only thought was that she hoped none of it would drip onto the floor when he carried her to their room. He thrust one last time, ensuring that there was nothing left to spill in her and so that she could feel his power and love.

"Now, my naughty mate, we will adjust your covering and you will get in the car and behave yourself. When we get to the main house, you will stay in the car until I get you out and take you to our room."

"You're going to carry me over your shoulder, aren't you?"

"Did you behave well enough to either walk in at my side or be carried in my arms as my cherished mate?"

"No, Marco," she admitted.

"You're right, you did not. So, I will take you as my claimed, naughty mate. Our pack will see their new mistress is spirited but that their alpha is her master."

He let her up and helped her adjust the bedsheet so that it was secure and nothing was showing. He helped her into the car, leaned down, and kissed her.

"Never forget, my Catherine, that I am the dominant one and that I love you with every fiber of my being."

She reached up to bring his mouth back to hers and returned the kiss.

"I'll try not to forget that you are alpha. But you need to know even when you are punishing me that I never doubt your love for me. Just please don't let my willfulness cause you to doubt that I love you just as much."

He smiled. "I promise, my Catherine. And as you know, I am a man who keeps his promises."

CHAPTER SEVENTEEN

They drove onto the grand courtyard, which had once served to allow horse-drawn carriages to easily maneuver and now served as driveway in front of the stunning main house.

"Marco?" she pleaded softly.

"No. I am hopeful that a small dose of humbling will cause the lesson you should have learned this day to be retained."

"I may never forgive you."

He chuckled. "Ah, my sweet mate, when I have mounted you and brought you to orgasm several times, you will remember it is you who needed to be forgiven and will beg me to do so."

They drew up in front of the villa and were greeted by what Catherine assumed to be the majority of their pack as well as those who worked in the large house. She would have given anything to be able to sink down into the roadster and not have to endure the embarrassment she knew she was going to feel. As Marco walked around the car and helped her out, her eyes pleaded with him to allow her a little dignity.

"No, my Catherine. You will accept your punishment."

Catherine knew that shoeless, any kick she tried to deliver would do nothing to deter him, but she refused to simply be made to submit in front of her new family without at least showing them some of her spirit. She meant to let them know that while their alpha may be all powerful, that he had a mate who was his equal. She stood on her tiptoes to offer her mouth to him for a kiss, which he was happy to accept. She drew back her foot and kicked him soundly in the shin.

She was rewarded by his quick intake of breath, indicating that her blow had at least inflicted as much pain to him as it had caused her foot to deliver it.

Marco growled and Catherine felt the sound surround and envelop her, causing wildfire to race through her veins and her pussy to become wet and needy. She heard those who were watching gasp at her outrageous, at least by their standards, behavior. She took small comfort in knowing that she had made her intended point.

Catherine saw him bend into her hips and hoist her over his shoulder. He had barely settled her over his broad frame when he landed two sharp swats to her still stinging backside.

"Catherine, these are your people. I had thought to introduce you to them before taking you to our room, but apparently you continue to choose to indulge your temper. My people, this beautiful creature draped over my shoulder is your mistress, Catherine. She is spirited and fills my heart with joy. I know you will make her welcome when she is allowed to rejoin you."

Catherine closed her eyes and considered all the ways she might kill him. She shook her head. Even as angry as she was, she knew she didn't want him dead. She didn't even want him hurt. What she wanted was to become one with him. There it was, the truth she'd been avoiding. She wanted to be a wolf. She wanted to share his life, to give him children, to watch them grow up in this magnificent palace.

Even from her vantage point she could see their home

was incredible. She smiled; it amused her that she was finding the use of the plural possessive pronoun to come easily to mind.

Marco went up the stairs and headed down a long hall filled with beautiful frescos and artwork. He paused only long enough to open a door and close it behind him. He set her down on her feet. She could feel him controlling his anger. She tried to move past him and he blocked her way.

"What did I tell you about striking me?"

"That I wasn't to do it and you'd spank me if I did," she said with growing agitation.

"Then you admit that you knew that if you kicked me, you would be due a spanking?"

"Marco, I was angry. You provoked me. I want these people to at least like me and you humiliated me."

"I thought to bring the lesson home both to you and our pack that you are mistress here now, mate to me and that you will mind me."

"And for those women brought up in this way of life, I'm sure it must be somewhat easier. But I've been on my own most of my life. I've answered to no authority other than my own for a long time. Even you said that you understood it was difficult for me and it is."

"But you understand that your former way of life has come to an end for you. Regardless of whether you choose to transition to a wolf, you are my mate and must learn to function effectively within the parameters of our society."

"I know that. I even accept that, but I'm not always going to get it right. My first reaction is to fight for what I want or know to be right, not to listen to my mate and accept his word as law."

"But my word is law," he said sternly. "For you and for the rest of our pack. I cannot be seen allowing my mate to run roughshod over my authority. You have done nothing all day but defy me. I thought you were starting at least to reconcile with the idea that you will submit to me."

"And you promised you wouldn't let my willful nature

make you doubt my love for you," she accused.

Realizing she was on the verge of tears, he kissed her and smiled. "I do not doubt what you feel for me. But I will not allow you to continue to defy me and endanger yourself."

"The only danger I've been in is not being able to sit down for the rest of my life and having eternally tender feminine parts, although that's not the worst thing that can happen to a girl," she said, trying to lighten the mood. "But I am trying. You have to admit, bringing me home wrapped in a bedsheet and then tossing me over your shoulder and swatting me was a bit over the top even for you."

"And you must admit that you knew I would spank you for kicking me. You are mine, Catherine. Do you agree?"

"Yes, but..." she said, her irritation increasing as he refused to see her point of view.

"There is no but—only yes or no. If you choose not to obey me to stay safe, I will take other measures to ensure it is known that you belong to a powerful alpha who would kill anyone who tries to harm you."

"What measures?" she asked, her own anger now rearing its ugly head.

Marco pinned her to the wall and quickly stripped the bedsheet away from her. He opened the fly of his trousers. She felt him lift her off the floor. He used the wall for leverage and without ever releasing her, he slowly lowered her back down and onto his engorged and hardened staff.

"Oh, God," she managed to moan as she clung desperately to him.

"Wrap your legs around my back."

He growled with satisfaction as she did so. He grasped her bottom and began to raise and lower her on his cock.

"Yes," she moaned as she began to forget that she had ever been angry with him.

Marco continued to move her body up and down as he thrust into her, causing her to cling to him as she climaxed. In the back of her head Catherine knew that she should be more concerned about what he would do when he had spilled himself in her. She knew he was angry. It even briefly crossed her mind that she was most likely going to be spanked again, and her passion lagged for a moment.

Catherine could feel him sense her loss of focus on their lovemaking as he drove harder into her now, holding her steady so that his cock jackhammered her pussy. She was no longer capable of coherent thought. All she could do was glory in the power he had over her body and the way her entire being seemed to sing in harmony with his.

She felt him ratchet up the intensity yet again as she climaxed and then felt another one immediately start to form. He had the ability to make her come repeatedly in rapid succession. Her pussy spasmed around him, trying desperately to keep him inside and force his cum to fill her.

Finally, she felt him begin the tempo and speed she had come to expect before he took his own release. She nuzzled his neck and threw her head back, reveling in his embrace. She was not prepared for the sharp nip he gave the base of her neck between the hollow and the beginning of her collarbone. It was brief but somewhat painful. She started to protest as he began to release her.

Instinctively Catherine realized he had not bitten her hard enough to break the skin or start the change process. But it did bring into sharp relief what it was she wanted. She didn't know all of the details of how the transition worked or what all it entailed, but she knew enough about her own feelings to know she wanted to be one with him. She brought her hands up to his head, kissed him with same kind of possessive passion with which he always kissed her, and then pressed his mouth to the same location he had nipped.

"Harder," she whispered.

He raised his head and looked into her eyes. She knew that he could see everything—her understanding, her acceptance, and her love.

"Are you sure?"

The constant rhythm with which he fucked her never ceased and had rendered her speechless. She could only nod. Once again, he drove into her, urging her body to give him more. As she reached the height of her climax again, Catherine felt him take hold of the place on her neck he had nipped before. Only this time, it was no nip he inflicted but a deep and savage bite. He began to thrust even harder into her, making her scream not from pain but from the unrivaled ecstasy he was giving her as she began to feel his cock pump his essence into the depths of her sheath. Her pussy clutched at his cock, urging every drop of his cum to spill.

When they were both finally still, he lifted her off his cock and set her on her feet but kept her pinned to the wall. He reached between them and righted his trousers, closing the fly. He removed his silk handkerchief and dabbed at the bleeding wound before kissing it reverently.

"My beloved Catherine, I have no words for the gift you have given me this day. I am glad that we are already home so that when the change starts to come over you, we will be able to take care of you. I will send for the doctor in Milan so he can be here from the very beginning of your transition. And while I will entrust your physical care to him, I will be by your side until you are safely delivered from the change."

"Is it that bad?" she asked, the first small inkling of fear creeping into her voice. She had been sure of her choice, but now realized the consequences of that choice were far greater than she may have actually considered.

"To watch it is a terrible thing to behold until the virus gets the upper hand and starts to take over. On the other hand, those who have been through it say they felt as though they had a long nap from which they awoke with a tremendous hangover."

"And you wonder why people don't sign up to be changed? Will I be able to shift like you did?"

"Yes. It takes time to learn and practice. But once the hangover goes away you will feel better and more in touch with your body than you ever have. And your libido should increase," he said, chuckling.

"I haven't heard you complain about the state of my libido."

"I haven't. I have yet to find you anything other than wet and willing."

She giggled. "Well, you'll just have to try to keep me satisfied."

He laughed. "I have yet to knot and tie you, my Catherine. I will have no trouble keeping your naughty libido in line."

She touched the mark on her neck. "This sucker is going to leave a nasty scar, isn't it?"

"I would not call it nasty, but yes, the scar will be prominent. It will let any wolf know that you are mate to an alpha and that harming you in any way will result in grievous bodily harm to the one who does."

CHAPTER EIGHTEEN

Marco swung her up in his arms and carried her to their bed. Catherine saw it was an incredible masterpiece of antique Italian furniture. A huge four-poster bed that looked to be even bigger than a regular king-size.

He laid her down gently into the soft, yielding mattress. He picked up the phone next to the bed and said something in Italian she didn't understand.

"Marco, this thing is a work of art." Catherine sat up to get a better look at her surroundings, noting that even though the bed was soft, sitting was still uncomfortable. "This whole room is amazing. And did you pick this mattress so that when you take your well-spanked mate to bed she would be more comfortable on her back?"

He chuckled. "Well, and I fear often-spanked mate."

"Not funny."

"Perhaps. But you are in charge of whether or not you get disciplined."

"Pfft. We both know I'm not always going to do what you tell me." She reached for a robe that had been lying across the bed and put it on.

"Yes, we do; and we both know that even when you are being disciplined you become aroused."

"As do you," she said pointedly.

"Indeed. But your mere presence inflames my lust."

She rolled her eyes and snorted.

He grinned at her. "I'm glad you like the room, but you are free to change anything in our room or in the house that you feel would better suit you."

"Are you kidding me? You don't mess with an iconic design and interior like this. It's stunning... and it's all real, isn't it?"

Marco laughed. "It is indeed, but it is your home now so change whatever you like. There is a large warehouse with furniture and other things and if nothing there suits you, buy whatever you like."

"Just like that, buy whatever I like?"

"Yes, my Catherine, whatever you like." He leaned down and kissed her. "I want you to be happy. You have given me so much. I do not want you to ever regret your choice."

"I never had a choice," she said softly. "From the moment you touched me, I was lost. I realized you were everything I'd ever wanted. I should tell you, there hasn't been a boy born in my family for many generations."

"My Catherine, although ours is a wholly male-dominated society, female children are rare and are revered. But I will tell you as long as you and our children are healthy and safe, I will be the happiest of men."

There was a soft knock on the door. Marco called for the person on the other side to come in. Giovanni, beta for the DeMedici pack, entered the room.

"Catherine, this is Giovanni. He is beta to our pack and my most trusted friend."

Giovanni approached Catherine, taking her hand in his and rubbing his forehead against the back of it before kissing her hand. "Mistress," he said with great reverence. "We are all so glad our alpha has finally found you and brought you home."

"Thank you, Giovanni. Between you and me, he didn't give me much of a choice."

Giovanni chuckled. "Of course not. He is alpha. His word is law."

"So he tells me," Catherine said, smiling. "But between you and me... I'm not buying it."

"Your mate is as spirited as she is beautiful, my alpha. I wish you both the happiest of pairings." He turned to Marco. "The doctor you requested should be here shortly. Both of you look to be in good health and fine spirits. May I ask why you sent for him?"

Catherine pulled the rolled collar of the robe away to reveal the fresh wound. She knew that Giovanni would have been able to see the area as Marco brought her into the villa. Understanding the importance of marking, Catherine was certain Giovanni would have made note of its absence earlier.

"I see. You do us the greatest honor, Mistress. It is no small thing to leave your humanity behind. Shall I send Valentina and some of the other women to attend your lady?"

"Yo, Giovanni?" He turned back to her. "Best to ask me if I want attending and if so, by whom."

"Catherine," Marco growled quietly. "You will not use the sharp side of your tongue to Giovanni. He is beta to our pack and only sought to see to your comfort. Apologize."

"So tell me, Giovanni, what are the chances he won't spank me this close to the change?"

Giovanni chuckled and shook his finger at her. "Do not seek to place me between the two of you, Mistress. I will always side with our alpha."

"Geesh, a girl can't catch a break."

Marco growled and Catherine felt his annoyance growing.

"Your alpha has no sense of humor. That being said, I do apologize. Marco is right, being snarky with you was uncalled for. But if I'm not going to be feeling good, I'd rather not have people around me I don't know. I'm sure I'll be fine with just the doctor."

Marco put his arm around her and kissed the top of her head. "You will not be just with the doctor. I will be at your side until you have completed the transition."

Catherine looked up and saw the concern on his face. She turned to Giovanni.

"Perhaps you could create some problem requiring his assistance. I fear if you don't he may scare the hell out of this doctor… or is he one of us?"

Giovanni smiled. "He is one of us, Mistress. It is helpful to have a doctor who is familiar with our differences from humans."

"That would make sense. Thank you, Giovanni. Please let everyone else I look forward to meeting them dressed in something other than a bedsheet."

Giovanni smiled and left the room.

"So… how do I know the change is starting?" she asked quietly.

Marco stretched out on the edge of the bed and pulled her into his embrace. "You will feel a chill and then warm up very quickly. Your surroundings will be on a sort of soft focus and you will pass out. Then I will keep watch over you until you wake."

"With a massive hangover."

"Yes, but we will be prepared to help with that as well."

"How long does it take?"

"It depends. In cases such as yours, where the person making the transition wants the transition, usually just a few days, although I will insist that you follow the doctor's orders regarding your recovery."

"Does Giovanni take bribes?" she giggled.

He chuckled. "No, and he tells his alpha if his mate tries."

"And does Giovanni have a mate?"

"He does indeed. Valentina. I fear the two of you will get on all too well."

"What do you mean by that?"

Marco smiled and kissed her. "Valentina has a penchant

for misbehaving. I fear the two of you will inspire each other."

Catherine giggled. "Sounds like my kind of girl."

"That's what I'm afraid of."

Catherine explored their room while Marco made a few phone calls necessary to the running of the vineyard. The room was truly a masterpiece with opulent furnishings. The bath was a good size and the free-standing tub and shower massive. Both looked like they could easily hold more than two people. The small adjacent room was a well-appointed walk-in closet.

"Marco? What are we going to do with my loft in SoHo?" she said, standing in the doorway.

"What would you like to do? We can keep it and perhaps try to get to New York annually."

"Do we ever have business in New York?"

He nodded. "Occasionally."

"Could we keep it and offer it to members of our pack to use to vacation? I hate the idea of selling it or subletting it, but I also know it is expensive to maintain just because."

Marco crossed the room and folded her into his embrace. "Just because it would contribute to your happiness is all the reason I need."

She looked up at him, prepared to make a sarcastic retort when she realized he was speaking the absolute truth. She hugged him close and pulled his head down, capturing his mouth with hers. "God, I love you," she said.

He smiled. "And I you, my Catherine... who didn't think she wanted to be my Catherine."

"You are never going to let me live that down. And oh, God, Griffin saw it as did others at the hotel."

"As I said, the stories about the DeMedici pack's glorious American mistress will grow to legendary status."

"No one knows about the train, do they?"

"Some know I had to chase you down and caught up with you there. The rest they will surmise as you are here with me now."

"I don't suppose the odds are that I can just peacefully die during the change."

"No, my Catherine. I fear you will have to wake and take your place as my mate."

"I can tell you this... I'm going to stay up in our room when I can't sit down comfortably."

"You will not," said Marco sternly. "It is your place to help guide and watch over our pack. That you cannot do from our room. When you have a sore bottom you will simply add a pillow to sit on."

"The hell I will. You have already caused me enough embarrassment."

"You forget—your women live within the same parameters as you. It is not uncommon to see at least one woman needing the extra addition of a cushion."

There was another knock and Marco called for the person to enter. A lovely woman with dark hair, light olive skin, and smiling eyes entered the room.

"Marco, Gio wanted you to know the doctor has arrived. He assumed you'd want him set up in here, but wanted me to double check."

She turned toward Catherine and approached her. As had Giovanni, she took Catherine's hand in hers, rubbing her forehead against it before kissing it.

"Greetings, Mistress. I'm Valentina. Giovanni is my mate."

Catherine smiled. Valentina's words were carefully measured and respectful, but she could sense a kindred spirit behind the demure façade.

Catherine turned to look at Marco. "You were right to be afraid, my love. Be very afraid. Valentina and I are going to be the best of friends and cause all kinds of trouble."

"Do you really think so?" Valentina asked, sounding all too eager.

Catherine's smile grew broader. "Count on it. Let me get this pesky change behind me and we'll see what we can't get up to."

Marco rolled his eyes. "Giovanni and I will need to come up with a plan designed especially to deal with naughty mates who conspire together."

"Pfft," Catherine said, dismissing Marco and making Valentina giggle.

"Valentina, go back down and let Gio know he was right to assume I want Catherine in our bed."

She hugged Catherine. "I wish you the easiest of transitions and I will see if I can't come up with something for us to do when you have recovered."

Valentina left the room before Marco could respond.

"You do know that within the hour, every woman within our pack will know that their alpha's mate is not in the least bit afraid of him."

"And should they want me to be?"

"No," he admitted. "The best mistresses are strong and capable. Their acceptance of their mate's authority is seen and received as a great gift. As Gio said, they are already glad that you are with us and the women will be more so now that they have a leader. Although be careful you do not lead them into too much mischief. Remember that their mates will hold them accountable and in the same manner I hold you."

"As long as you ensure that they get forgiven the same way I do, I'm sure they won't mind."

Marco laughed. "That is between a man and his mate and is not something into which I pry."

Another discreet knock came on their door, to which Catherine responded. It was Giovanni again.

"I have the doctor with me."

Catherine stepped forward. She thought she might as well start letting it be known that she was not under Marco's thumb.

"Don't just stand there, let the man in."

Giovanni opened the door and ushered the man in.

He looked at Marco. "May I approach your mate?" he said with great respect.

"Excuse me, Doctor? I'm your patient and what he wants has little to do with it," snarked Catherine, who was beginning to think that managing other people's expectations was going to be more difficult than managing Marco himself.

"Forgive my mate. She is new to our way of life and fails to understand that a male wolf does not simply approach an alpha's mate—especially when said alpha is already concerned for her safety. And you have my permission to do whatever is necessary to help make my mate's transition as easy as possible."

It was Catherine's turn to roll her eyes as Giovanni tried to stifle a laugh.

She turned toward him, "Seriously, Giovanni, you need to invent something to take his mind off this."

"I fear, Mistress, you are your mate's only concern at this time and his attention will not be diverted," Giovanni said, smiling.

"Then send Valentina back up here. I'm sure she and I can think of something."

Marco laughed at the somewhat confused look on the face of his beta. "I fear I should make an apology to you, my dear friend, ahead of time for whatever mischief my mate leads yours into. They met and much like when I first caught her scent, they recognized each other immediately."

Giovanni shook his head. "You couldn't have been fated to a nice quiet girl who thinks only to please her mate?"

Both Marco and Catherine laughed in unison. "I fear not, old friend."

Giovanni shook his head and then his finger at Catherine. "I suppose then I shall go and enjoy the relative quiet of the next few days as you transition." He departed the room.

The doctor approached Catherine. "How are you feeling, Mistress?"

"Actually I'm a bit chilled."

Marco and the doctor looked at each other knowingly.

The doctor walked over to the bed and began to remove things from his bag.

Valentina poked her head in the room. "Mistress?"

"Valentina, please, it's Catherine."

Valentina grinned. "I saw you were wearing Marco's robe and noticed you didn't seem to have anything with you. I brought you one of my nightgowns. I thought you might be more comfortable."

"Thank you, Valentina. That was so kind of you. I think I'm going to grab a quick shower and put it on. I have enough time for that, don't I?"

"Perhaps, but I think it advisable that either Valentina or your mate accompany you in case you get dizzy."

"Valentina," Marco said softly, "go downstairs and let Gio know I am not to be disturbed unless it is an extreme emergency and let the rest of the pack know their mistress is beginning the change."

Catherine could see Valentina was worried. "Tell the women a new day is dawning and then make sure someone has a big plate of scampi ready when I wake up."

Valentina rushed over and hugged her new friend. "You will have all of our thoughts and prayers."

Marco went with Catherine into their bath and stayed with her as she showered and then put on the beautiful silk nightgown.

Marco saw her tremble and sway a bit as the nightgown settled around her. "Dizzy?"

"Yes. Is it starting so soon?"

He nodded. "Often when the change is initiated by being marked, the transition is accelerated."

Before she knew what he was about, Marco swept her up in his arms and carried her to their bed, where the doctor had set up an IV. Catherine turned her head as the doctor inserted the needle and then lay back in their bed.

For all her bravado, she was glad when Marco stretched out beside her and held her close. The last words she heard before she lost consciousness was Marco telling her he loved her and would be waiting when she opened her eyes.

CHAPTER NINETEEN

Catherine drifted through time and space. She caught glimpses of previous lives with Marco. He didn't always look the way he did in the present, but she knew it was him. She remembered when in her dreams she knew he needed her and had found her way to his side. Now, she saw that he had been tortured and on the brink of death. She understood that it was her presence that had allowed him to escape the pain and focus on surviving. She saw Griffin burst into the room to save his friend and then a rather debauched night in Germany after Marco had recovered.

Catherine was also able to see the night Marco had first caught scent of her. She vowed to try to remember to tease him unmercifully about the little waitress he had planned to bed that evening as well as the degenerate night he and Griffin had spent after Marco had been captured, tortured, and almost killed.

When the memories, for she knew that's what they were, were unsettling or disturbing, she could feel Marco beside her and hear him whispering to her in Italian. She found his presence, even in the abstract, to be comforting.

Right before she began to ascend to a level of consciousness she saw a loop of all of their lives and in each herself being spanked and fucked by Marco. The memories made her giggle. She realized somewhat later that it was her own giggle that woke her.

• • • • • • •

Marco watched over Catherine for three days. The doctor had tried to get him to rest or even eat, but the alpha of the DeMedici pack had been unrelenting. He would remain at his mate's side. The doctor was able to observe that even when she rested comfortably she seemed to take solace from him. When the virus racked her body or she seemed in pain, Marco was able to soothe her discomfort by whispering in her ear and nuzzling her. The doctor felt he would always remember the devotion that Marco had shown to his Catherine.

• • • • • • •

Catherine opened her eyes. "Marco?" she said, reaching for him.

"I am here, my Catherine. Don't try to move. Let the doctor examine you first."

"Is it over? Jesus, my head hurts. I want two bottles of water, a regular painkiller, and a banana. Then I want another shower."

Marco looked at the doctor, who nodded. Marco helped her sit up but kept her cradled against his powerful torso.

The doctor took her vital signs and checked her eyes and her lymph glands and pronounced her through the change.

"But you must rest for a few days, Mistress, nothing too stressful or that causes your body to exert itself. While you are through the change, your body is weak and needs to recuperate before…"

"Before what?" asked Marco, who seemed overly concerned.

The doctor looked decidedly uncomfortable. Catherine

giggled again.

"I believe he's trying to tell you that you can't consummate our pairing and that I have a free pass on getting spanked for a few days."

"I wasn't going to say quite that," stammered the doctor, glancing furtively at Marco.

Catherine began laughing. "Jesus, don't make me laugh. It hurts my head." She elbowed Marco in the ribs. "Worst two hangovers in my life and you are responsible for both of them." She reached next to her and picked up the house phone. "*Prego*—can you get me Valentina? Thank you."

"And how am I responsible for both? Arguably this one because I marked you as mine, but the other?"

"Was from drinking way too much DeMedici wine with Sera. By the way, can you send her another case of our best? She loves it but it's much too expensive for her."

He chuckled. "Of course, my Catherine. I will have it delivered and let her know she is to phone when she is low and another will be delivered. And why did you send for Valentina?"

There was a knock on the door and the subject of Marco's question popped her head in.

"You are awake? That's wonderful news. It's spreading throughout the villa and you can't hear it, but your people are very happy. What can I do?"

"Two things. First get me a couple of bottles of water, some non-prescription painkillers, and a banana."

"Done!" said Valentina cheerfully. "And two?"

"Start thinking of things that I can do to drive Marco nuts for the next few days; apparently I have a doctor's excuse to avoid spankings!"

Valentina laughed with her mistress, Marco shook his head and rolled his eyes and the doctor tried to make himself as small as possible.

Within a few minutes, Valentina had reappeared with the requested items and Giovanni in tow. Catherine sat up, taking one of the bottles of water, taking the pills and draining the water.

She giggled and looking at Marco, peeled the banana in a most provocative manner, causing Marco to growl, the two women to burst out laughing, and Giovanni to invite the doctor to leave the room and make himself comfortable downstairs where lunch was being served.

"Valentina," Giovanni called. "Unlike your mistress, you do not have a free pass on getting your pretty bottom spanked and my palm is beginning to itch like it does when it has been too long since it got to do just that."

Valentina looked at Catherine, who indicated she should leave with Giovanni and calling after them, "Killjoy!" She turned to Marco. "You won't let him spank her, will you?"

He kissed her and chuckled. "I think because she came when he called he will not get after her. But let that be a lesson to you before leading your ladies into waywardness. It will most likely end up that all who participated are sitting on extra cushions the following day."

Catherine pulled down the last side of the banana and then licked back up it to the top before putting it in her mouth and running her tongue all around it. Marco's eyes were riveted to her display. She nibbled and licked the banana in the same way he had felt her suck his cock the few times he had allowed it. He felt his cock quickly becoming uncomfortably hard.

"Catherine, quit playing with your food."

Her eyes danced with merriment. "What would you rather I played with?" she asked lustily as she placed her hand on his growing erection.

"You heard the doctor," growled Marco.

"I barely mind you, and you spank me when I don't. What do you think I'll do if it's someone who doesn't have the ability to do that?"

Marco drew her to him and pulled her atop his body so his length was pressed against her.

"He may not, my beloved, but I will enforce his orders. While I am glad to see you rapidly recovering, you will do as he says. Know this, if you are well enough to misbehave, I will deem you well enough to be spanked for doing so."

"As I said… killjoy."

Marco leaned down and captured her mouth in a passionate kiss. Her surrender to him made him groan with pleasure and frustration.

"I missed you, my beloved."

"I didn't miss you at all." She kissed him and nipped his lower lip. "For I was never alone. It's not just that I could feel you physically here with me, but we have spent many lifetimes together and I got to see glimpses of most if not all of them."

"So you know you truly are my fated mate."

"Yes," she purred, "but we need to have a little chat about that waitress in Florence."

He laughed. "Once I caught your scent, I thought no more of her. I wanted only you and will only want you to the end of my days."

"And I mean to have a little chat with Griffin to thank him for saving your life and to find out more about one steamy night in Germany."

"He will never betray me. For his mate awaits him as well. Know this, my Catherine, it is the way of alpha males to enjoy women until they find their fated mate. From that point forward they see and want no one else."

While the banter between them had been teasing, she could see he was serious.

"But what if something were to happen to me?"

"The mates of fallen alpha males are forever protected by their pack. They are given the same honor as a dowager empress."

"But what about the men…"

"I fear they rarely last more than a year without their mates. So have a care with your safety, my Catherine."

"I don't intend to live without you either, so no more going off to war without me."

He smiled. "I will do my best to honor your request, but

you will never be allowed to go to war."

Catherine popped the last of the banana into her mouth, chewed and swallowed it.

"Not as good as what I would rather have had my mouth around, but between it, the painkillers and the first bottle of water, I'm feeling better. I do want to take a shower. Want to join me?"

Marco laughed. "You are determined not to mind the doctor. But I am just as determined you will. I will come with you to make sure you don't get lightheaded in the bath, but your libido will have to wait a while before it is satisfied."

Marco got up and helped her to her feet.

"We'll see about that," she whispered as they headed for the bath.

Once inside, Marco set her on the vanity bench. Catherine briefly wondered how many other DeMedici mistresses had sat there over the centuries deciding how best to entice their mates. Catherine discarded the nightgown, crossed to Marco, and wrapped her arms around him, rubbing her body along his back and finding her own ability to growl seductively.

He turned around, smiling. "Behave yourself. Do you feel you can be safe in the shower?"

Thinking quickly, she said, "I am feeling a little unsteady, can you get in the shower with me?"

"I can, but you will not have your way."

Marco removed his own clothes and then helped her into the steam shower. Catherine purred as his hands ran down her wet body possessively. He had been right when he'd said her libido would increase. She wanted him; no, that wasn't right... she needed him. She turned in his arms, rubbing herself along his body, this time his front, and giggling as his cock started poking insistently at the juncture of her thighs.

"Enough, my Catherine. Not until the doctor says it is safe for you to exert yourself."

Catherine jumped up, wrapping her legs around his waist and rubbing her hardened nipples on his chest then leaning back to offer them to him for suckling.

"Then don't fuck me hard, just make love to me where you stroke me past the point of being able to think. You were right, Marco, as the hangover is quickly fading, I feel more alive than ever before and I need desperately to feel your cock deep inside me. Please?"

• • • • • • •

Marco looked down at his mate. She was never more alluring that when she was offering herself to him flushed with desire. Her nipples grazed his chest like sharpened daggers. He could feel each ridge and whorl on their surface as they skimmed over him. He could feel her sweet essence leaking out of her slit and reaching the head of his rampant cock that seemed to have developed a mind of its own and was determined to bury itself in her wet, wanting sheath.

Knowing he should not give in to her wanton entreaties, his lust overrode his good sense and he leaned down to take her nipple in his mouth. Her sigh of exultation and rapture was his undoing. He latched on to her and began to greedily suck and nip at her nipples, locking his hands under her ass to keep her in place and nibbling between her breasts as he hungrily took her into his mouth and pleasured her.

He felt her arms wrap around his head, encouraging him to continue what he was doing. He nipped and kissed his way up the column of her throat and along her jawline, going up one side and then down the other. Reverently he kissed her quickly healing mark. His cock was becoming increasingly engorged and he was finding it difficult to focus in order that the knot would not form. It was a battle he was fast losing as he listened to her sighs and growls of pleasure.

If she wanted him buried in her, there was no better way to accomplish that than sinking his knot into her and tying her to him. The initial breach was always painful for the woman, but the actual rocking motion of being knotted and then being tied to one's mate was peaceful and deeply satisfying.

He forced her legs from around his waist but swung her up in his arms before she could protest too loudly. He thought about drying her off, but decided the knot that had now begun to rapidly form was not something he wanted to explain. She would resist the initial breach, but once accomplished he knew Catherine would quickly accommodate it and then would glory in the ecstasy that came with it.

He plundered her mouth as he carried her to their bed. He knelt down with her, laying her gently on her back and slipping in next to her. His cock twitched and trembled, seeking its targeted destination. He rolled her over onto her back and nibbled his way down her body. She writhed and moaned as he seduced her into a place he had yet to take her.

She climaxed for the first time as he wrapped his lips around her clit and sucked hard.

"Oh, God, Marco," she cried, lost in her own pleasure.

He continued to suckle and nip her pleasure bud until he felt her body getting close to the edge of a second orgasm, then he removed his mouth, nuzzled the engorged nub with his nose, and plunged his tongue into her dripping slit. Again he felt her body arch upward, seeking even closer and more intimate contact. His cock now throbbed with necessity and ached in a way it never had. Knotting this woman, his mate, was all his cock or he had ever wanted.

She exploded again, screaming his name as he continued to tongue her. Without giving her any respite, he began to lick and nibble his way back up her body. He quickly replaced his tongue with his fingers and stroked her. She moved her hips in nature's oldest rhythm to match his stroking. He continued to finger her until yet again she was on the cusp of coming.

Once he had settled himself between her thighs, he

cupped her ass, whispered his love for her in her ears. Her body once more came apart and he surged forward, forcing the large knot past the entrance to her sheath and burying himself within her. This time the scream was part pleasure and part pain.

He stilled himself inside her.

"Shh, my Catherine, I know the breach was painful, but be still, my love, and let yourself grow used to the fullness you feel."

Marco remained motionless as her body accommodated him and his knot was pulled forward and down, making her sigh with immense satisfaction. He caught his breath as he began to swell within her, tying her to him. As the knot formed the perfect seal, Catherine's eyes rolled back in her head and she orgasmed yet again.

"What the hell," she said with a mixture of lust and wonder.

Marco noted there was no rancor in her voice. Her legs came up to intertwine with his and she nuzzled and kissed him.

"That, my beloved, is the knot."

He began to roll his hips forward—in essence rocking within her. She came again for him, sighing his name. He rocked her repeatedly as he brought her to orgasm after orgasm. Each time she clung to him and called his name. Never did she try to retreat from him or dislodge the knot. Finally he felt his cum start to rush up from his balls, through the knot and start to gush within her. He had never climaxed as hard, as long, or as much as he did as he continued to bathe her pussy with his seed. Her sheath continued to contract around him, ensuring it got all he had to offer.

When at last he had finished, he raised his head to see her beautiful face reflecting back to him all the love he felt for her.

"Are you all right?" he said softly, brushing the hair from her face.

"All right? All right doesn't even begin to cover it. That was... I don't even have words for it and I don't want you to uncouple from me. I love feeling your power and strength. My pussy is going to hurt like hell when you do, but I can deal with that."

He chuckled. "It's good you don't want me to withdraw, for I couldn't without badly injuring both of us."

"Does it always hurt like that when you enter me with the knot?"

"Unfortunately, yes, but..."

"I can deal with that too. It was pretty brief but oh, my God, when it got even bigger once it was inside, I thought I would pass out from the pleasure. How often do you get those?"

Marco nuzzled her. "In the presence of my willing mate, it is more that I have to suppress them than encourage them to form."

"Have you been doing that up until now?"

"Yes. I have wanted to knot and tie you to me from the first moment I caught your scent."

"You talked about tying and just now about not being able to disengage without hurting both of us... does that last long?"

"Usually at least an hour but more often than not two to three hours. I can roll over so that you are on top."

"No. I quite like having you on top in general and especially this. This is amazing. I think I should get at least ten free passes on misbehaving because you made me wait for this."

He laughed. "I take it then, my most beautiful mate, that you will not object to taking your alpha's knot on a regular basis."

"It had better be on a frequent basis. Oh, my God, it still feels... blissful. Do all male wolves get knots?"

"In wolf form, yes. In human form, only the alphas."

"Good thing you're an alpha then. I'm telling you if I found out about this and you couldn't do it, I'd leave you for the first alpha I could find with a good-sized knot."

Her eyes danced with mischief, merriment, and love.

"Seriously, Marco, I've never felt anything that even compares to this. Do you have any other tricks up your sleeve?"

"Only one."

"As good as this?"

"Better."

"Doesn't exist," she said with confidence.

"Knotting you from behind. It's deeper, the rocking more pronounced and longer, and my release even larger and more forceful. And the tie itself can last up to eight hours. Most couples who engage in rear knots sleep spooned and tied together."

Catherine purred in a pleasured and predatory way. "You'll have to show me that as well."

"I will, my Catherine. You are sure I did not hurt you too badly?"

She giggled. "Let me put it this way, can you do it again in the morning?"

"Yes, mate, I can knot you again come morning, although I'm not sure this is what the doctor had in mind when he told you to rest."

"Why ever not? I'm lying in bed, I'm not moving around, and I'm quite sure when you finally move away from me, I will fall asleep completely sated and happy. Although that's always how I sleep with you—safe, secure, sated, and loved. I think I have become very used to that."

"Then I shall endeavor to ensure that is how you sleep for the rest of your life."

They spent the rest of the time talking with Marco explaining the ins and outs of their vineyards and other businesses and what he would expect from her as his mate. When he finally was able to withdraw from her, she was understandably upset and uncomfortable when her pussy was no longer stretched by him.

"I think my mate dislikes having an empty pussy," he

whispered, allowing her to roll to her side and spooning around her.

She giggled. "I'm afraid, my mate, you are correct. I find I have become somewhat addicted to having you inside me and my pussy is bereft at your leaving."

"Tell your pussy that my cock will knot her again in the morning and once more breach her core to tie her to me."

"Promise?" she said languidly, barely suppressing a yawn.

"I promise, my Catherine," he answered, kissing her shoulder before he too gave in to sleep.

CHAPTER TWENTY

As was his usual routine, Marco awoke as the sun began to rise. Catherine was nestled against him and fussed as he sought to extract himself from their bed without waking her.

"Where are you going?" she asked sleepily.

"Not far, sweetheart. I was going to call down to have something light sent up and speak briefly with Giovanni."

"Knot first, eat and speak later."

He laughed. "No. First I get something more than a banana into you…"

"But I really liked that banana I didn't have to peel. As I recall it spent a great amount of time in me and I didn't like not having more of it."

"Enough, mate. You will eat something, I will speak with Giovanni and the doctor will examine you to ensure that your wanton behavior last evening did not cause me to do you damage."

She rolled over to face him, wrapping her leg over him, using one hand to draw his mouth to hers and grasping his already engorged cock, actually feeling his knot for the first time.

Marco groaned and lightly swatted her backside.

"Hey, you're not supposed to do that."

"I told you if you were well enough to misbehave I would deem you well enough to spank. One does not touch her mate's knot unless she is ready to be breached by it."

"You're the one who's not getting on with it. I've been pretty clear since I woke up that I wanted to be knotted and tied again."

"I will not have the doctor, or anyone else for that matter, in here or on the phone when I am tied to you. Behave yourself or you may well find out how it feels to be knotted and tied on a well spanked backside."

Catherine pushed at him and began to pout. She knew it was immature, but it was the only thing she could think to do. He laughed at her as she pouted.

"Such a naughty mate," he said, continuing to laugh. "I will ease your ache in due course. Never forget the knot is painful to me until it is lodged and sealed within you."

"Well, that helps some to know that."

Before he knew what she was up to, she leaned down, kissed the knot, and licked down to the edge of his cock with a quick swirl of her tongue around the head. He was not quick enough to grab her as she jumped out of bed and ran toward their bath.

"Catherine DeMedici, you should count your blessings that you have just transitioned. Otherwise, mate, you would find yourself face down over my knee."

"Yeah, yeah," she laughed from behind the door. Then she opened it. "Not that I'm complaining, but you just called me DeMedici… do we not have weddings?"

"Not a typical human wedding. We take our vows, which we will do, but it is customary for the alpha's mate to take his last name and we will have rings."

"Will mine have a really big diamond?" she teased.

He laughed. He realized she filled his heart with such joy that he laughed often. "As big as you want. Do you want a wedding?"

She crossed back toward him. "It doesn't have to be a wedding per se and I don't really have anyone except Sera that I'd want to be there. But I'd like some kind of celebration with cake and food."

He caught her and pulled her into his embrace, swatting her backside with a bit more sting than he had earlier. "Catherine, you are Italian now—there is always food."

She laughed. "And fireworks... the kind in the sky—not the kind that you light up in my body."

"We will have fireworks. Anything else?"

She wrapped her arms around his neck and pressed herself to him.

"Actually, all I really need is you," she whispered.

"That, my beloved, you have. Now put on one of your nightgowns and get back into bed."

"I don't have any nightgowns and even if I'd brought one with me to Italy, you brought me home naked in a bedsheet, remember?"

"Yes, I remember. As I recall when I brought you into our home for the first time you had a freshly spanked bottom and a pussy filled with my cum."

Catherine blushed profusely. "Yes, I remember. And some day, Marco DeMedici, I will have my revenge. And I still don't have any nightgowns."

"Have you checked our closet?"

She couldn't quite read his face. She turned and went to the closet, opening it. Where once there had only be Marco's clothes, now there was an array of women's clothing for every occasion. She walked in to get a closer look. She gasped. Designer labels and upper end brands only. Everything was in her size and eclectic style in hues suited to her coloring.

"Marco... how... when?"

"When you were transitioning and with the help of your friend Sera. She went and selected everything and I had one of our people go to Florence to bring them home. Valentina was insistent that she would arrange our closet. I'm quite sure she gave you the lion's share of the space."

Marco loved that Catherine seemed unaware that she

was naked and that everything about her pleased him and caused his cock to harden even more and his knot to grow larger. He joined her in their closet and reached for something to put on.

"Tell me why you get clothes and I have to put on a nightgown?"

"Be grateful that I am allowing you to wear anything at all. Keep in mind, mate, I prefer you naked when we are alone in our room."

"What's the matter?" she said, closing on him. "Is the big bad wolf afraid he can't keep his hands off of and his big bad knot out of his more than willing and very wet mate?" she said, drawing her hand between her legs and then tracing his lips with the silky evidence of her arousal.

Marco sucked her fingers into his mouth and hauled her up close to him with one hand, swatting her exposed behind with the other. She yelped.

"That is the last time I will warn you, mate. Now cease your playing. Put on a nightgown and go get back in bed. I will not warn you again. Bed, my Catherine, now."

She grabbed one of the beautiful silk nightgowns and drew it over her head. "I much prefer when you want me in bed so that you can ravish me."

He chuckled. "So do I. And it isn't that I don't plan to ravish you again this morning should the doctor pronounce you no worse for our lovemaking last night."

Catherine went back to their bed and sat on the edge. Marco walked out, finishing dressing. As he put a beautiful braided leather belt through the loops of his trousers, he said to her, "In bed, Catherine, under the covers. Behave yourself." He crossed the room and picked up the house phone. "Could you send the doctor and Giovanni up to me? Luca? Yes, if says he needs to see me. Also send up espresso and biscotti for me and ask the doctor what might be good for Catherine."

Within short order, people descended on their room. A young man who resembled a high-end male model was the only one Catherine didn't recognize.

"You must be Luca," she called to him.

"Yes, Mistress," he said as he crossed to her and paid homage as had the others.

"Luca?"

"Yes, Mistress?"

"Could we make it Catherine? Especially in our bedroom with me in a nightgown sitting in bed. Mistress seems a wee bit formal."

"Yes, Mist... Catherine."

"Good boy," she crooned.

Marco growled low.

"Oh, hush," she said. "He's not an alpha and doesn't have what I want. Now could you get this over with so I can have what I want?"

"What is it you need, Catherine? I will get it immediately," said Luca.

"My mate is walking the razor's edge she likes to traverse," rumbled Marco.

"I could be more explicit but that would really piss you off... you know and embarrass you in front of our pack members?"

Marco caught her meaning and began to laugh. "Touché, my *tesoro*. Giovanni, I didn't think this through. Let's the three of us step outside to give the doctor and his patient some privacy."

"Of course, Marco. Valentina will be up momentarily with your breakfasts."

The three men stepped out, leaving Catherine alone with the doctor.

"Just so you know, you are to tell him I am perfectly fine and fit to do anything I see fit to do."

The doctor smiled at her. "But that you are yet too weak to withstand any kind of correction?"

She laughed. "Yes. I'm so glad we understand each other."

"You, Madonna, are going to keep our alpha on his toes.

You should know that I owe Marco DeMedici everything. I was a medic. I was with Griffin when we got him back from those bastards. He should have died. All the time we were transporting him and as he recovered, he repeated one thing over and over… Catherine."

"He never told me that."

"I don't think he knows," said the doctor. "No one else—man or wolf—could have survived what he did. I have always believed the only thing that kept him from succumbing to his injuries, both physical and mental, was you. And for that, Madonna, those of us who call him alpha will always serve you. However, I will not allow you to endanger yourself."

With that he proceeded to take her vital signs and to perform a thorough exam.

•••••••

Marco had stepped outside his room to speak privately with Giovanni and Luca.

"Luca, you wished to see me?"

"Yes, Marco, I need to know if you approve the business plan that Griffin and I have proposed. Your Welsh wolf has a keen mind for business and already we are seeing that the workers at the new vineyard are happier and more productive. I hate to bother you, but I need to know how to proceed."

"I must confess, Luca, that I have thought of little else than my mate. I trust both you and Griffin. If you both think the business plan is the way to proceed, I will sign off on it without reading it. If it fails, it falls on me."

"Yes, Alpha. I understand. Your mate is captivating."

Marco smiled as Luca turned to leave. "Oh, Luca…"

The young man faced him.

"See that a case of our best wine is sent to Catherine's friend Sera in Florence. Make sure that whomever delivers it lets her know she is to call when she gets low so that we can keep her well supplied."

Luca grinned. "Yes, Alpha."

As Luca left, Giovanni turned to Marco. "How may I assist?"

"My Catherine has a younger sister named Shannon. She has gone missing. Speak with Griffin to get the information he got from an unscrupulous private investigator named Salvatore. Ensure that Salvatore knows I am aware of what he had planned for my Catherine. If he is still in Italy when I come out of seclusion with my mate, I will kill him."

"I take it we are going to try to find the Madonna's sister?"

"We will find out what happened to her sister one way or another." Marco smiled. "So, she is the Madonna already?"

"I'm afraid so. My Valentina sang her praises and it is obvious that she has already brought you tremendous joy. The doctor was quick to chime in that he believes she had a hand in bringing you back from the edge of death. I told Luca to call her Mistress until I had checked with you."

Marco laughed. "No, I always knew she was destined to be the Madonna. She is exquisite, isn't she, Gio?"

Giovanni laughed with him. "That she is, but you are right, she and Valentina are going to create all kinds of mischief and mayhem."

"The best mates are always the most spirited, are they not, old friend?"

"I fear it is so. I will leave you to enjoy your time alone with your mate."

"Thank you, Gio. See that cook sends up regular meals and simply has someone knock when they are left outside the door."

• • • • • • •

Catherine felt him enter the room before she saw him. She was surprised at the way her heart leapt with delight that he had returned.

"Marco, make him stop fussing."

"I will do no such thing, my Catherine. You will do what the doctor feels is needed."

"Your mate is a remarkable woman. She seems to have made a complete recovery and your loving care of her last night seems to have restored her to perfect health. I would have no trouble releasing her care completely to you." He began to disassemble the IV equipment. "You, however, my Madonna, should know that also means should your mate deem you in need of correction he is free to do so."

There was a knock on the door and Valentina stepped in. "I brought you breakfast as well as some water, fruit, crackers, cheese. All things you can munch on as you are hungry and able," she said, giggling.

"Valentina," Marco scolded.

"Oh, hush, she's just being a realist. She knows I plan to take advantage of my wolf physiology and raging libido and fuck your brains out, not to mention that whole knotting thing you promised me," Catherine said, laughing.

"I'm going to be leaving now," Valentina said, escaping quickly. The doctor followed her.

"All right, my Catherine, you have had your fun and embarrassed me in front of the ranking members of our pack. You are done now."

"Maybe. Then again, maybe not."

Marco growled at her, irritated, but with an underlying seductive tone.

"I'm willing to call us even…" she said, hopping out of the bed, flinging off the nightgown, and launching herself into his arms, "if you are willing to take me back to bed and knot and tie me to you."

"You must eat, my Catherine, in order to truly regain your strength."

"How about we move everything to the side of the bed, you knot me, and once we are tied we can nibble and then fall back asleep."

"And the next time we wake there should be an actual meal for us to eat and you will eat before I pleasure you yet again."

She leaned and rubbed against him. "And is it such a chore to pleasure me, my mate?"

He chuckled. "It is, but I am a generous man and therefore am willing to sacrifice myself so that our pack may have its beloved Madonna."

"I don't deserve that title."

"You do. You are beautiful beyond compare, smart, already protective of our people, and you have made your mate, their alpha, the happiest of men. You, my Catherine, are a Madonna of the first order. Now come to bed, mate, your service of my knot is needed."

She giggled and practically ripped his clothes off before pulling him into bed on top of her. Marco wasted no time in knotting her, bringing her repeated orgasms and then flooding her womb with his seed. This time as she laid tied to him, he rolled over on his back closer to the food and they proceeded to nibble their way through the offerings and talk about things of little consequence.

It was only toward the end of the tie that the cloud of sadness washed over Catherine.

"We will find her," he said quietly. "I have set Giovanni the task of gathering the information from Griffin as well as ensuring Salvatore has told us all he knows and ensuring that Salvatore leaves Italy. We will have someone follow him to see if he will take us to his masters."

"With everything else going on, you still take steps to find my sister. No wonder I love you so."

"As I have said, I will do whatever it takes to ensure you are safe, happy, and well loved."

This time as he rolled her to her back in preparation of withdrawing from her, she resisted his uncoupling from her.

"No."

"Yes, my Catherine, we will sleep, eat, and then I will fuck you long and hard until your pussy will welcome respite from my cock."

"Never happen," she said. "But I will agree only if you agree to knot me from behind tonight so that we can sleep tied together."

He kissed her and nibbled on her bottom lip. "I will agree to your terms, but you drive a hard bargain."

She snuggled into his embrace and was blissfully asleep within moments.

CHAPTER TWENTY-ONE

Catherine spent the next two days in a lovely sexual haze with her new mate. That Marco was a skilled lover she had learned the first time he took her into his arms, but he was also creative and seductive as hell. Catherine had come to find the feeling that permeated every fiber of her being when he called to her was almost as addictive as his knot.

They spent their time not actively engaged in pleasuring one another talking, sharing the stories and secrets of their lives as well as planning for their future.

On the last morning of their scheduled seclusion, they were tied together with Marco on his back and Catherine happily ensconced on top of him.

"So tell me, mate, we spoke some time ago about children..."

He chuckled. "And you fear that as an egotistical member of a male-dominated society that I would only be happy with sons."

"It did occur to me," she agreed. "And that was short-sighted and judgmental of me. I should have known that you would love any children that came from our union regardless of gender. But I never asked you how many children you wanted."

"As many as you will allow," he admitted quietly. "I am not unaware that the greater burden of children falls on their mother—both before and after their birth. But I swear to you I will not be a distant or uninvolved father as I see often among humans. Ours is a society where children are cherished and both parents are involved in their lives."

"Then the DeMedici dynasty shall continue for another thousand years at least for I want lots of children. And I expect you to give them to me. But I have to tell you I will be hoping for sons."

He quirked his eyebrow at her and she giggled.

"I wouldn't wish you as a father of a girl on my worst enemy, much less my own child."

"How can you say that?" he asked, somewhat outraged.

"Are you kidding me? Some young wolf pup comes sniffing around your daughter and he may well end up seasoning a keg of our wine."

"I would nev—" His protest was cut off by Catherine laughing at him. "That is enough out of you, mate. And I will trust you to raise our daughters to be…"

"Careful how you finish that, mate," she said with a feral gleam in her eye.

"As I was about to say before I was interrupted, to be just like their mother. And if he is worthy, I will tell her mate precisely how to handle her."

"They'd have to be an alpha for that to even be possible," she sighed contentedly.

Marco laughed. "Our daughters will be the most coveted in our society and could only be truly happy with an alpha mate. As for our sons, they too will be highly desirable."

"How does that work? I know women aren't allowed to lead a pack… yet. But does the oldest inherit the title or what?"

"Only an alpha male can lead a pack. If all of our sons are alphas then tradition is that the eldest is his father's heir apparent. However, it is not law and I would designate whichever son or son-in-law that I felt best able to lead and protect our pack."

Catherine was quiet for a moment. "I think it is not an easy task to be alpha and lead one's pack."

"But the rewards are many if one is blessed with a mate such as mine."

She giggled again. "Yeah, you say that only because you have me tied to you. We'll see how you feel later today when we have to return to reality."

He chuckled and fondled her backside. "I say that in anticipation of taking you to bed tonight and tying you from behind again."

Catherine blushed and nuzzled the hollow of his throat. "That is a rather dreamy way to sleep, is it not?"

"That it is."

He was quiet and Catherine looked over her shoulder to see that the sun was well above the horizon. "I'm going to have to share you today, aren't I?"

He nodded.

"They're going to be so happy to have you back that you will barely notice you have a mate."

The swat he delivered to her backside was swift and painful, making her yowl both from the sting and from not being anticipated.

"Never will anything come before you. Never forget that. And it will be you they are so happy to see. Me they've known forever. You are new and exciting and already have made their alpha happier than he ever dreamed possible. Your women will look to you to lead them."

He rolled her onto her back and captured her mouth as he withdrew from her. As had become her custom, she fussed at her loss.

"You, my Catherine, are a mate beyond compare and I am the most fortunate of men to call you mine," he whispered.

"So what's the dress code around here?"

"Whatever you deem it to be."

"Ah, good. Then to each their own and I get to play with

all the things Sera picked. She did a really good job."

Marco smiled. "Not in my mind... there are way too many clothes, especially as I prefer you naked and flush with desire."

She giggled and kissed him. "When it's just the two of us, I prefer that as well."

With that he scooped her up in his arms and took her into the shower with him. After they were dressed they started out the door and Marco felt Catherine hold back.

"What if they don't like me? What if they resent this newcomer absconding with their alpha?"

"They will not. You are my mate and they already love and respect you. Giovanni, Luca, and Valentina I am sure have all been singing your praises. You will see."

He took her hand and led her down the hall and to the grand staircase that led up from the foyer. The foyer itself was filled with people... their people.

Before either of them could say a word, a great cheer went up and people began calling greetings... not just to Marco, which she had expected, but to her as well. Calls of Madonna rang through the vast space and Catherine found herself on the verge of tears.

Marco leaned down and whispered to her, "And you were worried they wouldn't like you. They are enraptured by you as is your mate."

They went down the stairs and Catherine found herself swept away from Marco and into the main dining hall, which was enormous. She looked back over her shoulder to see Marco's head bowed in quiet conversation with Giovanni and a man she didn't know. The latter didn't worry her much as she didn't know anyone outside of Giovanni, Luca, and Valentina, who quickly stepped up and took her place beside her.

Catherine had always been good at networking in social situations and even though this was now her home, she approached it in the same way. She made small talk and listened more than she talked. She finally got to what

Valentina said was their table for meals.

She and Valentina went through the buffet. Catherine was amazed at the amount, complexity, and diversity of the items offered. Catherine took many samplings to be enjoyed.

"This all looks so good. I'm going to have to be careful or my curves will turn to fat," she whispered to Valentina.

"Ah, you don't know—between your new wolf physiology and your increased sex life, you don't really have to worry about what you eat. If your Marco is anything like my Giovanni, you'll work it off at night... and in the morning."

She and Catherine were both laughing as they went to sit down with Luca.

He stood as they approached. "Madonna. Valentina."

"Oh, lord, Luca, I thought we settled that I was Catherine. I'm not big on titles, especially in my own house. Even if said house is a palace. This place is so beautiful and so full of life."

"The household staff, especially the housekeeper, chef, and main groundskeeper, are going to want to meet with you. They will now look to you, as Marco's mate, for how you want things run," he said.

"Either of you have any complaints or know of anything that needs fixing? I'm a hands-off kind of manager. The grounds are spectacular, this house is like a well-loved and cared for museum, and our chef isn't being paid enough. I think they just ought to keep doing what they are doing."

Valentina and Luca agreed with her.

Catherine smiled as she felt Marco's presence before he actually joined her. He brushed her cheek with his lips as he sat down.

She turned to him and pulled his face to hers before kissing him passionately to the cheers of the room.

"I don't think so, buddy. There will be no perfunctory kissing in this relationship," she quipped with her eyes dancing merrily.

Marco laughed at her boldness. "As you wish, my Catherine. But do not protest when I sweep you up in my arms to carry you back to our bed to have my way with you."

"Would it do me any good?"

"None whatsoever."

They both laughed and were joined by all those who had overheard.

"What were you and Giovanni discussing and who was the other man?" she asked him.

"That is a discussion best served for my office after breakfast."

"Is there news of my sister?"

"Yes, but eat your breakfast first, then we will adjourn to my office."

"I'm not hungry. Tell me now," she said stridently.

His rumbled reply did not surprise those who knew him. "After breakfast. Let the man who drove all night to be here at least put something in his belly."

"I'm sorry, Marco. It's just…"

"I know, my beloved. There is news and it isn't necessarily bad news. Your sister yet lives."

Catherine breathed an enormous sigh of relief. "Thank you. Thank you," she whispered, kissing the hand he had used to cover hers.

"Eat, Catherine. If I know our alpha he has let you have little of either food or rest these past few days," teased Valentina.

"Valentina," admonished Giovanni.

"Hush, Giovanni," interrupted Catherine. "You cannot fuss at Valentina for speaking the truth." Turning to Valentina, she continued, "But you are wrong. He gave me plenty of rest and food when he had me tied to him."

Marco, Luca, and Giovanni spit their beverages as Valentina and Catherine laughed together both at her outrageous statement and the men's reaction.

"Now, my mate and alpha, we are even," teased Catherine.

Marco shook his head indulgently. "See that it is so, mate. Giovanni tells me that our people are most anxious to hear us take our vows. What do you say to this evening? Gio already checked with you friend Sera and she has said she is available."

"Then I say no time like the present if it won't inconvenience anyone."

"I have a small confession," said Valentina softly. "I sort of already put a plan into motion. I'm not trying to usurp your authority, but I've done all the party planning until now and I knew everyone was anxious to see the two of you officially paired."

Catherine laid her hand on her new friend's. "You have done nothing but try to help. I will need you to continue to assist me. I've never done anything like run an estate of this size. You've seen my new wardrobe, anything appropriate for a quasi-wedding?"

"Oh, yes," Valentina sighed. "Your friend wisely included the most beautiful ivory lace gown. It would be beautiful. And there is a DeMedici veil if you choose to wear it."

"Wait a minute. This one," Catherine said, pointing to Marco, "promised me rings for both of us and that mine would have an enormous diamond."

"And they will arrive later this afternoon," said Giovanni.

Catherine whirled to look at him and then back to Marco.

"I did let you sleep sometime, my mate. I selected our rings from those we had here at the estate. If you do not care for yours, you can choose another or have one made."

Catherine felt tears welling in her eyes. "I'm sure it will be beautiful and I will wear it with great pride and pleasure." She leaned across and kissed him. "Thank you, my Marco."

"You are most welcome, my Catherine," he said, smiling and returning her kiss.

They finished their breakfast with Luca, Giovanni, and

Valentina asking her about her life and how Marco had finally run her to ground. Catherine found herself telling them the entire story including his having to run her to ground on the train.

"Oh, your sister will love to hear that," said Giovanni. "Will any of your siblings be here?"

"Stefano and his mate and Tony are in route as is Griffin. Gia is too far gone in her current pregnancy and Aidan feels it would be unsafe for her to travel, which of course caused Gia to throw a tantrum. I did the Irishman no favors when I let him run my baby sister to ground."

They all laughed save Catherine, who merely arched her eyebrow at her mate but held her tongue on the subject. Most everyone came by to welcome her and wish her well as they left the dining room. Once they were alone, Marco and Giovanni accompanied her to Marco's office.

A tall, handsome, middle-aged man stood as they entered the room. He doffed his cap. "Madonna, you are most welcome. We are so happy Marco has found you and brought you home."

"Thank you, but please call me Catherine. You have news of my sister?"

"I do. As you may be aware Marco's friend, the Welsh wolf, questioned that snake Salvatore extensively. He was able to determine when and how your sister was abducted. As we suspected she was taken to be sold at auction to the highest bidder. We have been since that time trying to find out where she was taken from but have so far been unsuccessful. Your mate had me reach out to Salvatore to try to see if I could ascertain any additional information and to tell him his business would not be tolerated in Italy and that if he was still within the country when Marco returned from his seclusion with you that Marco would kill him."

Catherine smiled at her mate. "Ever the charming alpha."

All three men chuckled.

"As I was saying, at that point we simply sat back and

waited for the rat to pack his bags and scurry back to his masters and the back alley from which he was sent. He did so, and we discovered a vast network of such abductions. They haven't been used regularly or with any frequency until recently. With the declining number of female shifters available, finding women who can be turned seems to have become a preferable way to obtain a mate especially for those who are too wealthy or too unscrupulous to be bothered with reputable means. We will be trying to infiltrate the organization to obtain additional information."

Marco stepped forward and shook his hand. "Thank you, Paulo. We will continue working until we can find Catherine's sister and bring her home to heal."

"I hate to be the bringer of bad thoughts," interrupted Giovanni, "but if she is already mated, what will you do?"

"If she wants to leave, I will ask her alpha to release her and if he refuses, I will bring charges against him before the Ruling Council."

"And if that doesn't work?" asked Giovanni softly. "If he isn't abusing her... and I am sure, Madonna, that you would think that any forced pairing is abuse, as would my Valentina... they will never agree to dissolve the union."

Catherine gasped. "You mean she'd be stuck with this bastard?"

"Calm yourself, beloved. If the Council will not intervene then I will challenge the wolf to personal combat. If he lacks the courage or honor to fight me, we will go to war."

Nothing was said until Catherine managed to utter, "Do you mean you'd risk yourself and our people for my sister?"

"Yes, but more for you," he said softly.

"Giovanni, talk to him. She's my sister and I love her but there has to be some other way than violence."

"Not always, Madonna. If she is your sister then she is important to this pack. We will gladly follow our alpha to bring her home. We would do the same for any member of this pack. If you harm one of us, you harm us all."

Luca nodded. "She is pack, Madonna."

Catherine shook her head. "I don't understand. You let your sister get run to ground by her mate..."

"But he was her fated mate. He did not buy her from me. When a man challenges his fated mate to run, it is only because he is certain of her, who she is and that she is simply being difficult... much like the current Madonna of the DeMedici pack."

Catherine laughed in spite of herself. "So say you all?" she asked.

"So say we all," replied Marco as the others nodded.

CHAPTER TWENTY-TWO

Catherine found that Valentina had preparations well in hand for the evening. She was helping with some last-minute selections regarding food setup when she was told her friend Sera had arrived. Catherine rushed out to greet her.

"Oh, my God, Catherine, you look amazing."

"Sera, it's great to see you. Thank you for coming on such short notice."

"Are you kidding me? Thanks for inviting me. I'm glad to see you so happy because I've been having the most amazing time. An all-expense shopping spree for you and then your man has them send me the things I was interested in when I wouldn't let him pay me for my time."

Catherine laughed. "That's my Marco. I have found he always finds a way to get what he wants... including me."

"Yes, as I recall you wanted nothing to do with Marco DeMedici and were quite adamant about that."

"What can I tell you, he's rich, handsome, and great in the sack."

"Well, that would certainly do it for me," she giggled. "This place is every bit as mind-blowing as I've heard."

"And you haven't seen the interior, the gardens or had

anything to eat."

"Yes, but I did get the case of wine with instructions that I was to order more when I needed it."

They were walking up the steps to the house, when another motor was heard and Catherine saw Griffin pull up.

"Hang on tight, Sera. I need to go see Griffin."

Griffin smiled at her broadly. "Catherine, it's good to see you."

She ran down the steps, throwing her arms around him and hugging him close.

She whispered in his ear, "I owe you a debt I can never repay for saving him from those butchers."

"You repaid that debt in full when it was your presence that drew him back from abyss. He lived for you, Catherine."

"Fine, then I want to know more about that rather debauched night the two of you spent in Germany."

Griffin could barely conceal his shock that she had any knowledge of that night.

"When I was transitioning, I saw Marco and me together during many lifetimes and a brief snippet of the two of you in Germany."

Griffin laughed. "No, if I tell you, should I ever find a mate, he will tell her. So my fair Catherine, my lips are sealed."

She linked her arm through his. "Come and meet my friend Sera."

"The woman you were with when Marco finally spotted you."

"Finally?" Sera asked, having overheard his comment.

"Yes. Marco had seen Catherine in his dreams for years. So when he finally spotted her at the restaurant, he wasted no time in trying to court her. I understand she was not all that impressed at first."

"He would be awfully hard to resist for most of us, but Catherine says he's great in the sack."

Griffin laughed and linked arms with Sera as well. The

three of them entered the house together as Marco came out of his office. Before he could object to Catherine walking arm and arm with Griffin, she had left Griffin to join her mate's side and kissed him, whispering, "I missed you."

"And I you," he responded.

"And how long has it been since you last saw one another?" Griffin asked with a huge grin.

"Far too long. At least several hours," said Marco.

"Two," said Giovanni. "They have been apart a little less than two hours."

Sera and Griffin laughed. Sera turned to Griffin. "Ain't true love grand?"

"Yes, and apparently all-consuming."

"Careful, Griffin. My Catherine has a rather nasty habit of evening the score when she thinks she has been wronged."

"Giovanni," said Catherine. "Would you be a dear and ask Valentina to join Sera and me up in Marco's and my bedroom?"

"It would be my pleasure, Madonna."

"Madonna?" asked Sera.

"An honorary title for the head of the family's wife… me!"

Sera giggled and whispered to her, "He didn't waste any time, did he?"

"What can I say… he's that good," she whispered back.

They ran up the stairs together.

• • • • • •

Marco watched them go before turning to Griffin. "Any other news?"

"On Shannon? None. But I did get the information to your brother Tony in Rome. He said he'd put out feelers for you."

"I appreciate you coordinating this for me. With

Catherine transitioning, my focus has had to be elsewhere. I owe you."

"Consider it a wedding present. She is truly glorious, Marco."

The alpha of the DeMedici smiled. "She is and is well worth the time it took me to find her and to bring her home. Now come, Luca is anxious to meet with us."

They were entering his office as Valentina walked past them, headed up to Catherine and Sera.

"Valentina, will you take my ring up to my mate. I have hers and wanted her to have mine."

"Of course," she said brightly.

"And did Gio arrange for the fireworks?"

She grinned. "They will be able to see them from the space station."

"Those are to be a surprise, Valentina."

"Yes, Alpha," she said, running up to join her friend.

"Think she'll tell her?" asked Griffin, nodding to Valentina.

"I doubt it. She wants our ceremony to be special as does everyone else in the pack. The surprise will delight Catherine."

"I heard Giovanni call her Madonna?"

"Yes, our pack has already fallen under her spell as well."

"This does not bode well for you, old friend," said Griffin, grinning. "I fear your mate will never be a quiet and demure mate. In fact, I think she may well be an alpha."

Marco laughed. "You are right on all accounts. My Catherine will never be the sweet submissive many alphas want. She herself is an alpha although hasn't recognized it yet. I plan to spend the rest of my life enjoying her wild spirit."

"I'll remind you of that the next time she tries to break your nose."

They both laughed and went to join Luca in Marco's study.

• • • • • •

Valentina joined Sera and Catherine in the latter's closet.

"Sera, this is Valentina. She organized the closet and I suspect helped put together the shopping list. Valentina, this is Sera who did all the shopping."

"You did a wonderful job," said Valentina. "I think everything you picked is perfect, especially the ivory lace with the sweep train."

Sera grinned. "I didn't want to assume, but I thought it might be nice to have just in case."

"It's gorgeous," said Valentina. "Have you pulled it out and looked at it, Catherine? It may be the most beautiful gown I've ever seen. And if you want, I know where the DeMedici veil is kept. It's been in the family for centuries."

"Catherine, if it goes with the dress you have to wear it. What a wonderful tradition. Besides it's the only time a woman can wear a veil and not look like an idiot."

"I'll run and go get it."

"Thanks, Valentina. And thanks for all of the work you've done putting this celebration together. Sera and I will be out on the balcony. Grab the veil then come and sit and put your feet up."

"Back in a flash," Valentina called as she sailed out the door.

"They seem to have taken you in remarkably quickly."

"I make their fearless leader happy and he loves me, that's all they needed to know. I was worried they would resent the American woman just sweeping in… but they didn't."

"I have to say I was still a bit concerned until I saw your face. It's so obvious that you're happy and madly in love as is he."

Catherine nodded. "Yes, I am very lucky."

Valentina rejoined them with the most exquisite veil made of a gossamer-like silk with a small lace detail on the edge. The color was a perfect match for the gown. She put it on the bed and then joined Sera and Catherine on the balcony.

"I checked with the household staff. They assure me they have everything under control."

"Why does that not surprise me?" laughed Catherine. She poured wine for her friends and looked out over the vineyard. The view from her balcony was commanding and magnificent.

The three women spent the afternoon chatting as if they were old friends merely needing to catch up with one another.

The ceremony was to be at sunset with dinner, feasting and dancing to follow. They watched as a beautiful ceremony site was set up, as well as an outdoor dining area and dance floor. In addition horses had been groomed and carriages cleaned and shined so that guests could take a moonlit ride through the vineyard.

Catherine shooed both women out of her room about ninety minutes before the ceremony was to begin and asked that Valentina show Sera to her room. She was sitting on the edge of their bed when there was a discreet knock.

A man who could only be one of Marco's younger brothers stepped in.

"I'm Tony and you must be Marco's Catherine."

"So he keeps telling me," she said, smiling and getting up to greet him.

He took her outstretched hand and used it to draw her into a hug.

"My big brother has always been able to get the most beautiful women, but with you, he has outdone even himself."

"And you would be his youngest brother and one of two who did nothing to stop him from forcing your little sister to run. Shame on you," she chided.

He laughed. "Marco warned me you weren't a fan of some of our traditions. You and Gia will adore each other. I plan to be home for a few days. I'm hoping you, Marco, and I can talk."

"Have you heard something about Shannon?"

"Nothing specific, but a rumor. I want to talk to you before pursuing it. But let us talk of happier things. My brother will be annoyed if I have done anything to dampen your mood. And you know what he's like when he's annoyed."

"Yes, but somehow I doubt he takes you over his knee."

Tony laughed. "You are correct. That he reserves only for his beloved mate."

"Pfft. He keeps telling me that as well."

Tony turned serious for a moment. "You don't doubt that you have his whole heart, do you?"

She reached over and touched his arm. "Not even for a moment."

He leaned down and kissed her cheek.

"Welcome to the family, Catherine. We're all so happy he finally found you. Now I can set myself up as the consolation prize since he's off the table so to speak."

Catherine's smile grew broader. "You are no consolation prize, little brother. And any girl who doesn't see that is blind, stupid, and beneath your notice."

There was another discreet knock and one of the household staff, who introduced herself as Maria, asked if she could be of assistance getting the Madonna ready.

"I'll be with Marco at the altar. I'm telling you as I'm sure you will only have eyes for my brother."

"I fear, my dear Tony, you are right. For me, he eclipses all others."

CHAPTER TWENTY-THREE

Catherine slipped into the ivory lace gown. It had a sweetheart neckline, corseted back, and was lined with a gossamer fabric that seemed to have been made from the same material as the several hundred-year-old DeMedici veil with the lace edging. Lace that was reminiscent of the gown itself. The gown was fitted as though it had been made specifically for her and hugged her body to just below her ass where it flared out slightly.

Catherine drew her hair back from her face but left it mostly hanging long in loose curls that Maria was able to coax into a reasonable style into which she attached the beautiful, silky veil.

"The alpha sent these up for you," Maria said as she offered Catherine a pair of baroque pearl and diamond drop earrings.

Catherine could not suppress her gasp.

"They're gorgeous. They're real, aren't they?" she said, taking them from Maria.

Maria giggled. "Yes, Madonna. The alpha would only send the best for you. You look so beautiful. If he could love you more than he already does, he would when he saw you."

"Thank you, Maria. Is there anything I should know or do? No one has said anything to me."

"He will claim you and you accept his claim by acknowledging him as your mate and alpha."

"Sounds simple enough. What if I fuck it up?"

Maria giggled again. "Then say what is in your heart. It is obvious to all of us how you feel. We won't care. Just accept his claim. I think he would be very cross if you did not."

"Thank you, Maria, for helping me. You and the rest of the staff will get to enjoy this evening, won't you?"

"Absolutely, Madonna. All of the real work is done, except for serving dinner. We will have plenty of time to relax, dance, and celebrate." Maria came forward and hugged her. "We are all so happy you are here."

Catherine returned the hug. "Me too," she whispered.

Catherine checked herself in the mirror one more time and had to admit that Sera had done an outstanding job picking a gown that was perfect for the evening. She slid Marco's ring on her index finger so she wouldn't have to worry about losing it and headed out in the hallway. She was surprised to find Griffin waiting for her.

"Marco wasn't sure if you wanted or needed anyone to take you to him at the altar…"

"Planning to sacrifice me to the Gods, is he?" she said, smiling at him.

"I think when he gets you on your back, Catherine, it will not be with the thought of doing you harm."

She laughed out loud and realized how tense she had been.

"He didn't send you up here to walk me down the aisle, he wanted you to make me laugh and relax so I could enjoy myself."

"I fear you know our Marco all too well. He did indeed and to ensure there wasn't anything you need or that you didn't have a train ticket tucked away somewhere."

Catherine blushed, rolled her eyes, and laughed again.

DELTA JAMES

"No, I think my running away on trains is over. You don't think he could pull a plane over, do you?"

"No, but he could bribe someone to stop it on the tarmac or fly it back to the airport."

She searched his face and realized even though he was smiling, he was dead ass serious. She shook her head. "Go join the rest of them. I don't want anyone to think that my decision to join my mate is anyone's but my own."

"They'll never believe you. Marco has been telling them for years you existed, he would find you and bring you home as his mate. And here you are."

"I know. Pathetic. I'm just stupid in love with him."

"That's all right, Catherine. He loves you even more, as do the rest of us." Griffin leaned into her and kissed her cheek.

She gave Griffin time to get out to the garden, took a long, cleansing breath, and walked down the stairs to join herself formally to her mate. She saw him waiting under the pergola that had been strewn with beautiful white roses and other soft pink and cream flowers. Valentina handed her a bouquet that was simple and elegant.

She saw nothing but Marco. She was struck once again at the sheer masculinity and sexuality that seemed to roll off of him. Catherine planned to enjoy the evening's festivities. However, when her most feminine parts began throbbing as they always did in his presence, she knew a part of her would be wanting them over with so she could feel the intensity of Marco's possession and love.

She stifled the giggle that threatened to rise from the depths of her soul. She knew he would know she was thinking of the night to come when she would be alone with him. He would know that by the time they got back to their room that her pussy would be aching with her need for him to fill her.

He held out his hands to her. She placed hers in his and he drew her to him, kissing her deeply.

"I missed you, my Catherine. You look even more

beautiful than you did this afternoon."

She whispered to him, "Bullshit, all you're thinking is how long we have to stay down here before you can take me upstairs and get between my legs to rut."

He chuckled and growled low in her ear. "And you, my mate, are thinking about the same."

There was no priest or officiant. As alpha, Marco basically presided over his own ceremony.

"Catherine Livingston, I, Marco DeMedici, claim you as my fated mate now and forever."

"And I, Catherine, formally accept your claim and declare you to be my mate and alpha for all time."

Marco pulled her into his arms and kissed her with a quiet passion that caused their friends and pack to howl and holler at the moon that was rapidly rising over the lake set behind the pergola.

The kiss had barely ended before a dazzling display of fireworks began. Catherine laughed with delight as did many others. The show lasted for about a half an hour and was as impressive as any she had ever seen.

They spent the evening with their friends and pack eating, dancing, and celebrating the night away.

Catherine made the rounds of their guests, all under Marco's watchful eye. She watched him as well and would smile when their eyes met.

"Still afraid she's going to bolt?" asked Griffin.

"No," Marco admitted. "Afraid she isn't real."

Giovanni laughed and said, "Your Madonna is real, Marco and appears to have been here all her life. If I didn't know she had just transitioned to a wolf I would swear she has always been one with us."

Marco nodded. "She does seem to have always been here. I am finding it difficult to remember when I didn't wake with her in my arms."

"Valentina said that our pack feels the same... as though she has always been here."

At long last Marco scooped his mate up off the dance

floor and carried her back to their room to the sound of her laughter and the well wishes of those who had celebrated with them.

• • • • • • •

Catherine laughed and nuzzled Marco as he carried her up the stairs.

"You do know that I'm quite capable of climbing a staircase, right?"

He looked at her questioningly.

"You are forever carrying me up them either cradled in your arms or slung over your shoulder."

Marco laughed. "The latter only when you are being a naughty mate and need to be shown the error of your ways."

He entered their bedroom and set her down, closing and locking the door behind her as he pressed her into it.

"You know," she drawled, "the last time you had me up against our bedroom door you stripped me naked, impaled me on your cock, and fucked me before you bit me."

He looked down at the mark he had left on her that was rapidly healing. He bent his head and kissed it with great care and feeling.

"As I recall, I only nipped you until you pulled my head back down and indicated your wish to be marked and claimed by me."

"I know," she said softly. "I think I wanted that more in that moment than I've ever wanted anything."

"As did I."

He backed away, drawing her with him and toward their bed, which someone had turned down.

"Do you like your ring, my Catherine?"

"Are you kidding me? It's gorgeous. I thought the earrings were stunning, but they pale in comparison to this. It's old, isn't it?" she asked, looking again at the large pale pink diamond surrounded by baroque pearls and white diamonds.

"Very. It was brought to the property when the pack first came to live here."

Catherine shook her head. "I love having something that is that old and has been with our family for so long. For it to stand testament to the eternal love I have for you." She giggled. "Gawd, that was a bit much."

Marco chuckled and kissed her hand. "Perhaps, but the beauty of that ring pales in comparison to she who wears it."

Catherine reached up and stroked his cheek before running her finger down the strong column of his neck as she began to unbutton his white linen shirt.

"You do know, Catherine DeMedici," he started with a voice that was deep and heavy with lust, "that I am the dominant partner and it is I who decides when we will make love."

"You may be the dominant partner and I may have to submit to your authority, but if you think I'm not going to fuck you whenever I want, you've got another thought coming."

She pulled his shirt free from his trousers before unbuckling his belt, sliding it from its loops, and flinging it across the room. She opened his fly and slid his pants down past his strong, muscular buttocks and hard thighs. With her dress made and fitted to her body as it was, she knelt down to help him step free and was eye-to-eye with the hard evidence of his need for her.

She smiled and drew off his briefs and was confronted with his engorged cock, which seemed to be twitching with its own need. She flicked her tongue over the head and heard him groan in response. She looked up into his face and saw him smiling as his hand gently grasped her head and directed her to do what he wanted.

Catherine licked down the top of the column of his staff and then back along the sensitive underside. She opened her mouth to express some disappointment that there was no knot, but found her mouth filled with the enormity of his member. Slowly Marco began to fuck her mouth. She had quickly learned with her mate that she didn't so much suck him off as he fucked her mouth instead of her pussy. Often times he withdrew at the last minute only to mount her quickly so that he came inside that part of her that seemed made for that purpose alone.

Even so, she enjoyed using her mouth and tongue to pleasure him as he so often pleasured her. Catherine had come to know that her needs would always be well attended. Marco seemed to know her so intimately and how to coax her body to respond even if she was angry or exhausted.

He fisted her hair and brought her up from her knees. Marco unfastened the elaborate barrette in her hair, freeing both it and the veil. The veil fluttered to the floor as Marco moved his hands down her back and untied the corset strings, loosening her gown and sliding it off her body.

As her breasts were revealed, he sighed contentedly and reached up with one hand to grasp a nipple as his mouth captured the other. Catherine swayed against him. He had a way of fondling her that made her literally go weak at the knees. She could hear the muffled chuckle as his mouth, full of her areola and nipple, was busy suckling.

He tugged her dress down past her derriere and then gently pushed her onto the bed. He removed her dress completely only to find her stockings held up by beautiful garters and that she had on no panties whatsoever.

"Naughty mate," he said, grinning up at her. "That you have been uncovered in this manner indicates a wantonness that will need to be seen to frequently."

"I was hoping you'd think that," she said, teasing him.

He removed her shoes and stockings before kissing his way back up the inside of her thighs as he closed in on that place that most held his attention. He smiled as he caught scent of her increased arousal, the swollen lips of her labia, and her engorged clit. As he had with her nipple, Marco latched on to her distended nub and suckled, causing her to throw her head back and writhe under his assault.

"Marco," she growled softly as she came.

He kissed his way up her mound to her belly and up once again to engage her nipples. He had no more than taken one in his mouth that he plunged two of his fingers into her heated channel, making her arch up into his hand and come a second time.

"Marco, please," she cried.

"Such a greedy mate. Most women are happy if their lover can make them climax once. But mine not only wants numerous orgasms but wants most of them done by my cock stroking her pussy or better yet being knotted and rocked."

"Right now she wants her mate to shut up and fuck her," she growled low, making him laugh.

He stood ensuring he was between her legs and caught her buttocks in his hands, lifting her so that she was at the perfect height for him to surge forward, ramming his cock deep within her and making her climax yet again.

Marco strengthened his hold so that she couldn't move and began to thrust with a hard, rhythmic stroke. He enjoyed watching and feeling her come apart in his hands. He held her in such a way that she could do nothing but act as a willing vessel for his lust. He continued to ram his cock into her over and over. Her orgasmic spasms only inflamed his need.

Catherine began to respond as she did when knotted to him. One climax followed another as if they were waves lapping upon the shore, one barely retreating before the next surged forward.

She reached up and covered his hands with hers before trying to grasp his powerful forearms to pull him down on top of her. He rutted within her for more than an hour. She wailed her need and he did nothing but stroke her further into ecstasy. She began to notice something different in the way his cock felt as it seemed to hit her cervix. Her rational mind failed her, but her body remembered—he was forming a knot as he fucked her.

She surrendered to his mastery and could tell he recognized it. He growled in a seductive way and she could feel and hear his call throughout her entire body. As once more she crested the top end of an orgasm, she felt the fully formed knot force past the entrance to her pussy and lodge in its place.

She felt her body relax and her legs wind around him as he slid them both fully onto the bed, grabbing a pillow for her head as he lay down upon her, grasped her buttocks once more as he began the timeless need of his kind to rock his mate until he spilled his seed deep within her before tying her to him for several hours.

Catherine clung to him as she always did as he rocked her through a series of climaxes and as he began to fill her with his cum. She felt the hard contractions of her pussy that coaxed every last drop of his seed from him. When at last he finally stilled, she sighed with great contentment and satisfaction.

"I love you," she said as she kissed, licked, and nipped him.

He chuckled. "That is a good thing, my Catherine. I love you even more and you are now mine for all time."

"Haven't I always been?" she asked softly.

"Yes, but you were being difficult when first I caught scent of you."

"Not my fault," she said defensively.

"How do you figure that?"

"You hadn't knotted me…"

Marco laughed. "Then it is entirely my fault."

"Entirely," she agreed wrapping her arms around his neck.

Marco took hold of her buttocks and rolled to his back, keeping her sealed to him but placing her where he knew he could coax her into napping. She would have need of her rest when she could get it for he meant to make their first night as a legally recognized mated pair memorable.

CHAPTER TWENTY-FOUR

Catherine woke as the sun cleared the eastern horizon. Marco was spooned around her with his arm draped over her waist and his hand resting over her mons. He had promised, or was it threatened, to ensure she would never forget the night of their bonding ceremony. He had been as good as his word.

After first using her mouth for their pleasure, he had spent most of the rest of the night with his cock lodged in her pussy, either stroking long and hard without the knot, or knotted and tied to her. Three times he had been actively fucking her, forming the knot as he did so and then forced it into her to claim her as she climaxed.

Catherine knew she was going to be sore. She also knew that he had planned it that way and that everyone in their pack would know. She giggled and felt him nuzzle the back of her neck.

"What is it that pleases you so this fine morning?"

"Other than waking up with me wrapped in your arms?" she said, sighing and wiggling backward to get even closer to him.

"That should now be normal for you. It will be a rare morning you do not find yourself so, or already underneath me having your pussy plowed."

She giggled again. "You do know I'm going to be sore as hell from you, don't you?"

He chuckled in a distinctly masculine and satisfied manner. "And are you complaining about that? Should I apologize?"

"If I did, you'd probably spank me for lying about it. You damn well know that I got far more pleasure from you than you did from me last night."

"No, my beloved, a great deal of my pleasure comes from pleasuring you and feeling you surrender yourself to me completely. Should I have them bring you breakfast in bed so you can stay up here to rest and recuperate today?"

"And let you have bragging rights? Oh, hell, no," she teased. "I'll walk down those bloody stairs if it kills me."

"You may be downstairs, but it has yet to be determined if I will allow you to walk."

He exited their bed and then lifted her up to take her into their shower.

Catherine couldn't remember a time the fragrant steam had felt so good. Marco held her steady and gently washed her body, taking great care and lingering on her breasts and between her legs.

He dried her off gently and helped her to dress. She sat on their bed as he dressed and wondered at how different her life was going to be. That it was going to be better with him was not even a question in her mind. Marco made everything better. Even the knowledge that her sister had been abducted and most likely forced into a pairing with an alpha not of her choice was made easier knowing that they would see it through together.

Her dark thoughts started to cloud her face, but she pushed them away. Shannon was strong. She would endure. And she was, as Marco and those of their pack who knew pointed out to her, a member of the DeMedici pack and they would find her and make those who harmed her pay. She meant to urge Marco to end the practice of kidnapping women, wolf or human, and forcing them into lives not of their choosing. She knew there was human trafficking on a global level and meant to see they got involved in those causes as well, but felt in this limited area they could be a part of the solution that ended the problem.

"What troubles you, sweetheart? Thinking of Shannon?"

"Yes. But Marco, you should know that you were right—sharing the knowledge that something had happened to her with you helped lighten that burden. And then the way you committed your resources…"

"Our resources," he corrected.

She smiled. "Yes, committed our resources to bringing her home makes me hopeful for the first time. Tony said he wanted to talk to me so I do want to do that."

He kissed her tenderly. "You may do whatever pleases you… within reason."

"I take it that means running off and getting on a train is out."

He smiled ruefully. "It does indeed."

"Killjoy. But I'm sure Valentina will have thought of something."

He rolled his eyes and then joined arms with her as they walked down the stairs and into the dining room. Catherine saw that Valentina had brought Sera to their table and that she was engaged in some kind of spirited discussion with Luca.

"You go sit down. I will bring you a plate. Is there anything in particular that you have a taste for?"

"Other than you? Although you didn't let me taste as much as I'd like last night. And anyway, isn't that beneath an alpha of your standing?"

"Far from it. How the alpha treats his mate sets the standard for the rest of the men and is reflected throughout the pack."

"Then all our women are in for a treat."

"As are the men if their mates reflect the response of their Madonna. Of course the pack will be retiring earlier in the evening and getting up much later so that my men can enjoy their mates as I do mine."

She blushed but laughed at his teasing.

Catherine walked to the table and all the men stood.

"Okay, guys, that has got to stop. You don't stand when Marco comes over. I get it… you respect me. Now just sit down and relax."

"My brother seems more relaxed than I have ever seen him. Relaxed is not a normal state of being for Marco," said Tony.

"That, little brother, is because he is newly mated to his Catherine and likely she took full advantage of his devotion last evening."

"Stefano, enough," said his mate. "Do not embarrass Catherine."

"Don't worry about it, Louisa," said Catherine. "I've already grown used to hearing the DeMedici men tout their own prowess in bed. But I wonder, Stefano, if Louisa would attest to your abilities in that regard. I can assure you that your brother's legendary status as the ultimate lover is greatly deserved and vastly underrated."

Stefano seemed a bit outraged at both her tone and her words.

Griffin pounded the table, laughing. "Well said, Catherine."

Marco set a plate full of tantalizing food in front of her and sat down beside her.

"Your mate," said Stefano in a scolding tone, "should learn her place where other alphas are concerned."

Marco stilled her retort before saying, "In case you missed it, brother, my mate is an alpha in her own right and you sit at her table. Perhaps it is you who needs to be reminded of his place."

"And perhaps," said Catherine sweetly, "the two of you could just take them out, put them on the table, and measure them to settle the dispute."

Marco and Stefano looked at her in outrage. The others

at the table all began laughing riotously. The two brothers looked at each other and joined in the humor.

"It would seem, sister, I underestimated your strength and resiliency. You will need both to survive being mated to Marco," said Stefano with affection in his voice.

"Perhaps, but it was his strength and virility I enjoyed throughout the night."

Stefano laughed. "You, my brother, married a spitfire. And you, my love," he said, turning to his mate, "do not need to emulate her."

"I don't know," she said sweetly, "she seems to be having a great deal of fun and is already much loved and respected by her people."

Stefano took Louisa's hand in his and brought it to his lips. "As are you and most of all by your mate."

Catherine glanced at Sera, who appeared to be fascinated.

"Don't you just love male displays of testosterone?" Catherine said to Sera.

"Actually on the way here, I was worried that you might find life out here too quiet for your liking, but after the party last night and this morning's shenanigans, I'm beginning to think you'll have far more fun out here." Sera looked directly at Marco. "You do plan to continue to spoil her rotten, right?"

"The most spoiled rotten mate in history. And you, Seraphina, are always welcome here at the villa. Besides Catherine will be in and out of Florence. I sit on several boards that are mostly about the arts. I have asked Catherine to take on those duties for me and she has agreed."

"Well, damn. I got a good friend and an endless supply of DeMedici wine out of the deal," said Sera.

The rest of breakfast was finished with laughter and fun. Sera made her apologies but said she had a new guest booked into her bed and breakfast and needed to get back to Florence. Catherine accompanied her to her car and hugged her close.

"Thank you for coming. I know it wasn't a normal wedding…"

"Girl, if not-normal gets you all of this and a man who is clearly head over heels for you, sign me up for not-normal. I thought it was just wonderful."

Catherine smiled. "Me too."

They hugged again and Catherine waved as her friend drove off. Catherine felt Tony's arm go around her.

"I like your friend. Think she'd like Rome?" he said conversationally.

"Doubtful," said Luca as he joined them. "But the villa isn't far from Florence and the new property even closer. I may have many times I need to be in Florence in the next several months."

Catherine watched them eye each other wearily. "Enough, boys. Sera is my friend and under my protection. If she falls for either of you, fine, but she will not be forced to accept a claim by either of you."

The two men grinned at each other.

"You gained one helluva of Madonna for your pack, Luca," said Tony.

"That we did, Tony. But she is now your sister."

"And God help all of us when she meets Gia. Poor Aidan and Marco may have to have new straps made. I need to leave for Rome no later than tomorrow morning and I want to talk with Catherine and Marco."

He clasped Luca on the shoulder and headed back to the main house.

Tony found Marco, Griffin, Catherine, and Giovanni in Marco's study.

"Tony?" Catherine said hopefully.

"Good, you're all here." Tony fished out his wallet and took out a picture. "Could this be Shannon?"

Catherine took the picture from his hand. The woman who stared back had been beaten and was tied up, but the look on her face was pure defiance. There was no doubt in her mind, the picture was of her sister, Shannon.

She hugged Tony. "Yes, that's Shannon."

"I am surprised by your reaction," said Tony. "Griffin and I were fearful that seeing the picture, if it were her, would upset you. But Marco knew better. He said confirmation that she was alive and her spirit unbroken would lighten your heart." He kissed her hand. "My brother has mated himself to an extraordinary woman, has he not, Griffin?"

"He has indeed," replied the Welsh wolf.

"What do you know?" whispered Catherine.

"Not much. She was taken, as you suspected, in Florence. Apparently she got away from them once but before she could get to safety they had her again. Whoever the head of the organization is thought she had something special and has had her protected somewhere while he prepares her for a live auction in the next month or two."

"Prepares?"

Tony smiled and took her hand. "Yes, they want her cuts and bruises healed. They don't want her beauty marred nor do they want her spirit diminished. Griffin was able to get this from Salvatore. They think she is more valuable to them."

Catherine looked at Marco. "But talking to Stefano it seems that you're kind of the odd duck wanting a mate who isn't submissive."

"It is not as common," he replied gently. "But there are those that believe spirited mates are the best for alphas and then there are some alphas who live to break their spirit. These bastards won't give a damn which kind is bidding."

"Marco," she started.

He reached her quickly and comforted her with his embrace. "Shh, my Catherine. We will find her. Griffin, I fear I am going to need your help."

"You have it."

"And you have mine and the backing of the pack in Rome," said Tony. "These bastards are shipping girls in and out through our city. Lorenzo, he is alpha of our pack, is none too happy about it. I persuaded him to do nothing until I talked with you. He did say he was amenable to follow your lead and wanted me to assure you that we are at your disposal."

"The first thing," said Marco, "is to find where the auction is being or was held. If it hasn't been held then we will simply use Griffin as a shill and purchase your sister," he said, looking to his old friend, who nodded. "If she has, we will try to track down the buyer and see if he is willing to be reasonable."

"If not?" asked Catherine quietly.

"Then my patience and willingness to settle this peacefully will have reached an end. We will get your sister back."

"So say we all," said Griffin.

Catherine's eyes welled with tears as each of the men in the room nodded.

"Thank you," she said with great depth of feeling. "I am in your debt."

"No," said Tony with a grin, "your mate is. And that's far better because he's very, very rich!"

He waggled his eyebrows at her, making her laugh.

"Beyond your wildest imagining, little brother."

"I think he means you," said Tony to Catherine.

"I do indeed," agreed Marco.

Catherine took hold of his hand, brought it to her lips, and kissed it.

CHAPTER TWENTY-FIVE

The new few months flew by as Catherine took on the role of mistress or Madonna, as her people called her, to the DeMedici pack. She also, at Marco's urging began to serve on the boards for two museums, the Bargello and the Uffizi, where both directors enjoyed a discreet smile and laugh with her.

It was while she was in Florence for the day that Tony managed to get away from his duties in Rome and meet with her at the DeMedici hotel. He was able to relay the information that Shannon remained unsold. Those who held her were trying to build an enormous bidding war. She was being held in one of the country houses of one of the packs in Eastern Europe. Through Griffin and Marco's intelligence contacts they had been able to track her location.

"Lorenzo has had dealings with this pack before. He was a bit surprised that they had participated and wanted to know if Marco wanted him to try to negotiate or if Marco wanted to do it himself. I've got a call into Marco."

"Tony, give me the information. I'll call them."

"While my brother cherishes and values you above all else in this life, I fear this alpha will only talk to another alpha… another male alpha."

"Does Lorenzo have any idea whether they might give my sister back?"

Tony shook his head. "He really doesn't know. He was surprised that they had been involved at all much less were in the running to purchase her."

"Why do you keep saying they instead of he? What aren't you telling me?"

"You aren't going to like the answer. We think this pack may have gone feral."

"What do you mean feral?"

"I'd rather we were at the villa to explain."

"Fuck it, Tony. I want the information. Give it to me. I'll take it home with me and talk to Marco."

Tony laughed. "No, you won't. You'll call the bastards yourself and when they won't speak to you, you'll curse them up one side and down the other. And that will do nothing except earn you a soaped mouth and a trip over my brother's knee. I can only imagine how difficult this must be for you, but you must allow us to do this in the way that gives us the best chance at success."

"You know, little brother, you are neither pack nor your brother, Marco, I'm thinking the rule about my not striking out at pack or Marco doesn't extend to you."

Tony laughed again. He and Catherine had become close. "Can I be there when you try that argument on him?"

She smiled ruefully. "No. We both know it will fail and I'll end up having trouble sitting down. If you don't get hold of him, will you at least come home with me this afternoon so that we can talk to him?"

"Yes, sweet sister, I will come home with you mainly because I now worry without someone to remind you that you are mate to a powerful alpha you will do something that will get you in trouble."

"Pfft," she said, dismissing his concerns, but knowing he was right.

When they hadn't heard from Marco by the time

Catherine was ready to head for home, Tony joined her on the helicopter that made short work of the trip back to the villa. They landed and ran up to the house.

Catherine smiled as she saw him. It didn't seem to matter how long or how many times they were together, her heart always seemed to skip a beat, her nipples would harden, and the place between her legs would begin to pool moisture. There was no question about it—the Madonna of the DeMedici pack had a decidedly lustful relationship with its alpha.

Marco swept her into his embrace, twirling her around with his arms locked under her ass and kissing her passionately.

"God, I missed you," she said. "I swear if you'd showed up at the hotel I'd have blown everything else off just to have the chance to blow you."

Marco laughed—a sound laced with more than just a trace of arousal. "Shall I knot you from behind tonight, my Catherine? Would you like that?"

He allowed her to slide down his torso.

"Yes, but only after you have stroked me long and hard. I want to wake up in your arms tomorrow morning feeling sore and well used."

He kissed her again before turning to his little brother.

"I take it you have news you didn't wish to share with Catherine?"

"It isn't that I didn't want to share it with her. I feared she would not wait for you and would inflame the situation and/or put herself in danger."

"In other words," said Catherine archly, "he didn't trust me not to fuck it up."

Marco's swat to her backside was swift and hard. "Catherine," he growled, warning her.

"Well, he didn't," she said sullenly.

"Watch your tone as well, my Catherine, lest you end up finding out how it feels to be knotted from behind when your beautiful bottom is a deep shade of red."

"Yes, Marco," she said, nuzzling him. "But he could have told me."

"And most likely he assessed the situation correctly and you would have made things worse. That is not what you want, is it, my *tesoro*?"

"No."

"Then apologize to Tony and we will all go into my study."

"But…"

"If you can't or won't apologize, then I will send you to our room where I will decide how to deal with you after I have talked with my brother."

"I'm sorry, Tony. I'm just…"

Tony crossed to her and kissed her on the cheek. "I know, Catherine. We're fine… and your mate is far too strict with you. You should run off with a handsome beta who would only lavish you with love and affection."

She giggled and Marco growled. Tony had a way of always finding a way to make her laugh. And if he could piss off Marco in the bargain, he considered it a good day.

"Yeah, that would be a problem. You see… I'm seriously addicted to that whole knot thing."

"Catherine!" Marco admonished her.

Tony laughed. "Oh, come now, Marco. That's fairly tame for your Catherine when she's getting even with you."

Marco shook his head. "You are of little to no help, brother."

"Perhaps. But your mate adores me, don't you, Catherine?"

"I do indeed," she said, linking her arm through his, but wrapping her arm around her mate's waist.

They walked up to the house and entered Marco's study.

"As I told Catherine, we have been able to confirm that Shannon has been taken to the country estate of one of the packs in Eastern Europe."

"Tony says they think they've gone feral, but he won't tell me what that means."

Catherine watched a look pass between the two brothers.

Tony continued, "Lorenzo knows the alpha a little and was surprised that he would have participated in such an operation. Lorenzo said he would speak with the man either as a way to introduce you or on your behalf."

"I want to talk to this bastard," Catherine said heatedly.

"And you, my mate, can take yourself up to our room and wait for me. If you start to fuss, I will call Giovanni to escort you upstairs and you can take off your clothes and wait for me with your nose in the corner."

"Marco…"

"Catherine, one more word and I will summon Giovanni."

Marco looked down at her.

"I'll go. It was nice to see you, Tony. Your brother can be a real jackass when he tries."

Marco growled as she left the room.

• • • • • • •

Catherine grabbed Valentina's hand and dragged her along as she ran up the stairs. Pulling her into the room, she closed the door behind them.

"Catherine?" said Valentina, her voice filled with concern.

"What the hell is feral? I mean I know the meaning of the word, but what does it mean when someone says a pack has gone feral?"

"There is no chance the DeMedici pack will ever go feral. Marco and Giovanni would never allow it."

"That's great," said Catherine exasperatedly. "But what the fuck does it mean?"

"If a pack has gone feral, the ranking member structure has become irretrievably broken. Often times a beta has killed the alpha and seeks to take over."

"What would it mean for a woman entering that pack?"

"Why do you want to know?"

"Valentina, please."

"If she was brought into such a pack, it would mean that she would be kept as a breeder. Feral packs do not take mates in the way we do. They will bring a new female into the pack, generally young and of child-bearing age. Several members, usually the ranking members, will breed her on a regular basis. Even once she has conceived they will continue to use her for their pleasure until it is dangerous for the baby for them to do so. Once she has delivered the child, either they determine the father and she is mated to him or the child is placed in a nursery for the pack to raise and the whole horrible process starts over. Generally there are only a few women, one will be used by the three ranking members and the others will be used by the rest of the males."

Catherine stumbled as she grabbed the bedpost for support. "Oh, God," she cried softly.

"Should I get Marco?"

"No. I just needed a moment."

"Why did you ask about a feral pack?"

"Tony thinks my sister may have been placed in one pending her sale."

"Catherine, I'm so sorry. I'm sure Marco will find her and get her out of there."

"Thanks, Valentina. You'd better leave. I got sent to my room and I doubt Marco meant for me to have company."

Valentina hugged her. "I don't care. If you want me to stay, Gio can just be mad at me too."

"What greater love for a friend than that she would put her butt on the line for you."

"You'd do the same for me."

Catherine watched the door close, then stretched out on their bed and began to quietly sob.

• • • • • • •

"I appreciate that you didn't give her the information that would have caused her to get herself into even more trouble."

"This is hard for her, Marco," said Tony.

"I know, but she also needs to obey me, especially when I have warned her to cease and she continues on."

"But, Marco…"

Marco laughed. "And this, little brother, is why beta males should never mate with alpha females."

"She may be a handful, but she does love you."

Marco smiled. "That she does. Almost as much as I love her. But you were right not to give her the information. She would have called him."

"Lorenzo warned me that he was a stickler for protocol. A female calling him and challenging him, there's no way he would have been willing to listen."

"What did Lorenzo think the chances were of his giving her up?"

"Not very good. As I said, he thought it was out of character and so for him to have done it, he had to have been desperate. And the rumor is that he has lost control and his pack has gone feral."

"In that case, tell Lorenzo not to risk his relationship with the man. We may need it later. Give me the information and I will take it from here."

"Only if you promise not to punish Catherine."

Marco laughed. "You don't even live here and have taken up her cause. I knew the women would all fall in behind their Madonna but I hadn't counted on the men. At this point, I wouldn't want to put it to a vote with them."

Tony laughed as well. "I'll leave the information with you. If I can trouble you for a ride back to Rome?"

"Of course, helicopter or car?"

"I'd love to take one of the vintage roadsters, but I'm needed before then. You aren't the only one with a misbehaving woman. One of our girls is going through a rough patch. I've got her on weekly maintenance and she is due tonight."

"Ah, the work of a beta is never done," Marco chuckled.

"It's different though, you know? I mean I've played around with spanking girls for fun and pleasure and now as beta for our pack, but they say it is different when the woman is your mate."

"It is," said Marco. "Because you're involved on a more intimate level, as are they."

"But they don't seem to like being spanked. I get why I'd get aroused, but why do they?"

"It isn't the pain or discomfort that makes them aroused. It is the dynamic of surrendering themselves to your authority. When a woman is spanked for discipline, it hurts. It can be difficult to do what you know needs to be done in order for your mate to be secure and happy. And it's harder on your mate. She is upset that she has disappointed you. The more powerful and spirited the woman, the more satisfying the surrender."

"Spoken by a man who has a spirited powerhouse of a mate."

"It is the pain that forces them to cry and to release their guilt and allows balance to be restored." Marco smiled again. "Catherine's surrender is the most exquisite feeling in the world regardless of whether or not I had to force it from her by having to discipline her."

Having anticipated that Tony would need to get back to his own pack in Rome, Marco had asked the helicopter pilot to wait. The two brothers walked to the helicopter, embraced, and Tony got in to head back to his home.

Marco watched them take off. He then turned toward the house and contemplated how to deal with his mate. He had been looking forward to her return from Florence, although as Giovanni had pointed out, she had only been gone since this morning. Marco smiled and shook his head. There was no doubt in anyone's mind, he was madly in love with his mate.

He went into his study and finished up some work. It

was good to let her have some time to consider her behavior and how he would react to it.

Marco had decided to simply put her over his knee to warm her backside and scold her. Not a true disciplinary spanking but enough to remind her that she was subject to his authority and when she misbehaved, there would be consequences. Like most strong-willed women, his Catherine needed consistency and to know that she could depend on him.

He left his study and headed into the kitchen to ask the chef if he'd prepare dinner and have it delivered to their room. Marco ascended the stairs. He opened the door expecting to see her sitting either on the settee or on the bed. She wasn't. He checked their walk-in closet where she often undressed and did not find her there. He knocked on the door to their bath and there was no answer. He tried the door and found it locked. He called for her and there was only silence. He put his shoulder into the door, thinking her hurt, but when he was able to force it, Catherine was nowhere to be found.

CHAPTER TWENTY-SIX

Catherine knew that Marco was annoyed with her behavior and contemplated how best she might avoid a spanking. The more she thought about her sister being bred by a group of men repeatedly, the more angry she became. When she saw Tony and Marco headed out for the helipad, she made her decision.

She closed and locked the bathroom door and then ran down the stairs. As she had hoped, she found the information Tony had brought to them in Marco's office. She thought about copying it down and leaving the original, but decided it was better if Marco had no idea where she was headed. She grabbed the piece of paper and quietly slipped from the house and headed to the garage.

She thought about taking one of the sports cars for their speed, but decided that one of the Range Rovers was probably a better choice and harder to track. She chose one without the DeMedici logo emblazoned across the doors, got in, and took the back drive to leave the property. She knew she wouldn't have a lot of time and needed to make the most of the head start she'd given herself.

She made it off the property, turned off her phone removing the battery, and turned on the Range Rover's navigation system. She checked the storage compartment between the seats. The small handgun was still there, was loaded, and there was extra ammunition. She plotted the address for the location for the pack that was said to be holding her sister.

Marco and Tony were wrong. She had no intention of calling this so-called alpha and asking to speak with her sister. She planned to confront this mangy pack of hyenas, firearm in hand and get her little sister. She was certain that Marco would be furious but that he would keep them safe once they had returned to their vineyard. After all, the damn thing was a fortress.

The nav system indicated she had an eight- to nine-hour drive if she averaged sixty miles per hour. Catherine intended to do better than that. She meant to keep to the main highways as much as she could. Catherine drove through the night and tried not to think about how angry Marco was going to be when they were finally alone in their bedroom. She had no doubt that she would need an extra cushion to sit comfortably for days after her return.

She figured by now Marco had been able to speak with Tony and would have a good idea where she was going. Depending on what kind of transportation he was able to put together he might be able to arrive around the same time she did. Private flights were heavily restricted so she hoped he'd be limited by how much time he could fly and how much he would have to drive.

Catherine's plan was not to go in through the front door. She meant to slip in from behind, find her sister, and get out. If she had to confront the alpha and his pack, so be it. She had already determined that she was willing to harm and even kill anyone from this foreign pack who tried to stop her or to harm her sister.

Catherine hoped that as her sister had been turned she would have been able to learn to shift. She smiled, remembering Marco teaching her to shift and the amazing sense of freedom and power she felt when in her wolf form.

She and Marco would often run through the vineyard on a full moon before going back to their room to make love for the rest of the night. They had become famous amongst their pack for not being seen before ten on a morning following a full moon.

Thinking of Marco always caused her nipples to harden and her pussy to begin to ache for his presence. She smiled and shook her head. The power he had over her never ceased to surprise her. She'd always enjoyed sex and had always achieved orgasm easily. But never had she come just from being penetrated. She laughed; no, that wasn't what Marco did. He didn't use his cock to penetrate her pussy. He mounted and then possessed her. He demanded her surrender and she gave it—mostly willingly but when needed, he would force it from her.

She'd made good time. The sun had yet to creep over the eastern horizon when she arrived at the estate's border. She took out the aerial maps and studied the best direction from which to approach. Catherine found a cluster of trees and overgrown bushes. It appeared to back up to the estate's boundary. She backed the Range Rover in. She planned to pull some of the overhanging branches down in front of the vehicle to help hide it from any passing, casual observer. She backed in so that if they were being pursued when they got back to the vehicle, she could slam it into drive and they could make a clean getaway.

Catherine took the handgun, checked that the safety was on, and tucked it into the back of her jeans and pulled her sweater down over her waist. Catherine headed toward the house at a good pace. She wanted to at least be inside before the sun started casting light all over the property.

She stood next to the house and listened intently. It didn't appear that the house was awake or even beginning to stir. Catherine used a pocket knife she had to jimmy the lock on the door and let herself in. She closed the door so it wouldn't be noticed and then made her way to the stairs and climbed up them quietly.

Looking around, Catherine could see that the furniture was covered with protective drop cloths. She listened again and could hear no signs of life whatsoever—no sounds even from an HVAC system. Quietly she moved throughout the house. She tried the light in the small powder room. Nothing. As she made her way through each room in the downstairs she became convinced the house was abandoned.

She walked through the rest of the house with her gun drawn, but found no signs of life. She checked out several of the fireplace mantels and found thick dust. She was quite certain no one had been here for months.

She was headed out of one of the upper back bedrooms when she could feel his presence. Marco was here. And more than that, Marco was pissed.

"Catherine," he bellowed as he climbed the stairs.

"Up here, sweetheart," she called as she headed toward him. "I don't think anyone has been here for months."

"Catherine DeMedici." He pulled her into his arms, his mouth descending on hers in a fiery kiss as his hand connected smartly with her backside.

"Ouch," she said as his tongue invaded her mouth.

When he'd finished kissing her, he set her back on her feet away from him. "Do you have any idea how much trouble you're in?"

Catherine decided the best defense was a good offense. "I thought my sister was being held here."

"And you were going to what… talk them out of her?"

"I'm not stupid, Marco. I brought a gun." She showed it to him.

He laughed as he took it from her. "You meant to confront an entire pack of wolves with one little handgun?"

"Well, uhm, I was hoping I wouldn't have to use it at all."

"Valentina told me she explained to you what a feral pack means… you thought they'd just give up a breeder?" Marco turned from her as Giovanni approached.

"Nothing, Alpha. No one's been here for months." He looked at Catherine. "Did Valentina know what you planned?"

She shook her head. "No, I pulled her into our room and asked her what a feral pack was. That's all, Gio. She knew nothing else. Please don't be angry with her."

"I will take your word for it." He turned back to Marco. "Shall I take the men home and leave you to deal with your very naughty mate?"

"Thank you, Gio."

"I think we should all go home together," said Catherine, only half teasing.

Marco scowled. "Would you like them to all witness your punishment? At least the spanking portion?"

"No…" she cried.

"Then they will go home, leaving their precious Madonna in my care for her correction."

Giovanni smiled. "You should probably wait until we are well away from the house if you do not want us to overhear the wailing of your mate."

"If I wait that long, she may have forgotten why she is being spanked."

"You can remind her as you're administering it. I find that to be useful with Valentina."

"My Catherine will not have any doubt in her mind when I am through with her exactly why she was punished and why she will not want to ever do it again."

"I will leave the Madonna in your capable hands."

Catherine watched with some dismay as Giovanni and the rest of their men took their leave. It suddenly occurred to her that these men had come prepared to fight to keep her and her sister safe and to rescue them if needed. They had been prepared to bleed and die for her.

"Oh, God, Marco, those men, you, Giovanni—all of you could have been hurt or killed."

"Yes," he said evenly, "which is why I intend to ensure I do not see this behavior again."

"But you're going to wait until we get home."

"No, my Catherine. As I didn't wait on the train, I will not wait here. I am going to take you downstairs into what looks like the old library. There was a chesterfield couch, which should work nicely. I'm going to strip you naked, put you over my knee, and turn your bottom bright red so that we will need to steal a pillow from this house for you to use on the ride home. I will also be wrapping one of these furniture coverings around you and taking your clothes. After you have made me believe you are truly sorry for your behavior, I'll put you over the back of the sofa to mount and fuck you until you are reminded who is alpha and who is not. Once we are home, I will take you to our room and strip you of the furniture covering and you will stand in the corner. I will attend to any business that had to be neglected due to your foolhardiness. When I have finished that, I will come to you, lay you across the edge of our bed and you, my Catherine, will get the first taste of leather from me."

"Marco, no. I know I shouldn't have done this. And I realize now that because I didn't stop to think through all the ramifications, especially as it pertained to our pack, I put other lives in danger. I want you to know that was never my intent."

"I do believe you. You have gone way too far and your realization is a little too late. Come, Catherine, it is time you paid a penance for your disobedience."

"Please?" She didn't want to beg, but she knew he had every intention of punishing her in precisely the manner he had laid out.

Marco said nothing but took her by the hand and led her down the stairs to the abandoned library. They entered the room and Marco swept the furniture cover off the beautiful oxblood-colored sofa. He sat down without turning her hand loose and said simply, "Strip."

"Marco…"

"Catherine, either you accept my authority and your punishment with the grace I expect of you, or after I have finished fucking you here, I will use my belt to leave several welts across your bottom to ride home on."

He tugged her gently, but she knew there was no escaping Marco's wrath. And if she were to be honest with herself, she knew he was right and that this punishment was well deserved. She stopped but before he could even emit a warning growl, she began to undress, folding her clothes neatly and placing them on the other end of the couch.

"I know I was wrong and I do accept your authority and my punishment," she said as she draped herself across his lap.

Marco ran his hands over her bottom. "My beautiful mate," he said before raising his hand and bringing it back down in the first of what she knew would be many hard swats. "I intend to ensure you never put yourself in this kind of danger again. Protecting our pack does not fall in your scope of responsibilities, but you do not endanger them recklessly either," he said as he spanked her harshly.

His hand rose and descended over and over, spreading heat and pain as it landed. He overlapped the blows so that she was quickly squirming, moaning, and trying to keep from crying. Even though she knew the spanking was well deserved, that knowledge did not lessen its intensity.

It wasn't long before she could no longer refrain from kicking her legs and crying out. Neither seemed to deter Marco's determination to make this spanking more painful than any he had delivered before.

He took time and care to thoroughly cover her entire bottom as well as her sit spots and the upper portion of her thighs. Catherine struggled to loosen his grip or lessen the pain. She accomplished nothing. She finally began to beg and plead with him. He said nothing but continued to paddle her already well-colored backside. Finally she capitulated to him. She went limp over his lap and began to cry in huge racking sobs.

Marco finally ceased his onslaught. "I think, my Catherine, that you begin to see the error of your ways."

"Yes," she cried.

"Up you get. I want you to lean over the back of the sofa with your legs spread."

Catherine let him help her up and she moved into position. This she thought was worse than having to stand in the corner. It was more overtly sexual and there was really no place at all to hide or to focus and not feel the full weight of her punishment.

She was finally able to choke back her sobs to just muffled cries.

Marco stepped behind her and she could hear him unzip his fly, feel his cock spring free and begin to probe between her legs for her sheath that was ready to receive him. She felt his cock stop with the crest of the head just inside her labia.

"Marco?" she said, pleading.

"Are you ready to be forgiven, my Catherine?"

"Yes, please. I'm sorry."

"Very well," he said, his tone beginning to soften, some of the anger being replaced by his growing lust.

She felt him grasp her hips firmly and press her down and into the back of the sofa as he thrust to his hilt, his pelvis impacting her very red and very painful bottom. Catherine braced her hands on the seat of the couch in front of her and began to be overcome with desire for the man who had punished her and now was going to take her to the heights of pleasure as he forgave the behavior that could have caused so much pain and destruction.

Marco plunged in and out of her, pummeling her pussy with his cock, his powerful thrusts driving home the lesson he had first imparted to her backside with the spanking. Catherine felt her pussy begin to contract as she tumbled over the abyss into a powerful orgasm that shook her to her core.

Catherine was glad she had the couch holding her up. She knew if she hadn't, Marco would have to be holding her. Her knees had buckled and she had no strength left with which to stand. In the same way she had yielded to his authority as he spanked her, she now surrendered to his dominance as he fucked her.

Twice more he brought her to climax as she called his name and begged him to forgive her and to take his own release spilling himself deep inside her pussy. At last she felt his thrusts coming faster and harder. Finally, as he gave a mighty groan, Catherine could feel his cum gushing inside of her.

Catherine reached one of her hands back to him. He grasped her hand and then took it and leaned forward, resting on her back.

"Is my beautiful mate ready to go home?"

"Is there any chance she can have her clothes back?" she asked hopefully.

"No. Would she like to argue with me and earn a set of welts before we go home?"

"Thank you, I'll pass. Any chance I can avoid them when we get home?"

"No. What you did was dangerous to you, to those who came with me to rescue you, and to our pack in general. You could have ignited a war among the various wolf packs."

"I really am sorry. I didn't think, and I know that doesn't excuse what I did, but can you at least believe me that I wouldn't knowingly endanger our pack?"

Marco stood up and drew her up off of the couch. Folding her into his embrace, he whispered, "I believe you, but that will not keep me from welting you when we get home."

She nuzzled his neck, grateful that she could no longer feel anger rolling off of him in waves. "Yes, Marco."

He gave her the drop cloth he had removed from the couch and picked up her clothes. Catherine wrapped it around her as best she could, said nothing, and took his outstretched hand as they walked to the front of the house. Marco had asked one of their men to go get the Range Rover from its hiding place. He helped Catherine into it and then after walking to the driver's side, slid into the driver's seat and started the vehicle.

As he did so, he reached across and took her hand, bringing it to his lips.

"Do not fret, my Catherine. We will find her, we will bring her home, and those who did this will be made to pay."

CHAPTER TWENTY-SEVEN

They arrived home to a subdued greeting from their pack. They were all happy to see Catherine home safe and sound, but also knew their alpha well enough to know that Catherine was in serious trouble with Marco.

Similar to the first time he'd brought her into their home, she was wrapped in nothing more than the drop cloth from the couch. Marco stood and looked at her and instead of tossing her over his shoulder, scooped her up into his arms and carried her to their bedroom.

He set her down. "Do you remember what I told you I wanted you to do?"

"Yes, Marco. If you're going to go downstairs for a little bit, would it be all right if I took a quick shower before standing in the corner?"

Marco thought for a minute and nodded. "You may but only because you asked permission first and have been accepting of your punishment."

She stood on her tiptoes and kissed his cheek. "I know I've already said it, but I really am sorry. I didn't think. All I can say is she is my sister and I thought I could save her."

"But she wasn't there. Had you given me a little time I would have known that or known if she was there what kind of resistance we might be facing. This is not, as you Americans say, my first rodeo. I'm actually quite good at rescuing people."

"I know. Even those of us who don't know we need rescuing."

Marco kissed her forehead and patted her bottom, causing her to sharply inhale. He chuckled and admonished, "Be standing in the corner like an obedient mate when I get back upstairs."

"Yes, Marco. Marco?"

He stopped in their doorway. "Yes?"

"Do you have any idea where they've taken her?"

"Not yet, but we will. I have feelers out all over Europe. We will find her. It may take time, but we will find her. If she has even a quarter of her sister's strength, she will survive and once home will recover. Don't be too long in the shower, mate, I don't intend to be long."

She watched the door close and then went to take her shower. She washed away the grime and then went to stand in the corner. She hated standing in the corner, but had to admit, it was better than when he'd made her bend over the back of the couch.

As she had come to expect, she felt his presence before he ever entered the door.

"Good girl," he said soothingly as he entered. "Did the shower feel good?"

"Yes." She knew better than to turn around. "Are you still planning to use your belt on me?"

"Not my belt, Catherine, a strap. A lovely leather strap that has been taken care of for more than five hundred years. It has welted the backsides of the DeMedici Mistresses and Madonnas for more than five centuries."

"Maybe you ought to retire it."

"No, it has proven to be effective in bringing our mates to heel, and it will do the same with you. Perhaps not this time, but I will ensure it is used when necessary. Now come lay over the end of our bed."

"Marco…"

"No, Catherine, you have earned this and you know it. When I'm done, you crawl up on the middle of our bed on your hands and knees. I will join you and then breach you with my knot from behind before tying you to me for the rest of the night."

"You aren't going to breach me as I come?"

"Not this time. You will be even more aroused than you are now, but the breaching will not be as easy for you. You will be reminded once more this day who is alpha and who is not. Catherine?"

"Yes, Marco," she said quietly.

She left the corner and put herself in position over the edge of the bed. Even though she was tall, her feet did not reach the floor. She had barely put herself in position when she heard the thin leather strap slice through the air only seconds before it laid a line of fire across both of her ass cheeks.

Catherine bit her lip to keep from screaming. She barely had time to catch her breath before the strap cracked across her bottom again. She was certain she could feel the welts beginning to swell.

The devil's tongue, for that's what she had named it in her mind, came down to inflict a third wave of fire and pain. Catherine hadn't had time to prepare and this time she did scream his name pleadingly.

"Two more, my Catherine."

Another stroke, another weal. She bit the bedclothes to keep from screaming and fought to stay in position.

"Final one," came his soothing voice.

The last one seemed to cut across the other four and turn the burn into an inferno of agony. Catherine could barely catch her breath from her crying.

"Up on the bed, mate."

Catherine crawled onto the bed and knelt shakily on all fours. Marco growled seductively and she felt her entire body tremble. The throbbing pain began to morph into arousal. Marco walked around to the other side of the bed and crawled up onto it, keeping his body low as he growled and nuzzled along her sides and flank. As he passed her, she saw that his cock was completely engorged and the knot at its base fully formed.

Her breathing began to become erratic and shallow. Her skin was fevered and flushed as he whispered kisses along the inside of her thighs. She widened her stance and steadied herself. As much as she knew his breach would be painful, she welcomed it. She wanted to be knotted by him, wanted to feel his strength and power as he rocked her to repeated orgasms, to feel him flood her with his seed and then to fall asleep exhausted from his use tied to him until morning.

Marco reared up over her and pulled her to him. "Now, mate," he said as he thrust forward and breached her pussy with his knot.

Catherine heard him. What she was sure he thought was a warning to be prepared for him, her body heard as his command to orgasm and accept his knot as he mounted her.

His hands moved up from her hips and began to knead her breasts and play with her nipples as he rolled his hips, rocking them both back and forth.

She moaned and growled as he pleasured her. Her climaxes came one after another in wave after wave of increasing ecstasy. Marco rocked her harder with a primal rhythm. Catherine realized that her arms were giving way and she could no longer support herself.

"Just a little longer," he whispered.

"I can't, Marco."

"You can," he said as he wrapped a powerful arm around her middle to pull her closer and used his other arm to provide the strength she needed.

As exhaustion began to overtake her, she felt his cock surge forward and his cum begin to bathe the walls of her pussy as he filled her to what would be overflowing if his knot had not done its job and sealed her pussy, tying her to him. His cock continued to spurt inside her. She could feel every spurt of his semen and every throb or twitch of his cock.

When he'd finally emptied himself into her, he drew her close and laid her gently down on her side, spooning against her. Her welted bottom wanted her to protest but this was the thing she liked best—lying exhausted and sated in his arms and falling asleep listening to the sound of his heartbeat.

• • • • • • •

She woke to see the sun had risen and realized Marco was not lying beside and behind her. She raised up on her side. One thing she had learned early on was that sitting after he had spanked her was to be avoided if at all possible. Her pussy ached and pulsed, missing his cock being lodged up inside of her.

She smiled as she felt him returning to their room.

He opened the door carrying a tray filled with her favorite breakfast items. Another thing she had learned about being with Marco—once he had delivered her punishment, the forgiveness always followed. There was no residual anger, no recriminations, no snarkiness.

He leaned down and kissed her. "Good morning, my Catherine. I think you should rest today."

"Are you telling me I can't leave our room?"

"No, my love, I am recognizing that while your punishment certainly fit the level of your disobedience, I know that I was not easy on you. So, while I am not apologizing for disciplining you, I have also forgiven you, restored balance between us, and wish once more to dote on my mate."

She drew his face down for a kiss. "I love you too. And I agree with you."

"But," he said, "you are not to leave the house for the next week. You can be out on the patio, but I want to know where you are."

Instead of getting angry, she giggled. "I suppose I deserve that as well, and I will be a good and obedient mate."

Marco laughed. "Do not make promises you will never keep."

"Pfft. I'm going to tell Tony you're being mean to me and perhaps he's right, I should take up with a nice malleable beta."

"Another alpha perhaps, but you are far too fond of being knotted, my mate, to settle for a man who could not fulfill that need for you."

"Hmm… you could be right. I hear Griffin is available."

"I see that your punishment did little to curb your mischievous nature or sass."

"You like my mischievousness and sass," she teased, rising up out of the bed.

"That I do, my Catherine," he said, drawing her against him. "That I do."

EPILOGUE

Three months after Catherine's failed, dramatic rescue of her sister, Catherine sauntered out of their bath and smiled. Today was Marco's birthday. She had awakened him with what started out to be a blowjob, but which turned into his fucking her mouth as he came awake and then finishing with her on her back with her legs wrapped around him.

They had spent their day riding horses through the vineyard and celebrating with their pack. Catherine had located a vintage Rolls Royce Phantom and presented it to him at dinner. She had followed their meal with a fireworks display and then had absconded with her mate to the howls and hollers of their pack shortly after dinner.

They had spent several hours making love and simply enjoying being together.

"So, my alpha, do you want your birthday present?"

"You gave me the Phantom."

"No," she said dismissively, "that was for show and from the entire pack."

"Ah, so my mate's pussy is empty and she wishes for me to fill it yet again?"

"Pfft. We do that all the time. Not that I didn't and don't always enjoy it. But I have a present that's just for you…

just from me."

She crawled across the bed and straddled him. He lifted her breasts in his hands and rose up to suckle her nipples. She leaned back and moaned appreciatively.

"You need to stop that," she sighed.

He chuckled and continued to fondle her and was rewarded with her increased arousal.

"Why would I do that?" he said, his cock beginning to swell and become erect. "I think, my mate, you are ready to let me have my way with you."

"But I want to give you my present. The one that is just from me."

He lay back. "All right. You have my complete attention."

She scooted off of him, pulled on his shirt, and then threw him his pants.

"You need to come out on the balcony with me."

He pulled on his trousers and then joined her. The pack had been directed by Valentina—the only one who knew the secret—to look at the sky over the lake.

"Look there." Catherine indicated where she wanted him to focus his attention.

He ran his hand down her flank and ran his hand over her bottom lovingly. He looked to the point above the lake she had indicated and watched as the fireworks began again. The show consisted of symbols representing their time together and had almost finished when one last great display was launched. As the design revealed itself, a hush fell over the pack and they all looked to the balcony.

For once in his life, the alpha of the DeMedici pack was speechless, for the fireworks had revealed a baby carriage.

He said nothing but tears of happiness filled his eyes. He drew her into his arms and kissed her with reverence and passion. The silence that had descended on the crowd downstairs erupted into riotous noise and celebrating. Marco released her and presented her to their well-wishers.

Catherine giggled and said, "I told you I had a special

present for you."

"No, my *tesoro*. You are my most special gift and always will be. You are to take no chances with your health or that of my child. Disobey me and your bottom will once more be sporting stripes from my strap."

She shook her head. "You arrogant bastard!" she said, laughing at him. "You didn't get me in this condition by yourself."

He smiled and kissed her gently. "No, my Madonna, I'm quite sure you were an eager participant. You are always an eager participant even when standing in the corner with your bottom covered in red handprints. Do you know when the baby will come?"

"That's the thing about babies… they come when they choose regardless of what their alpha says…"

He shook his head. "Sounds familiar. I am all too experienced with dealing with that sort of behavior."

"But I'm pretty sure he or she was conceived the night we returned from my failed attempt to rescue my sister."

They both smiled.

"They say a child born of a knot between fated mates is destined for greatness," he said, rubbing her belly possessively.

"I'm not sure about that, but I do know that while my womb may be full, my pussy is very empty and requires this baby's father to come fill her again. Will you do that for me, my alpha?"

Marco laughed and swept his Catherine into his arms, carrying her back to their bed.

"Always."

THE END

STORMY NIGHT PUBLICATIONS WOULD LIKE TO THANK YOU FOR YOUR INTEREST IN OUR BOOKS.

If you liked this book (or even if you didn't), we would really appreciate you leaving a review on the site where you purchased it. Reviews provide useful feedback for us and for our authors, and this feedback (both positive comments and constructive criticism) allows us to work even harder to make sure we provide the content our customers want to read.

If you would like to check out more books from Stormy Night Publications, if you want to learn more about our company, or if you would like to join our mailing list, please visit our website at:

www.stormynightpublications.com

Manufactured by Amazon.ca
Acheson, AB

13573056R00140